JUN 2 6 2022

NO LONGER PROPERTY OF
SEATTLE PUBLIC LIBRARY

D1603268

A KILLING IN GOLD

A KILLING IN GOLD

RALPH COTTON

THORNDIKE PRESS
A part of Gale, a Cengage Company

Copyright © 2021 by Ralph Cotton.
A Ranger Sam Burrack Western Adventure.
Thorndike Press, a part of Gale, a Cengage Company.

ALL RIGHTS RESERVED
This is a work of fiction. Names, characters, places, and incidents either are the product of the author's imagination or are used fictitiously, and any resemblance to actual persons, living or dead, business establishments, events, or locales is entirely coincidental.
Thorndike Press® Large Print Hardcover Western.
The text of this Large Print edition is unabridged.
Other aspects of the book may vary from the original edition.
Set in 16 pt. Plantin.

LIBRARY OF CONGRESS CIP DATA ON FILE.
CATALOGUING IN PUBLICATION FOR THIS BOOK
IS AVAILABLE FROM THE LIBRARY OF CONGRESS.

ISBN-13: 978-1-4328-9794-9 (hardcover alk. paper)

Published in 2022 by arrangement with Berkley, an imprint of Penguin Publishing Group, a division of Penguin Random House, LLC

Printed in Mexico
Print Number: 01   Print Year: 2022

For Mary Lynn, of course

PART 1

CHAPTER 1

The Valley of Mexico

Arizona Ranger Sam Burrack stood leaning comfortably against an ancient bare juniper tree atop a rocky rise overlooking the small town of Vista Hermosa. With his battered telescope to his eye, he watched a tall figure riding a dapple gray at an easy pace from a northerly direction out of the lower hills surrounding the wide fertile valley. The ranger recognized the tall figure as former Indian Territory lawman Daniel Thorn.

A friend of his? Yes, the ranger believed so. He and Thorn had somehow carved out a friendship of sorts over the years, but those four horsemen fanning Thorn's trail gave him pause. He'd watched them for as long as he'd watched Thorn as they rode in and out of sight along cleared stretches of trail between broken boulders and scrub trees and cacti.

What's wrong with Thorn?

He had to wonder. The fact that Thorn did not seem to know the riders were there was cause enough for concern, Sam thought. Yet he waited and watched, drawing no conclusion, but with his Winchester resting in the crook of his left arm. With every fifty or so yards that Thorn traveled, he'd reach down and from memory adjust the small brass dial on his raised long sight.

Now that Thorn and the riders were inside Sam's shorter range, some seventy or eighty yards, he no longer needed the long sight; he reached down with a fingertip and closed it with a quiet *snap.* He also closed his telescope and slipped it into his duster pocket. Through the brush and rock that lay between him and the trail below, he'd seen a thin game path that appeared to run most of the way there.

Time to go to work.

He made an ever-so-slight sound in his cheek that caused his dapple roan stallion, Doc, to perk his ears just as slightly. With no fanfare whatsoever, Doc turned and walked over to stand beside him.

"Buen caballo," Sam whispered.

Without slipping his rifle down into its saddle boot, he gave Doc a rub on his nose, then led him by his reins over to the start of the game path and headed down.

■ ■ ■ ■

Humming "Sweet Betsy from Pike," a favorite song of his, Daniel Thorn stepped down from his saddle, pulled an apple from his duster and raised the big knife from his boot well. He scanned the area from under the wide brim of his black Stetson as he carved a slice of sweet Mexican Valley apple and popped it into his mouth.

He had just lowered the big knife to take another slice of apple when the four riders came suddenly around a huge boulder that formed a blind spot in the trail right behind him. With their four guns drawn and aimed at him, Thorn merely raised the slice of apple up to his mouth more slowly than usual.

"Can you believe this jake?" said the gunman near the center of the four. He gave a dark chuckle. "Hell, old-timer, don't let us interrupt you eating." He was a large man with a big red face.

Old-timer? This melon-head son of a bitch, Thorn mused.

"That's all right," Thorn said. "I'm about finished." He lowered the big knife to pare off another slice of apple.

The man gave a dark laugh, his Colt

aimed and cocked.

"You're right about that," he said. "You're finished, sure enough! Nobody with any sense stops on a trail this close around a blind turn. You're too close to see what's waiting to kill you!"

The four of them laughed.

Thorn gave a sheepish little grin. "Well, I guess I wasn't thinking straight like I should have been," he said quietly.

Stupid melon-head son of a bitch . . .

Thorn was thinking just fine and had stopped there for exactly the reason mentioned. Four men trailing him and he'd managed to catch them all by surprise, and they had a lowered opinion of him to boot.

"Yeah, I guess not," said the man with the big red face.

One glance at the red sashes around three of their waists had told Thorn that these were members of the Arizona Cowboy Gang. The one without a red sash kept his hat brim lowered. *Hiding his face? A good possibility,* Thorn thought. He'd kill him last, he decided, if this thing went the way he was confident it would.

Thorn popped another slice of the apple off the knife blade into his mouth, talking as he chewed. As he chewed and spoke, he reached the knife blade up and around to scratch the back of his neck with the pointed tip.

"What can I do for you fellas?" he asked.

His ease seemed to make the red-faced outlaw furious.

"When you get an itch, you've got to scratch it," Thorn said.

"Get rid of it!" the man shouted, waving his gun barrel at the big knife.

Thorn gave him a bewildered look, but stopped scratching. "All right! I'll get rid of it!"

Without hesitation, he raised his left hand and tossed the rest of the apple off the trail and into the rocks. As the gunmen watched, he raised his empty left hand for them to see.

"There, see? All gone," he said. He turned his empty hand back and forth.

Three of the gunmen laughed a little, but not the one with the red face. His hand tightened on his cocked Colt.

"Not the apple, you damn fool!" he shouted. "The knife! Get rid of the knife!"

"Okay!" said Thorn. "See, it's gone too!" He held his hands up and out — both of them empty.

The men looked around as if the big knife was hidden somewhere among them.

"The hell?" one said.

"I'm killing this worthless old jake," said the red-faced gunman.

"Careful," one of the others warned him. "I was told not to take this one lightly. To keep our eyes on him at all times."

"Whoever told you that can go straight to hell," the man with the red face said. "I'll show you how careful I'll be!"

He tried to raise his gun hand, ready to fire, but something stopped him, sudden and cold. He rocked back in his saddle before seeing the knife's bone handle jutting from the middle of his chest. All four gunmen stared at it as if having just witnessed a magician at work. Guns sagged. Eyes flashed all around. The man with the lowered hat brim stepped his horse back, and his black-handled Colt came down, uncocked.

Before the gunmen could gather themselves, Thorn's first pistol shot rang out. One outlaw fell, his gun flying from his hand. The next was a split second faster and might have gotten the drop on Thorn. But it didn't matter. Before Thorn could fire again, a rifle shot exploded from beside the trail and sent the man flying backward out of his saddle.

Thorn spun toward the rifle shot and saw the ranger step into sight as he jacked a fresh round up into his rifle chamber.

"Ranger Sam Burrack," Thorn said, "just the man I was looking for."

"Thought I'd give you a hand, Dan'l," the ranger said, keeping an eye on the fourth gunman, who sat perfectly still in his saddle. His black-handled Colt was back in its holster, and his hands were held chest high, his eyes still shaded by the brim of his hat.

"Ha!" Thorn said to the ranger. "Don't go thinking I needed a hand against four *miscreants* like these!"

"Make that *three* miscreants," said the fourth men. "I pulled back before it got serious." He slowly pushed his hat brim up to allow a better look at his face.

"Roman Lee Ellison," said Thorn, recognizing the young gunman. "Had I known it was you up under that feltwork I would have shot you just for keeping bad company." He looked Roman Lee up and down, feigning anger. "The hell are you doing following me with this coyote bait?"

Roman Lee lowered his hands and shrugged. "I was up in Happenstance drinking with some lonely women. A dozen Cowboys rode in and recognized me. I'm still one of them, you know." He gave a thin smile. "They said they were riding you down, Thorn. They invited me along. I figured you'd like seeing my smiling face if it all broke bad out here."

"Riding me down?" Thorn looked around at the three bodies in the dirt. "We see how *that* worked out, don't we?"

He walked over to the jittery horse standing beside the man with the big knife in his chest. When the man had fallen from his saddle, his right foot had stayed in the stirrup.

"Easy, boy," Thorn said to the grumbling animal.

He took the man's boot out of the stirrup and pressed his own boot down on the dead man's chest, above the knife handle. He yanked the blade out and wiped it on the man's bloody shirt and slipped it into his boot well.

The horse blew out a breath, stepped away, shook itself off and stood easier.

"Well, Roman Lee," Thorn said, looking up and west, judging the evening sun mantling the horizon, "since you've managed not to shoot any of your pals here, maybe you'll help drag them off the trail. I'll gather their canteens and see if the ranger will boil us a pot of coffee."

"I will do that," said Roman Lee, stepping down from his saddle.

The ranger began searching the trailside

16

for a good place to build a fire unseen.

"While we're at it, you can tell me why somebody wanted these Cowboys to ride me down," Thorn said as he replaced the bullet he'd used to kill one of the Cowboys. He tapped his Colt in Roman Lee's direction. "See if you can convince me that you have changed sides once and for all, and are now on the side of good and righteousness with folks like the ranger and me." He turned, tapped his gun barrel in the ranger's direction and slipped it down into his holster.

"I will do that too," said Roman Lee. "I might be an outlaw, but after riding with these Cowboys, I've come to realize that even among outlaws, there're both good and bad."

"Oh," said Thorn, "did that time the ranger here put a bullet through your gullet and stuck you in Yuma prison for a couple of years rehabilitate you after all?"

"Don't start on that, Dan'l," the ranger cut in, looking up from starting the fire off the side of the trail where he'd cleared a spot.

"No, that's okay," said Roman Lee. "The fact is, taking a bullet in the chest might have had a lot to do with the way I think of things these days." He looked back and forth between the two. "What the bullet through my chest didn't change, riding with the two of you in Bad River made up for. It just took me some time to mull it over."

"Don't go getting sentimental on us, Roman Lee," Thorn said. "Sam might shoot you again."

"That's enough, Dan'l," Sam said.

He stepped onto the trail, took a small coffeepot from his holdings bag and took two of the dead outlaws' canteens from Thorn on his way back to the fledgling campfire.

While the coffee boiled, their horses were moved off the trail out of sight. Then the three of them dragged the dead off to the opposite side of the trail and rolled their bodies over the edge and down the rocky slope. The outlaws' horses were unsaddled and stripped of all tack and bridles and shooed away. But a few minutes later, as Sam, Thorn and Roman Lee sat around a low campfire drinking coffee from tin cups, the outlaws' horses eased out of the shadows into the soft circling glow of firelight. Gradually they gathered closer to the three men, their horses, their coffee and their banter as wolves began their searching howls in the distant darkness.

"Well, come on in, fellas. Don't mind us,"

Thorn said.

The ranger topped up Thorn's cup and set the coffeepot off of the low flames. Roman Lee Ellison lay leaning back against his saddle, a wool blanket beneath him, his battered Stetson brim down over his eyes.

Sam studied Thorn for a moment across the flicker of firelight. "If you're all through talking to stray horses, why don't you tell me what brings you out here on my trail?"

Thorn gave a nod toward Roman Lee, as if to say that he might be listening.

Sam looked over at the tilted-down Stetson. "Roman Lee, are you listening?" he asked, loud enough to be well heard.

"I hear every word being said," Roman Lee replied. "But I'm not listening."

"He's not listening," the ranger said to Thorn.

"Yeah, so I heard," said Thorn. "If you don't mind, neither do I."

He reached inside his duster, pulled out an official-looking envelope and handed it around the fire to the ranger.

Sam gave him a questioning stare in the flicker of firelight. He gestured all around at the darkness and then down at the letter in his hand.

"This is a joke, right?" he said.

"All right, give it back," said Thorn. "I'll

tell you what it says and you can read it in the morning and suit yourself."

Sam withdrew the envelope before Thorn could reach for it.

"I'll just keep it, read it in the morning, *then* give it back," Sam said. He said to Roman Lee, "How does that sound to you, Roman Lee?" Sam stuck the letter inside his shirt and patted it.

"Sounds good to me," Roman Lee said quietly under his hat brim.

"All right, here's what the letter will tell you in the morning," Thorn said to the ranger. "It'll say I'm working on bringing down a faction of the Arizona Cowboy Gang that was all set to take over Clement Melford's bank in Bad River, and with it the members of the French business group that was siphoning off large amounts of both cash and gold from the mining operations across Mexico —"

"Who are you working for, Dan'l?" Sam asked, cutting in.

"We'll get to that later," Thorn replied.

Sam started to insist on knowing right then, but he would wait, he decided. Maybe that was too much to talk about in front of Roman Lee.

"All right," Sam said, "go on."

Thorn glanced at Roman Lee and lowered

his voice.

"That was good work you did in Bad River," Thorn said, half under his breath. He got up in a crouch and seated himself a little closer to the ranger. "I hope you won't mind, but I sort of let some people think that I might have had something to do with all of it —"

"Hold it there, Thorn." The ranger raised a hand. In the same lowered voice, he said, "I *sort of* did the same thing myself."

Thorn looked at him, confused.

"That's right, Dan'l," said Sam. "When I gave my report on Bad River to my captain, I told him you were a big help. Told him I might not have made it out of there, had it not been for you keeping me in the know on things."

Thorn looked even more confused. "You told him *that*?" he said.

"I did," said Sam.

"Why?" Thorn asked as if he couldn't believe it.

"Because it's true, Dan'l." Sam said. "If it wasn't true, I wouldn't have said it."

"Well, I know that," Thorn said, "but I didn't —"

"Don't start second-guessing me on it, Thorn," Sam said in a firmer tone. "You didn't have to tell me you were on my side,"

Sam continued. "I saw it in every move you made. A lot of men died at Bad River. I might have been one of them if you hadn't been backing my play without anybody knowing it. I saw what you were doing for me without you telling me."

"It seemed like the right thing," Thorn said.

"It was," said Sam, "and when you and Irish Mike Tuohy came along backing me with shotguns near the end, I knew it was going to work out." He paused, then said, "Anyway, I did the right thing telling my captain."

Thorn grinned at Sam. "Don't forget crazy JR Claypool," he said. "He sure came through in a tight spot."

"Yes, he did," said Sam. "I hope he's doing well."

"He is indeed," said Thorn. "He's *rich* now!" He laughed and continued. "Funny thing, how when you're poor and crazy, they chase you off the streets. But if you're rich and crazy, they name streets after you!"

"Anyway," said Sam, "I figured I owed you. If you're going up against the Cowboys, I'm with you as soon as I tell my captain about it."

"No need. The letter will tell you that the people I'm working for have already cleared it with your captain," Thorn said. He glanced again at Roman Lee and then said to Sam in almost a whisper, "Read it in the morning. They say everything looks better in the light of day."

"I'll read it first thing," said Sam. "But I have to tell you, I'm working on my wanted list right now. I can't break away until I've taken some hard cases off of Mexico's hands one way or the other."

"I understand," said Thorn. "I'll help you take them down if you want me to. If you don't want me to, I'll stand back out of the way and watch you work."

CHAPTER 2

Ciudad Esplanade, Mexico

The six riders wore masks even in the dead of night with no trace of the moon showing its face in a low cloudy sky. They stepped down from their saddles and led their horses along the soft-dirt alleyway. At the rear door of the large stone and adobe Banco Franco-Mexicano de Explanada, they stopped in the pitch-darkness and wrapped their horses' reins loosely around an iron hitch rail.

A moment later, without benefit of shadow or silhouette, a low, barely audible sound came forward in the black night. Only when a wagon stopped and a slight squeak rose from the brake handle did the waiting men manage to discern the outline of a large freight wagon. When one of the two wagon horses puffed out a breath, everybody froze at once and listened.

When it became apparent that the horse

had not been heard outside of their circle, the leader of the men, Nathan Catlow, nudged his accomplices forward, one and two at a time, until all of them somehow understood and gathered around the door as it creaked open. It was as dark inside the building as outside.

In the open doorway, a watchman whispered, "I was starting to worry you weren't going to —" He stopped with a muffled grunt as Catlow's hand clamped over his mouth.

The watchman didn't offer another word. He backed away as the men moved past him like ghosts until they all stood inside. Then the nervous watchman closed the door silently and took a candle and a round candlestand from inside his coat. He stuck the candle on the flat candlestand and lit it, crouching so as to hold it low, even though he had already pulled down every window shade in the bank's front windows.

In the dim light, Catlow looked around the cluttered storage room. Two of his men carried in feather mattresses. Two more carried copper wire and breaking tools. Catlow himself carried a plain wrinkled paper bag. A block away in the alleys on either side of the bank, men stood watching the bank building itself. At the sight of any light seep-ing from the window edges or the door-frame, everything would stop, and the burglars would disappear in the night like smoke.

Catlow motioned with his hand, sending his men about the jobs they were there to do. He watched them move away in the darkness, the already dim light growing even dimmer as they moved carefully through it.

All right . . .

In his coat pocket, Catlow carried three sticks of dynamite, which had been re-measured, compacted and rewrapped days ago in preparation. *All very professional . . .*

He smiled to himself, carefully gripping the small sticks. He'd been assured that they were designed to hold the exact amount of explosives needed to blow a reinforced steel safe wide open. He liked the thought of it.

Carrying the dim candle low at his side, he left the dark storage room and stepped through an ornate iron-and-wooden gate in the main counter. Behind the row of steel bars and brass-frame teller windows, he walked across shiny red tile through another door into a room he knew had once been twice its size. An iron-reinforced stone wall ran across its middle.

What a sight!

He closed the door behind himself. This

room needed no candles on a stand. Because there were no windows to let the light seep out onto the dark streets, the burglars had lit all six large lamps along the stone dividing wall, in the center of which stood a huge shiny steel door trimmed in brass. The door's main handle, made of solid brass, was the size of a captain's wheel on a medium-sized sailing vessel. Lamplight glistened and flickered in the reflection from the shiny iron. The men stopped doing their jobs for a moment and looked at their leader.

"As you were, men," Catlow said with a laugh.

The men each gave a nod and went back to work, stringing copper wire and moving heavy office furniture around. The men who'd brought in the feather mattresses laid them out on a long table and set a coil of rope beside them. Another man stood with one shoulder against the frame of a metal drill. With his opposite hand, he turned the big handle on the drill, putting bolt holes where he would need them to fasten a steel plate onto the door's mechanism.

Less than an hour later, Catlow and his men gathered by the door leading out to the room with the row of tellers' cages.

"She's a beauty, sure enough," the bank watchman whispered near Catlow's ear. "Won't be long, I suppose, till I get paid for my part in this?" he asked quietly.

Catlow patted the elderly man on his damp shoulder and smiled. "I haven't forgotten you, *mi amigo,*" he said.

He looked over at Kura Stabitz, better known as the Russian Assassin, who had shown himself in the rear door only moments earlier. "Kura, take care of my friend here as soon as the safe door swings open."

Kura looked at the watchman with the blank eyes of a corpse, then said, "I will take care of him, Cat."

His blank, hollow stare unsettled the watchman for a second until Stabitz gave him the slightest trace of a smile.

The watchman breathed relief. "I don't mean to hound you, Cat," he said.

"Don't call me by my name, you damned fool!" Catlow reprimanded him.

"I'm — I'm sorry, sir," the watchman said. "It's just —" He gestured toward Stabitz, who had just used the name.

"Forget it," said Catlow. He looked at the other men and motioned them backward, out the door. "Except you, Stabitz! Everybody else, get the hell out of here! I've got this part of it myself, unless one of you wants to do the honors!"

The men wasted no time getting out and heading all the way to the rear storage room, from which they had started.

Catlow chuckled to himself. With the wall lamps still lighting up the room, he unfolded a small sheet of paper he took from his hip pocket and looked at it closely. He read the five numbers written on the paper as he dialed them, going back and forth, precisely, one at a time.

There! That wasn't so hard!

He smiled and spun the brass handle until he felt the door give inside itself. *All right!* He took a step back, braced himself and pulled the heavy door open, revealing the dark, cavernlike inside of the safe.

Looking around, he saw that it was empty, save for a large canvas bag with leather seams sitting in the middle of the floor. He stepped right over, opened the bag, reached down inside and scooped up a handful of gold coins. Coins so bright, they seemed to draw lamplight into the dark safe and reflect it in a soft yet dazzling glow. *Holy Mother, Beth Ann!* He imagined that he could feel heat emanating from the coins, warming his face, his hands.

"Easy, Cat," he whispered to himself.

Picking the heavy bag up by its reinforced

leather handles, he walked through the open door and paused to pitch the coins from his hands in either direction, both inside and out of the otherwise empty safe.

He set the bag down beside the long table, on which the paper bag lay atop the two feather mattresses. He opened the bag and carefully removed the inner windup mechanism of an office desk clock. Suddenly, just looking at the little brass wheels and the windup key slot lying there before him caused his brow to take on a sheen of sweat.

Removing one of the sticks of dynamite from his coat pocket, he cut the end with his pocketknife, walked over and sprinkled a two-foot trail of the explosive dust on the floor. He set the open stick at the end of the dust trail and left it there. He closed the safe door and firmly turned the brass wheel clockwise. He pushed the table, which held everything else he needed, closer to the safe door and went to work.

Waiting in the small dark storage room, where they had come in, the watchman stood with the other crooks, growing more anxious by the minute. Inside and out, the big bank building sat as silent as a tomb, with the exception of an occasional muffled breath.

The grumble of a wagon horse at the hitch rail caused the watchman to step over and look out through a security peephole. But one of the gang pulled him back and whispered, "Stay away from there. It's just an alley guard checking the horses."

The watchman stepped back, but he had seen something that puzzled him. The silhouettes of the wagon and its team of horses were all that was left standing there.

"But — but, your saddle horses are all gone!" he whispered shakily.

"Yeah," the man whispered, letting go of the watchman's shoulder. "The alley guard took them away. We decided we'd all ride in the wagon tonight."

Stifled laughter rose and fell among the men. The watchman looked all around, baffled.

"You mean, ride the wagon with all the gold in it?" he said.

Again the chuff of laughter.

"That's right," the same man whispered. "Now shut up."

"But I'm staying here," the watchman said. "What about my share?"

"Don't worry about it," another voice whispered. "Both of you, shut up. Somebody's coming."

"It's about time" came a whisper.

"It'd *better* be Catlow" came another.

"Yeah, it'd better be. I got to go water my garden."

Again the chuffed laugh. This time a little louder until a slight signal tap on the door grabbed the men's attention.

"Cat?" a man whispered to the closed door.

"Yeah, open up," Catlow whispered in reply.

The door opened and Catlow stepped inside, carrying the lit candle on its stand. Behind him came Kura Stabitz, toting the heavy canvas bag of gold by both of its leather handles. Stabitz set the bag on the floor and Catlow handed the candlestand to one of the men.

"Hold it low," he said.

Taking the candlestand, the man held the flickering light down close to the bag of gold. "Ain't that nice?" He grinned, his face aglow in the radiance of freshly minted gold coins.

"All right," said Catlow, "let's get going here."

The man holding the candlestand gestured toward a pile of tools, leftover scraps of wire and rope the men had thrown over in a corner.

"Good, good," Catlow said. "Get this bag

of gold loaded up —"

"What about me, sir?" said the watchman. "I have to get my share!"

"You're right," Catlow said. He took a deep, calming breath and motioned Stabitz forward.

The watchman's eye gleamed with delight and anticipation.

Stabitz stepped in front of the men and shoved both hands down into the bag of coins.

"Hold up your shirttails," Catlow told the watchman, cupping his hands to illustrate.

The watchman looked confused but only for a second, then jerked his shirttails up from his trousers and cupped them in front of him.

"I know this is more than we promised you," said Catlow, "but we're taking good care of you, making sure you keep your mouth shut."

"I'll never tell a soul!" the watchman said.

He stared transfixed as Stabitz raised two large fistfuls of coins and held them above the watchman's cupped and waiting shirttails.

"My, oh, my!" the watchman said. "I brought a bag, but this will do just fine! For now anyway!"

His smile grew as Stabitz let the coins fall

into his waiting shirttails. "Never a word from me! I swear on my wife — I mean, my soon-to-be ex-wife!" he whispered, and laughed, actually doing a little quick-stepping jig. "I'm retiring first thing tomorrow. They will never see me again. But if you ever need me for some other job, I'll stay in reach. I'm your man!"

Retiring? Catlow and a couple of others gave one another a glance. Retiring first thing would be an admission of guilt! *Leaving his job, leaving his wife? Adios, you crazy old bastard.*

"You bet," Catlow said to the joyous watchman. "All right, then." He turned to everybody. "I say we leave here and go somewhere more accommodating." He looked at a man standing close beside him who was reaching to pick up the bag of gold. "Leave it," Catlow said. "Stabitz will get it."

The watchman settled down and looked around, confused.

"What about all the rest of the gold?" he said.

"Don't worry about it," said Catlow quietly, watching Stabitz step around behind the watchman's left shoulder.

The watchman chuckled, jiggling the gold in his shirttails a little. "I know you're not going to just leave it all here —"

His words stopped abruptly. The Russian Assassin had reached around him and slammed a long dagger into his heart, all the way to its hilt. He twisted the dagger back and forth to make sure it did its job. The men watched Stabitz sink into a crouch, cradling the watchman before dragging him over to the rear door. He laid the body with the feet toward the door and left the dagger where it was in the man's chest.

Good. Catlow nodded appreciatively.

Stabitz stood, smoothed down his clothes and checked himself for any blood, finding none as usual.

The men began to scramble for the coins that had spilled from the watchman's hands.

"Leave them," Catlow said.

He reached down into the bag and picked up a few more coins, which he pitched around the room.

Stabitz opened the rear door, letting in what little pale starlight had seeped down through the broken cloud cover.

Catlow blew out the candle and dropped it. "All aboard," he said quietly over his shoulder.

He watched the men climb into the wagon until Stabitz handed the heavy bag up to the men's waiting hands. Then Stabitz climbed up, and making sure Catlow saw him, he reached into the open bag and tossed a few coins into the dirt as the wagon drove away.

CHAPTER 3

Catlow carefully picked his footing along the alleyway behind the bank. He stayed close to the row of buildings, where the dirt stayed as solid as stone from foot, hoof and wheel traffic day after day. As he passed the alleyway where a guard still kept an eye on the empty streets, he gave a nod, signaling him that all had gone well. The guard returned his nod and disappeared deeper into the alley.

At the Hotel Majestuoso, where Catlow had taken a room for a few days, he slipped inside the ornate lobby as silent as a ghost. In a long wall mirror, he saw the reflection of the night clerk asleep at his desk behind the hotel counter. He eased up the stairs to his room on the second floor, overlooking the empty street. Inside his room he locked the door and walked to where an unopened bottle of American bourbon stood beside a tall porcelain drinking cup.

Come to me, my sweet strong darling, he said silently to the bottle. He looked it up and down, opened it and poured four fingers. "This could be a long, long night."

He raised the tall cup to the dressing mirror standing in front of him, said, *"Salud,"* and tossed back a large drink. And a moment later, he tossed back another and gave a bourbon hiss.

He was awakened before dawn when he felt his bed tremble, then settle beneath him. His first response was to sit straight up and say aloud, "What the hell was that?" Then he picked up his pocket watch from the small bedside table, looked at it, shook his head, then looked at it again.

If the tremor he'd just felt was what he thought it was, it was more than thirty minutes late.

What was that? he asked again, this time silently.

He wiped his bleary bourbon red eyes and held them open wide, then gazed at the watch, sure it must be wrong. He shook the watch and looked at it again.

The same time as before within a minute . . .

Okay, he reasoned. His pocket watch was right as always. He'd followed the instructions he'd received when he went by and picked up the timepiece mechanism in the paper bag. The mechanism had been set wrong. That had to be it.

As he thought about it, he heard the sounds of the Mexico City Fire Department bugles and drums blaring in the streets below. He stepped over to the window and looked down. Stray dogs raced along, howling and barking alongside and behind the team of fire horses. Behind the dogs, donkeys brayed and kicked and snapped their large teeth in the air.

Looking up the street to the front of the large bank building, Catlow saw no flames, no sign of fire other than a spiral of gray smoke rising lazily from around a window near the room where he knew the safe to be. People were gathering in the street, coming out of their homes with blankets draped around their shoulders.

Men wearing trousers held up by suspenders watched and spoke among themselves and assisted the fire department in searching all around the building for any sign of fire.

All right, Catlow decided. Maybe this was nothing to worry about, just a simple mistake. Any other time and place, a mistake like this would have meant nothing. But if you were robbing a bank! Catlow smiled to himself and looked over at the near empty bourbon bottle standing on the dresser.

"Ease up," he told himself.

Mistakes could happen. Yet even as he thought about it, he heard excited voices from outside the bank and went back to the window.

Looking down, he saw men carrying a gurney out of the building. He recognized the lifeless body with the knife handle sticking up from its chest. He took a drink out of the bottle and stood watching with an unmoved expression until he saw another gurney brought out, this one carrying a badly burned body, smoke still rising from it.

Damn! Who the hell is that?

He took another drink. *Damn!* He watched the gurney men carry their gruesome load to a waiting city hearse. *Damn!* He had no idea who this could be. His men were all accounted for. The watchman was dead, of course, already lying inside the hearse. *Okay . . .* That was all according to plan. He took another swig of bourbon and let out another bourbon hiss. He was going to go downstairs and ask some questions. That was all there was to it. Something wasn't right, no matter how you looked at it.

What was he going to do? He corked the

bottle and stood it on the dresser. He pulled on his trousers, shirt and boots and shoved a Navy .36-caliber pistol down behind his belt and smoothed his shirt down over it.

Check this malarkey out, that's what, he told himself, heading for the door.

Downstairs, there was no one at the desk. The clerk stood out front staring down the street at the fire equipment, the stray dogs, the donkeys and now two drunks dancing in the street to a single trumpet still playing aboard the fire rig.

"What's going on there?" Catlow asked the clerk as soon as he stepped out front beside him.

"Señor," the clerk said, "this is terrible!" He waved a hand at the gathered crowd. "Someone has killed the bank manager!"

"The bank manager?" Catlow asked. "I saw two people carried out."

"*Sí,* one was the night watchman," said the clerk. "The other was the bank manager! He arrived the same time as usual! Only to meet Mr. Death, who lay in wait for him!" He bowed his head slightly and crossed himself. *"Santa Madre de Dios!"*

"Gracias," Catlow said, and headed down the street toward the circuslike commotion.

The bank manager had arrived at the usual time? Which just happened to be when the mechanism was set to go off and trigger the mercury device that lit the dynamite? *Uh-uh.* Too much coincidence to suit him.

The time is already set. Don't touch the device no matter what! That was what he'd heard the man's voice tell him the day he dropped by his shop and picked up the paper bag with the striking device inside it. *No matter what,* he had insisted.

"No matter what?" Catlow whispered under his breath.

That son of a bitch had set the alarm for later than they'd agreed on. Why? Well, hell, that was easy. Someone the man worked for intended to kill the bank manager! Whoever had set the device had had no qualms about putting a noose around Catlow's and his men's necks. Killing a night watchman was not a big thing. It would be forgotten quick enough. But a bank manager, an upstand-ing man of the community? It would be remembered. Somebody would swing for it.

"Excuse me, señor," Catlow asked one of the fire crew in good Spanish. "What has happened here? I heard the noise. I saw smoking bodies. But I see no fire!" He spread his hands toward the bank as if in disbelief.

"Step back, señor," the man replied in

Spanish. As Catlow stepped back the man stepped back with him and spoke under his breath. "Say nothing to anyone, señor, but the bank has been robbed! I tell you only because I see you are an *Americano.*"

Catlow gaped at him for a moment. "The bank robbed! How can this be?" Catlow said. Again he spread his hands, looking shocked.

"Yes, it is so," the man said. "The safe was blown open and the manager arrived just as it happened. The gold is gone, all of it! All that remains are some coins that lay spilled on the ground." He pointed down the dark street where people were bent at the waist picking up coins, hiding their newfound treasure in their clothes.

Catlow took a deep cleansing breath, wishing he'd brought the bottle of bourbon with him. His men and the wagon had gotten away clean; if they hadn't, he would have heard by now. This job was still going okay. He would play it safe, lie low and leave on tomorrow's stage out of town.

He would join his men at the hideout they had chosen near the high desert town of Hermosas Flores del Desierto. *Beautiful desert flowers,* he translated to himself. Once there, rested and well-fed, in the safety of his fellow Cowboys, he'd look up the man

43

who'd arranged the killing of the bank manager.

He closed his eyes, almost feeling, almost smelling the sweet, heady scent of flowers wafting in on a desert breeze.

Oh, yes! He would look that man up. He'd blow that fool's head all over anyone or anything standing near him.

The ranger awakened before Daniel Thorn or Roman Lee Ellison, and he set to drinking a tin cup of hot coffee from a fresh pot he made. The letter Thorn had given him the night before hung from his hand. He'd read it at first light and once again only a moment ago, in case he might have missed something — although he knew he hadn't.

The next one to wake was Thorn. He opened his eyes but a slit and looked all around before raising his head or taking his arm from under the saddlebags he used as a pillow.

Sam watched from across the low campfire, familiar with this slow waking process from years of using it himself.

When Thorn completely opened his eyes, he faced the ranger, who held the letter up and tapped it on the air toward him.

"No longer than this is," Sam said, "you could have told me what it said last night."

Thorn sat up on his blanket and rubbed his neck. Raising his hat from where it lay covering his gun belt beside him, he set it atop his head.

"Top of the morning to you too, Ranger Burrack," Thorn said in an almost mocking tone.

Sam noted, when Thorn raised the hat from over the gun belt, that the holster lying beneath it was empty. Thorn now reached under his saddlebags, pulled out his long Colt .45, checked it and slipped it into the holster.

"So what about the letter?" Thorn said. "Anything wrong with it?"

He stood up, swung his gun belt around his waist and buckled it. As he tied the holster down, he looked sidelong at the sleeping Roman Lee and said, "Have you checked him for a pulse?"

"Not yet," said Sam. "Back to the letter. Nothing's wrong with it, but you could have told me what it said last night."

"You sort of made it clear you're the kind who'd rather *read* than be *read at,*" Thorn said.

Stepping over beside the fire, he reached down, took the letter back from Sam and read aloud, " 'Letter of Authority.' " He cleared his throat and continued. " 'This

45

document of authority, issued jointly by the Sovereign Government of Mexico and the Government of the United States of America, is issued: granting Daniel Thorn, an investigative agent for the Mexican Government, and Samuel Burrack, an investigative agent for the United States of America, full power of investigating, apprehending and legal prosecution of wanted felons sought by either or both governments on either side of the Mexico–United States of America border. This document of authority signed and dated' so on and so forth. 'BY: Generalissimo' so and so. 'Dated —' "

"I've got it," said Sam.

"Good," said Thorn. He grinned and asked, "How's the coffee?"

"It's tolerable," Sam replied, "unless you're looking for a grudge to carry. Get you some." He motioned toward Thorn's and Ellison's tin cups still sitting fireside.

"Obliged," said Thorn. "Did you boil enough for just yourself or for me and Roman Lee too?"

"I'm awake over here" came a sleepy voice from Ellison's blanket.

"Noted," said Thorn.

He wiped both cups out and filled them as Roman Lee sat up on his blanket and holstered his black-handled Colt, which had

46

spent the night on his chest. He stood up, having slept wearing his gun belt. He drew his Colt, fast and slick, rapidly cocking and uncocking it. He spun it forward and backward. Then he checked it and spun it backward again. This time it slid from his hand smoothly into its holster. He flipped the safety loop over the hammer.

Sam and Thorn looked at each other.

"There're times I miss being a youngster," Thorn said with a faint grin.

Sam didn't reply. He stood, slung the remaining coffee grounds from his tin cup and walked over to his bedroll to make ready for the trail. The other two took the hint and began making up their bedrolls while they drank their coffee. In moments they broke camp and rode away as the last purple streak of dawn faded into a blazing sunlit sky.

Before leaving, Roman Lee Ellison looked the three dead outlaws' horses over for any brand markings or scars that would easily identify the animals. Finding none, he made a loop in a lead rope, then dropped the loop around the neck of the bay that belonged to the red-faced outlaw before he'd caught Thorn's big knife in his chest. It stood to reason in horse logic that this bay horse was used to riding ahead of the others most of the time and was already their leader. If Roman Lee kept the bay riding beside him the other two would follow close behind, rope or no rope.

Watching Roman Lee put the bay on the lead rope, Sam and Thorn sat in their saddles, sizing up the young gunman, their wrists crossed on their saddle horns.

"What does that there tell you about our number three pistolero?" Sam said sidelong to Thorn.

"He's frugal with rope," said Thorn.

The ranger gave a chuckle and shook his head, turning Doc toward Roman Lee's horse string. Even though Thorn had made a joke of it, Sam knew the two of them had just witnessed the same thing. Somewhere in his life, Roman Lee had learned a lot about horses: how they act, how they think. It always paid to know as much as you could about the man riding beside you. They both knew that.

The two reined in behind the horses strung out a few feet behind their leader, the bay clopping along at the side of Roman Lee's horse, the lead rope drooping between the two of them.

"So I take it we're officially riding together now?" Thorn said. He rode his dapple-gray stallion, Cochise, beside Doc, Sam's dapple roan.

"Yep," Sam said, gazing ahead, "far as I'm concerned, we are."

"Good!" said Thorn. "Maybe now you'll tell me where we're headed today."

"Perrito," said Sam. He stared straight ahead.

"Little Dog?" Thorn asked. "No wonder you acted like you didn't want to say."

Sam looked a little surprised. "You already want to drag up?" he said.

"No, I'm good," said Thorn.

"What's wrong with Little Dog?" Sam asked.

"Nothing," said Thorn. "It's an awfully rough place —"

"They're all rough places," Sam said. "That's why we go there."

"I know it," said Thorn. "That's why I caught myself. Who are you after in Little Dog — I mean, Perrito?"

"The Smith brothers, Ludall and Larson," said Sam. "Ever hear of them?"

"Oh, yes," said Thorn. "I had posters on them, oh, must have been fifteen years ago, before they dropped out of sight altogether. I finally figured they'd died and gone. They're both old enough."

"No, they're both still alive," Sam said.

49

"Still alive and still killing every chance they get."

"Wait a minute!" said Thorn as a dark realization came upon him. "Do Ludall and Larson Smith happen to be Lude and Lars, the Cannibals of Mexico I read about a year ago? Some folks called them the Miner brothers because they were both miners by trade?"

Sam looked at him with a flat expression. "I'd say that's a good possibility," he said. "I read about them too. They outran a Mexican posse two years ago. They've been living a couple of days' ride out of Perrito ever since. A posse searched their adobe hideout. They found human bones and human flesh in the spring-house. There were bodies buried everywhere."

"I read that too," said Thorn in reflection. "They said it looked like some of the dead were still alive when they buried them —"

"These brothers are at the top of my list," the ranger said, cutting the talk short.

"Think they'll come in without a fight?" Thorn asked.

"I don't know," said Sam. "I don't have much hope they will."

They rode up beside Roman Lee and his three-horse string and continued on in silence.

CHAPTER 4

Eighteen miles south of Perrito at a low dip in the trail, the ranger, Thorn and Roman Lee came upon an ornate open-topped Mexican stagecoach sitting off to one side of a rocky stretch. The elaborate rig, an older trail coach, was of a kind seldom seen on these treacherous, unkept Mexican roads and byways. There was an iron jack under its right rear wheel, which held the rig level, even though the wheel had been removed and lay beside the trail.

"*Hola* the coach," the ranger called out in a sociable tone as the three of them and the horse string stopped a few feet away. He lifted his sombrero from his head and placed it on his lap.

"*Hola* to you too, traveler," called a woman, one of three hot, tired-looking passengers who stood up from a row of stones on the roadside.

She turned her gaze from Sam to Thorn

51

to Roman Lee, looked them up and down and said, "Thank God for the three of you. Maybe our luck is taking a turn for the better." She modestly clasped her gingham dress closed at her throat.

A nervous-looking Mexican coach driver straightened from where he crouched over the broken wheel. A short eight-gauge shotgun with a full four-inch-wide flared barrel leaned against the coach.

"Buenos días, caballeros," he said.

He deliberately avoided looking toward the shotgun and kept his hand away from the butt of a large French pistol in his belt. He waited for a second to see if the three men would reply in Spanish or English.

"Buen día," said Thorn to show an amiable attitude.

The driver looked relieved.

"You have a big problem, *sí*?" Thorn added.

"Not so big, I think," the driver said with a guarded smile. "My fellow driver rides one of the horses to Perrito even now to bring back a new wheel-hub sleeve."

Sam made sure the driver and his passengers saw the badge on his chest as he looked back and forth along the trail.

"How safe are the trails for you to travel by coach?" he asked the driver. Wagon and hoof markings were plentiful in the dust on the trail.

"Oh, señor," the man said, apparently feeling better at the sight of the badge. "It is worse than I have ever seen. I thank the Virgin Mother you have come to us. Three riders have come by twice and looked us over, seeing what we might have. This is how they rob travelers here. They are in no hurry. They ride by once, twice, sometimes three or more times until they know that *we* know as well as *they* that there is nothing we can do to stop them. Then they attack like a pack of wolves and take whatever they want. Many of us are never seen again after they are done with us!"

Hearing the driver talk, the male passengers, a pair of well-dressed Swedes, walked over to hear better. They shoved small pistols into their waists now that they saw there were lawmen here to help them.

The driver gestured toward the woman and spoke more quietly. "I hate to think what they would do to this poor helpless woman. They would rip off her clothing and use her over and over until —"

"Take it easy!" Thorn said in a strong tone, seeing the shame and humiliation on the woman's face. He looked at Sam, then back at the driver. "How long has the other fella been gone?"

"He should be arriving back here anytime," the driver said. "The Lobos will not
bother an armed man on a swift horse. They
only want a coach, one carrying mail and
cash. When they come back this next time,
they will strike."

"We'll just see about that."

Thorn stepped down from Cochise's
saddle. He led the big animal over closer to
where the flared shotgun leaned against the
coach. He picked the gun up, set it against
his shoulder and swung it back and forth,
aiming it at random.

"I have always wondered how it would be
to shoot somebody with one of these hog
snouts," he said.

The Swedes ducked slightly and huddled
together while the driver moved farther
away. The woman stood her ground, but
crossed her arms and continued clasping
her collar.

Thorn lowered the shotgun and hefted it
in both hands. "This thing is light as a
feather, but I bet it'll send a man's head flying twenty feet straight up, whistling on its
way!" With a wicked grin, he looked at the
ranger.

Light as a feather? All right, Sam thought.
Thorn was telling him the shotgun wasn't

even loaded.

"Dan'l!" Sam said in a firm tone. "Let's help Roman Lee get these horses out of sight and give these desperadoes a surprise when they come back." He looked at the driver. "With your permission, of course."

"Oh, señores, yes, *por favor*! Stay here with us as long as you can! Maybe if the Lobos see your badge . . ."

"Happy to oblige," Sam said. "Sometimes that's all it takes."

Thorn walked over and took the lead rope from Roman Lee. He gave the woman a smile and a touch of his hat brim as he led the horses past her.

"I'll just get these cayuses out of sight, and I'll be right back, ma'am," he said.

"It's Pearl," she said. "My name, that is. I'm *Miss* Pearl Whitcomb from Ohio." She looked expectantly at Thorn.

"May I say you have a lovely name, Miss Pearl?"

"You certainly may." The woman blushed, and her arms uncrossed slightly.

"I'm Dan'l Thorn, Miss Pearl," he said, walking on with the lead rope and the horses in hand. "And I'm going to be right back! Hoping you'll tell me about Ohio, a place I have always longed to visit."

"Oh, I'll wait right here, then!" the woman

said, growing a little bolder as Thorn walked off the trail with the dead men's horses.

"What's that all about?" Roman Lee quietly asked the ranger, referring to the shotgun, the woman and the way Thorn had suddenly taken on the airs of a gentleman, so unlike himself.

Sam shook his head. Roman Lee caught a glimpse of the ranger's big Colt slip from his hand into its holster when he raised his sombrero and put it back on. Stepping down from his saddle, Sam led Doc and Cochise into a strip of shade on the other side of the stagecoach.

"That's just Thorn checking things out," Sam said finally. "Leaving no stone of possibility unturned."

"We're going to wait here with these folks until the other stage man returns?" Roman Lee asked.

"I think we should, don't you?" Sam asked.

"Yes, of course, I do," said Roman Lee. "I'm just thinking I still have my red Cowboy sash." He paused, not sure what Sam would think of him wearing it if these thieves came back around. "This part of Ol' Mex *is* all Cowboy country," he added. "Everybody knows what the red sash means."

"Get it. Put it on," Sam said with no hesitation. "With my badge and your red outlaw sash, we might start these bandidos walking the straight and narrow."

Caballo Saltando Village, the Valley of Mexico

In his trail clothes, with a thinly woven Mexican blanket worn poncho style, Nathan Catlow stepped down from his saddle in the plush yard of Dutch-Portuguese jeweler Bidden Matelin. He surveyed Matelin's recently acquired adobe rancho as he hitched his horse to one of the three iron rings on an ornately carved hitch pole. He caught a glimpse of someone at a front window. A shutter pulled slightly aside for a moment, then carefully closed.

At the front door, Catlow waited only a few seconds after pulling the bell chain before Bidden Matelin himself opened the door with a wide friendly smile.

"My, my! Nathan Catlow! To what do I owe such an honor?" he said. He opened the door wider before Catlow could offer a reply. "Traveling alone, I see," he continued, scanning the yard.

"Yes, all alone," Catlow said. "I'm on my way home from Esplanade. Thought I'd mosey by and let you know how it all went back there." He tilted his head in the direction of Esplanade, far behind him. His voice dropped lower and he said, "It is all right to talk here?"

"Oh, yes, of course," said Matelin. "Here, please, come in!" He closed the door and motioned Catlow into a large sitting room. "Have a seat. Can I get you a drink?"

Catlow smiled. "You can always get me a drink," he said.

Instead of taking a seat, he remained standing, facing the man, his hand holding his hat against his chest.

Matelin looked back over his shoulder into the large sprawling rancho.

"Constensia," he called out.

"*Sí?*" a voice called back.

"Bring *mi amigo* a drink, *por favor,*" Matelin said. He pointed a finger, flashing a large diamond ring at Catlow, and said, "Bourbon, no?"

Amigo? We'll see, Catlow thought.

"You know it, amigo." Catlow smiled. He noted how Matelin's eyes kept sweeping across his hat. He could put his hat back on and show that he had no gun behind it, but he'd wait, let Matelin sweat a little. "We are friends, like you said, eh?"

"Of course we are," said Matelin. "Why do you even ask me such a thing as this?"

58

His look turned concerned. "Is everything all right?"

Catlow shrugged. "Yeah, it is."

A woman walked in briskly and he took the glass of bourbon from the silver drink tray she offered.

"I mean, I think it's okay."

He gave Matelin a cold stare until the woman left the room. Then he set the glass of bourbon on a small table beside a large leather chair.

"But you tell me."

He stared hard at Matelin but let his hat droop in his hand, showing him there was no gun hidden behind it.

"What are you saying?" Matelin asked, seeing no gun behind the hat, yet knowing how quickly Catlow could bring one up.

"The device set the dynamite off a half hour later than it was supposed to," he said flatly.

"*What?* That's bad," said Matelin.

He tried to outstare Catlow, but saw right away it wasn't going to work. Breaking eye contact, he tried to talk past what Catlow might have had in mind next.

"However, I have to say," Matelin went on, "I have heard of it happening on occasion. That's the bad thing about mechanical devices. You can't rely on them the way you can a person. Had you been there and set the charge off by hand —"

"Shut up," said Catlow in a tone that brought an immediate response.

Matelin froze. He stared as if wondering what Catlow would ask next.

Catlow looked all around the beautiful rancho.

"How many clocks did you have set to afford a place like this?" he asked. "How many diamonds and sapphires did you cut and shape and turn into necklaces? How many watches did you fix?" He grinned a flat, mirthless grin. "A lot, I bet, huh?"

He reached his hat over at arm's length and let it fall onto the leather chair. Picking up his glass of bourbon, he swirled it and took a long, strong sip. He let out a bourbon hiss.

"Look," said Matelin, seeing it would do him no good to keep denying his role in what had happened, "I was told that this wasn't intended to kill you. It was only to make sure the watchman was dead and the bank manager got blown to hell."

"I believe you, Matelin, *mi amigo*," Catlow said in a half-mocking voice. "Now, you tell me who was behind it, and we'll be all done here."

"All right," said Matelin, "here's the part

you're not going to like to hear. I have no idea who was behind it."

"I think you do, Matelin," said Catlow. "Whoever set it up knew that a death sentence awaits whoever killed the manager. But if it ever gets out . . ." Catlow shook his head at the thought.

"It won't get out," said Matelin. "The way it was planned and carried out, nobody will ever tie any of it to the Cowboy Gang. There's no way in hell. Trust me, Cat!"

Catlow took his time as if considering everything the way Matelin was explaining it. He swirled the last of the bourbon in his glass, studying it, then tossed back the last mouthful and set the empty glass on the table.

"You know your bourbon, Matelin," he said with a thin smile. "I'll give you that."

Matelin smiled. "Let me have Constensia bring you another," he said.

Catlow raised a hand, stopping him.

"No, I'm good," he said.

"Well, then," said Matelin, "I take it we're through here?"

"No, no, no," Catlow chuckled. "Far from it."

As quick as a whip, he stepped forward. His left hand grabbed Matelin by his string tie, silver bullhorns and all. His Colt streaked up from his holster, cocked, jammed up under Matelin's chin. They stood eye to eye.

"Tell Buck to lay down the scattergun and step on out here with us," Catlow said in a low, easy voice, almost a purr.

"Okay, *okay!*" said Matelin. "Buck, you heard him. Drop the scattergun and come out here right now!"

Something in the sound of Matelin's voice told Catlow that his bodyguard-houseman, Buck Stanly, was not holding a scattergun and that he'd already been told to pay no attention to any order having to do with Matelin's head possibly getting blown all over this new beautifully furnished hacienda.

Catlow heard the squeak of a door, and he swung his Colt from under Matelin's chin in time to put a bullet in Buck Stanly's face as the man came charging in, a big Remington held out at arm's length, firing repeatedly and wildly.

"Look at your bodyguard over there, Matelin," Catlow said, his Colt back under Matelin's chin, the barrel hot to the touch.

Blood and bone matter ran down a wall across the large room.

"You don't want that for yourself, do you?" he said in the same easy voice.

"No! No! I don't," Matelin said, sounding on the verge of vomiting.

"Don't you get sick on me, Matelin, *mi amigo,*" Catlow said just for the hell of it. He shook the terrified man. "Here's what you need to tell me if you don't want to die like ol' Buck there."

When the woman ran in to see what had happened, Catlow stepped back without letting go of Matelin's string tie.

"Oh, no! Oh, no!" she screamed, shaking her head.

"Tell her I'm not going to kill her," Catlow said to Matelin.

But the woman had heard enough to shut her up.

Good! Catlow said to Matelin, "Tell me the name of every man you even think might have been in on setting up the bank robbery."

"And — and if I do, you won't kill me?" Matelin said.

"What did I tell you?" said Catlow like someone losing patience with a difficult child. "I said I won't!" He shook him as the woman stood watching, terrified. "I won't kill you, and I won't kill the woman. Tell her I said so so she'll believe it!"

Matelin told the frightened woman in her native language. Catlow listened.

63

"Now the names," he said to Matelin. "And I mean every one of them."

"Okay! *Okay!*" said Matelin. "There are three men at the top of the Cowboy Gang. They have taken over and are running this gang the way they would run a big business! Catlow, you would not believe how large this gang has gotten! It's bigger than *Los Pistoleros.* Remember them?"

"Yeah, I remember them," said Catlow, lowering his gun barrel an inch. "But I haven't heard much out of them lately."

"It ain't likely you're going to either," said Matelin, breathing deeper, the gun no longer against his throat. "The Pistoleros own all the judges, politicians, lawmen and border gangs money can buy! They pay off anybody who gets too close to them. And that's how big the Cowboy Gang is getting!"

"I know we're getting big, Matelin. I'm one of our leaders out here on the trails, remember?"

"Of course!" Matelin said. "And nobody is better at what you and your men do. But you're wanting to know who might have it in for you and want to pin the murder of the bank president on you . . . ?"

"Yeah," Catlow said, giving all this some close speculation.

"Well, I'm just saying," said Matelin,

"when you get too close to the top, maybe the top doesn't want you there. Maybe some of these men want you dead. Maybe they all want you dead — except me, that is! Maybe it's the only way to get you out of their way." He slipped his hand slowly inside his shirt and brought out a folded piece of paper. "There're the three names, Catlow. But God help me if they ever find out I gave this to you."

"I wouldn't worry about that if I was you, Matelin," said Catlow, taking a quick glance inside the folded paper.

He would remember the three names easily enough. He put the list in his pocket. Then with a smile, he raised his Colt back up under Matelin's chin and cocked it.

"Wait!" Matelin shouted. "You said you wouldn't kill me! The woman either!"

Catlow looked at the trembling woman, who stood to the side listening.

"Bourbon, Constensia, *por favor!*" he said to her.

She looked at Matelin, frozen with terror.

"Do as he tells you! Do anything he asks!" Matelin said. As she hurried out of sight, he said, "You don't have to kill me or her either. You even said you wouldn't!"

"Yeah, but I was lying," said Catlow, almost whispering. "I'm going to kill you

65

and her. Is there anybody else here?"

"No!" said Matelin. "Listen to me! I've got all kinds of money upstairs in an unlocked safe in the bedroom closet. Take it and go!"

Catlow chuckled and said, "You can bet I will."

"No, wait. That's not what I meant!" said Matelin.

"I didn't think it was." Catlow chuckled again.

In Bidden Matelin's manicured front yard, the groundsman who had just arrived and started sculpting a hedge almost dropped his pruning shears when he heard the shot ring out. Following the gunshot came a long, harrowing scream as he saw the woman Constensia bolt out of the hacienda naked, running wildly along the walkway, half of a broken glass pitcher in her hand.

Her scream released the plea for help that tore from her throat. It stopped abruptly as a bullet roared through the open doorway behind her and opened a red spray from between her bare breasts. She slid lifeless to a halt.

The groundskeeper stood like a man entranced, staring at the unfamiliar horse looking back at him from the iron hitch ring. He'd lost track of how long he'd stood there, a scene of horror acting out before his eyes. Even as the woman lay dead on the walkway and a veil of gun smoke wafted out the front door, the man who walked out with a bag over his shoulder did so calmly, swirling a half-full glass of liquid in his hand.

Whiskey, sí, *it must be,* the groundskeeper decided as if it were important to know.

Still, without moving, he watched the man mount his horse and ride first to where the woman lay on the ground. He looked down at her naked corpse and shook his head, his gun hand holding the big Colt atop the bag that was now in his lap.

After a moment he gigged his horse forward, veering toward the groundskeeper. With barely a glance, he raised his gun hand slightly. The Colt bucked as he shot the man once through the head. He kept moving, riding the horse out of the yard at an easy pace.

CHAPTER 5

Stripes of afternoon shadow had stretched down and crossed the trail by the time the second coach driver returned with an iron sleeve for the wagon's rear wheel. No sooner had he gone to work on the wagon axle than Roman Lee came walking up the trail from where he'd been watching for the three bandidos who'd circled the wagon twice like vultures.

"Looks like our road agents are back," he said, "and they've met a couple of friends along their way." As he spoke he took the red sash from over his shoulder and tied it around his waist above his gun belt.

With a suspicious look at the red Cowboy's sash, the second driver started to stand up slowly. Roman Lee had not been at the wagon when the second driver arrived.

"Easy, now," said Sam, motioning the man back down to work on the wheel. "This man is with us. He doesn't ride with outlaws anymore."

"We converted him," Thorn said.

He stepped over and handed Roman Lee a canteen of tepid water. While the erstwhile outlaw drank, Thorn picked up the eight-gauge relic of a blunderbuss leaning against the wagon.

"If nobody objects, I might use this deck cannon."

"It's not working, señor!" the driver said in warning. "I must tell you: Do not depend on it. I keep it in sight only to show people we mean business. It is loaded, but it will not fire!"

"I figured that from the looks of it," said Thorn. "I won't depend on it. But I'd just like to see how well it will bust somebody's skull." He gave a grin. "Call it curiosity of my trade."

"I understand," said the driver. "It has been riding on this coach for over twenty years, loaded but never fired." He looked at Roman Lee and said, "Much like your young friend's Cowboy sash. If it will keep someone from killing you, show it to them. If you are lucky, they will fear it and leave you alone."

"Amen to that," Roman Lee put in.

"Did you ever cock it and point it at a

tree?" Thorn asked.

"*Sí,* many times years ago," the driver replied with a sad look. "Never would it fire. I cannot fire it although it is loaded, and I cannot reload it until it has first been fired."

"That's too bad," said Thorn.

He hefted the eight-gauge in his hand and walked to where Miss Pearl stood with a worried look on her face. Opening the coach door for her, he said, "Don't you be frightened, Miss Pearl. You just climb in here and lie down on the floor until bullets stop flying and it's safe to come out."

Sam looked away and shook his head. Roman Lee cracked a thin smile.

"Could I . . . perhaps watch from above the edge of the door — unless it gets too dangerous, that is?"

Thorn gave Sam a bemused look, then said to Pearl, "Of course you can, dear lady. We'd be honored." He touched his hat brim.

"Our company's here," said Roman Lee.

"Let's spread out," Thorn said. "We don't want one shot to kill all of us." He glanced at Pearl, saw the fearful look on her face and whispered, "I'm joking, of course."

Five riders came into sight up the trail, two abreast, three right behind them. They looked confident at the sight of the wagon still sitting up on the jack. But seeing the ranger, Thorn and Roman Lee standing there looking steely eyed and expectant, like they had been hoping for a gunfight all day, gave the riders pause.

Between the red sash around Roman Lee's waist and the badge on the ranger's chest, the bandidos' minds appeared to have changed at the last minute. They would keep riding and look for easier pickings farther along the trail. There was no shortage of day travelers with money on them. So instead of stopping as they might have intended, they continued slowly riding past, staring at the coach, its drivers. Inside the coach, Pearl and the Swedish businessmen stared back.

A couple of the riders turned their gazes to one of their own who also wore a red sash, who Roman Lee recognized as Rady Stolz. The two of them had joined the Cowboys around the same time.

"Roman?" Stolz said, reining his horse almost to a full stop. "Roman Lee, is that you?"

The other four riders drifted on past him, and Roman Lee didn't answer. He stood staring straight at Rady Stolz as the other four riders nudged their horses slowly forward.

"Think this one would be worth talking to

if he knows anything?" Thorn whispered sidelong to the ranger.

"He might," said the ranger, "but —"

"Good enough," said Thorn, hurrying three steps forward and drawing back with the heavy eight-gauge before Sam could finish what he was saying.

Stolz turned but he was unprepared for Thorn moving in so fast, stepping up atop his foot in the stirrup and standing balanced there for the split second it took to swing the short, heavy shotgun around and smack him full force across his face.

"Hey!" said Roman Lee.

Thorn stepped back and touched down as Stolz crumpled from his saddle and down his horse's side into the dirt. The horse spooked and bolted out along the trail, straight through the four riders, who had a hard time collecting themselves. They had to make way for the runaway horse or be trampled. As the horse raced through the four of them, they immediately turned and started firing from their saddles.

Sam, Roman Lee and Thorn had wasted no time either. As shots exploded back and forth between the two groups of gunmen, Sam's big Colt sent a man flying from his saddle. The downed man's horse, spooked by the flying bullets and explosions, took off in the same direction Stolz's had taken. Thorn saw Roman Lee spin in place as a bullet grazed his arm and thumped off the side of the coach.

Pearl screamed. Two more bullets caromed into the coach's rear. The Swedes shouted in their native tongue. Thorn, who had started to run and take cover, turned instead and ran to the knocked-out Stolz, who lay sprawled in the dirt. Another shot hit the coach. Thorn wrestled with Stolz's limp body and managed to get it propped loosely in front of him.

"Hold your fire!" he shouted.

Swinging the shotgun around with one hand, Thorn planted the wide flared barrel up under Stolz's chin. The four-inch diameter of the flared barrel covered most of Stolz's face. He stared mindlessly down into the barrel as if he'd lost something there, but the weapon served to help hold him up in place as Thorn shouted again.

"Hold your fire, or you'll gather his brains in a bucket!"

"Hellfire, hombre!" shouted one of the bandidos. "You started all this! What's wrong with you anyway?"

"Not a damn thing is wrong with me!" said Thorn. "If you think I won't kill this knocked-out jake, watch this!" He reached his big thumb and cocked the gun's loud hammer.

"Whoa now! Hold on!" a voice called out. "Don't shoot him. There ain't no need in that!"

No need in that . . . ? Sam thought.

Sam and Roman Lee looked at each other.

"Are you sure Rady Stolz is in the Cowboy Gang?" Sam asked.

"He is," said Roman Lee, "but these others are just wild desert bandidos. They wouldn't be saying that if they were in the Cowboy Gang." The bullet graze in Roman Lee's forearm bled steadily.

"That's what I thought," Sam replied. He directed his words back to the bandidos. "Then all of you drop your guns and haul out of here. Come back in an hour, and your guns will be lying in a pile. Now get going."

"What about our man there?" the same voice called out.

"Pick him up in town this evening," Sam said. "We'll leave him at the jail. We won't say the lot of you were here to rob anybody."

"Because we weren't out to rob you," the man said. "Anyhow, the jail is closed down, so you can't leave him there. He's an Arizona Cowboy Gunman in case you don't know what you're fooling with. We're not, but he is."

"We know he's with the Cowboy Gang," said Roman Lee. "So am I. If you force us to splatter his brains out, I'll tell the Cowboy Gang you made us do it."

The man speaking turned to the man beside him. "Damn, this ain't no simple matter, is it?" he said.

A silence set in. After a moment, the same voice called out, "All right, we're going to leave. But our guns had better be waiting here when we come back for them."

"I'm through talking, fools!" said Thorn. "Here goes this man's head."

"No, wait! I told you we're leaving! Right now!" said the voice. "I've never seen a bunch like this!" He looked at the two drivers, who had taken cover under the big coach, and shook his head. "You people are crazy. Every last damn one o' yas."

The ranger, Thorn and Roman Lee stood prepared for battle as the riders gathered their horses and men without another word. Thorn had lowered the unconscious Rady Stolz until he sat sprawled, leaning back against Thorn's shins, his head lolled to one side at Thorn's knees. Thorn had turned the shotgun upside down and stood it pointing straight down, the wide flared barrel covering a large portion of Stolz's skull.

"Gringo lunático," one man whispered harshly to another.

As soon as the bandidos had ridden out of sight on the upward rocky trail, the driver working on the wagon wheel hurriedly finished inserting the new metal-hub lining, packed the hub with heavy grease and wiped his hands on a dirty work cloth. With the help of the other driver, he wrestled the big wheel into place and pegged it there with iron holding rings.

Pearl and the Swedish passengers all stood outside the coach now as the two drivers lowered the big jack. When the repaired wheel stood soundly on the dirt trail, the three clapped and cheered. So did both of the drivers.

"All right, folks," Sam said, "we've burned a lot of daylight sitting here. Let's get rolling before those bandidos change their minds and come back wanting to fight us."

An hour later as Sam and the others made their way to Perrito, the bandidos came back toward them, their horses at a slow walk. They looked beaten and dejected, each with holsters and saddle boot empty. The rider in front held a hand up in a sign of peace. He looked ashamed at having to pass this close by the ones who had taken his and his men's guns, not even by force but by verbal threats.

Thorn let out a little chuckle under his breath. He reached over and prodded Rady Stolz, who was riding unsteadily between Thorn and Roman Lee.

"Let it go, Dan'l," the ranger said as Thorn shook Stolz by the shoulder.

"I'm not starting anything, Ranger," Thorn assured him. He shook the half-conscious Stolz again. "Just letting these jakes know we're men of our word." He called out to the bandidos as they continued on. "We left all your guns back there. Nothing'll happen to them unless a squirrel starts fooling with them. You know how bad a squirrel can get."

"Stop it, Dan'l," said the ranger.

"All right, I'm done with it."

Stolz managed to turn a swollen purple face to Thorn, then to his bandido friends passing by.

" 'S goin' on?" he slurred painfully. "Why'm I over here? They're all over there, goin' that way."

"It's a long story, Rady," said Roman Lee quietly. "Go on back to sleep. You'll feel better later."

On the ancient stone-paved street running through Perrito, the people who made their homes or earned their living in the few businesses remaining in the crumbling adobe town stepped out into the long evening shadows and watched the large coach and the riders file past. The hot, dusty array of travelers and horses looked straight ahead as they went, like survivors of some terrible trial.

They didn't stop until a faded wooden sign beckoned them to a shaded cantina. A few yards from the cantina, a stone wall encircled a community well. As they veered their horses over to the cantina's hitch rails, a boy stepped out from some thin shade, eager to take their horses to the well and water them.

The boy carried a water gourd dripping fresh well water and handed it up the ranger. The ranger thanked him, but instead of drinking, pointed him toward the three passengers as they stepped down unsteadily from the coach.

Thorn, who dismounted and handed the boy his reins, looked all around the nearly vacant town.

"Just the kind of grand welcome I always hope for," he said to the ranger as Sam stepped down from Doc and also handed the water boy his reins.

Roman Lee helped Rady Stolz down from

his horse, noting that the gunman was recouping well enough after the long ride into Perrito.

"Do you know where you are now, Rady?" Roman Lee asked.

Stolz held on to the side of his saddle for a moment but he looked pretty steady on his feet.

"I'm in Little Dog," he said. "I mean, Perrito." He looked at Roman Lee with two black eyes, one badly swollen. "I still don't know who hit me or with what."

Thorn walked over with the blunderbuss hanging in his hand.

"I hit you, hero," Thorn said, "with this." He shook the short, heavy gun in his hand. "If I hit you with it again, you think it'll help your memory?"

Stolz looked at Thorn long enough to realize he wasn't joking. "No, I'm getting it all sorted out now," Stolz said.

"Look who's coming here," the ranger said quietly to Thorn and Roman Lee as two gunmen approached down the middle of the dirt street. Each of the gunmen wore a red sash around his waist.

"Easy now," whispered Roman Lee. "I know these two. They're all right."

He took a step back, drawing Stolz along beside him just in case. Thorn didn't budge

79

an inch. Neither did Burrack. They stood and watched the two men walk right past them with a touch of their hat brims and stop in front of Roman Lee and Rady Stolz.

"What are you two deadly gunslingers doing here?" one man asked Roman Lee jokingly. "Thought you were up in Bad River living high."

Roman Lee grinned. "All that good whiskey, all them sweet women," he said. "I knew if I stayed any longer they would kill me."

"So you hightailed it out right away?" the man asked.

"I did about two months later," said Roman Lee.

They laughed.

The man looked at Stolz, at his swollen purple face.

"The hell happened to you, Rady?" he asked. "You look like somebody busted you in the face with a . . . Oh . . ." He let his voice trail off, seeing the blunderbuss in Thorn's hand.

"I had a run-in with a damn storekeeper," Stolz said. "He slipped around from behind and let me have it with a two-handed shovel! My head rang like a church bell the rest of the day." He gestured a hand toward Thorn. "Hadn't been for my pal Thorn here, I'd have taken another hefty wallop or two."

"Thorn, huh?" one man said, eyeing Thorn closely. "You look familiar."

"I wore a badge down in the Nations for a while, bringing in criminals, renegades and such."

The two men nodded, but made no comment.

"And my other pal here is Arizona Ranger Sam Burrack," Stolz said.

The street seemed to go silent. Even the water boy stepped out of the way. The two men looked the ranger and Thorn up and down.

"Yeah, well, I'm Bob Adams," one said, "and this here is John Jones."

They both stared at the ranger. Thorn cradled the blunderbuss with his thumb over the hammer.

"Jones and Adams. I've heard of you two," Sam said in a mock-serious tone.

They all laughed. Then Adams said, "Since we're below the border, I don't reckon it matters you're both lawmen unless you're here working under the Matamoros Agreement."

Sam was surprised, but he only nodded. He was used to having to explain the Matamoros Agreement, which allowed him to enter Mexico to arrest wanted men. Let them think that wasn't the case now.

Jones changed the subject. "Where's your sash, Roman Lee?"

"I wish you hadn't asked," said Roman Lee. "Truth is, it got wet this morning. I stood too close to the jakes."

Both Adams and Jones nodded stoically. "We have all done that a time or two," said Adams.

"All right," Thorn said. "Who do I have to arrest to get a drink in this town?"

At first the two Cowboy Gunmen looked taken aback, but then they got it. "For a drink? Arrest us both," said Adams. "We'll come along peaceful-like."

They all turned and walked into Perrito Cantina, where Pearl and the two Swedish businessmen had already taken a table, a huge travel trunk on the floor between the two men.

Sam drew Adams to the side and said in a more serious tone, "Bob Adams, I didn't want to say out there but I am here on business. There're two brothers here who have done some terrible things."

"The Smith brothers, I'm betting?" Adams said.

"Yes," said Sam. "I'm here to take them back across the border."

"That's okay with us," said Adams. "We

82

all know how it works. And we know you too, Ranger. We heard what you did in Bad River. You killed that thieving Cree Sims, kept him from taking off with all our French gold. You blew the hell out of the mine where he had it hidden and we all got a piece of it!"

He grinned. Then he lowered his voice and said, "By the way, my real name is Doan, Eli Doan. Jones's name is really Jones, but it's not John. It's Randall. I can say this because I know neither of us is wanted anywhere. Leastwise not on this side of the river." He nodded east in the direction of the Rio Grande. "Now, if you want to come here and take out the Smith brothers, you're welcome to both them brain- and liver-eating sumbitches."

CHAPTER 6

On the dark stone street, lit torches hung on either side of the faded welcome sign reading BIENVENIDO above the arched adobe door of the Perrito Cantina.

A trail-weary Nathan Catlow rode in from the west, having traveled with his horse by train out of Mexico City, avoiding the Valley of Mexico as much as possible. He was used to riding in alone at night.

Two torches proved to be the only real light in this remote little hill town. They stood like sentinels warding off whatever human, beast or demon prowled in off the rocky high desert.

He was almost out front of the cantina when one of his street guards stepped out of the greater darkness of an alley with a rifle in his hands.

"Boss," the man said quietly, "it's me, Fairday."

"*Hola,* Fairday," said Catlow, bringing his

horse to a stop outside the flicker of firelight. "What have we here?"

Catlow asked the same question of his street guards when he returned at night whether he'd been gone for the day or for far longer. Russell Fairday had expected the question and was prepared for it.

"From the top," said Fairday, "we have two lawmen, but neither of them is a legal Mexico lawman."

Catlow only nodded.

"One is Arizona Ranger Burrack," the street guard went on, "the one who blew up the mine in Bad River and shot Cree Sims down like a dog."

"Sam Burrack," said Catlow. "I wonder what brings him here. As far as Sims goes, I'd have killed him myself had I been there."

"Oh, yeah, me too," said the guard. "Anyway, the word is, he and a former Nations lawman, Dan Thorn, are here to take out the Smith brothers."

"Take them out?" said Catlow. "You mean, Burrack is here to kill them?"

"That's what everybody generally thinks he means by it, boss," Fairday replied. "And that's usually the way he takes out people. Thorn too, from what our people say about him."

"All right," said Catlow, running the

information quickly through his mind, "what else?"

"A couple of our newer men rode in here with them, Roman Lee Ellison and Rady Stolz. Looked like somebody used the side of Stolz's head to hammer fence posts."

"Does he know who he is?" Catlow asked.

"Seems to," Fairday said with a shrug, "as much as usual."

"Is he staggering, walking into anything?" asked Catlow.

"Not that I've seen," said Fairday.

"Keep him away from the well until you see he's walking straight," said Catlow. "He'll get all right in a few days."

"Will do," said Fairday.

"What else?" said Catlow.

"Just a couple of Swedish businessmen and —"

"Good!" said Catlow. "I've been expecting them!"

"And a woman," said Fairday. "They're all three staying at the hotel."

"And a woman," Catlow repeated. "Is she a dove?"

"No, just looks like a plain, ordinary woman," said Fairday.

"All right," said Catlow. He stepped down from his saddle and tucked a travel bag under his arm. "I expect everybody's staying at the Eagle Nest Hotel?"

"Except for Roman Lee and Stolz," said Fairday. "They took up with the rest of our bunch."

"All right," said Catlow. He handed the street guard the reins to his horse. "Take him to the livery barn for me."

"Will do," said Fairday, taking the reins. "But can I just put something to you?"

"Go ahead," said Catlow.

"Not to second-guess anybody, boss. But if we ever wanted to kill this ranger and this Nations lawman Thorn, well, this would be a good time to do it. We've got a lot of men here, and I understand there're more on their way."

"No, not right now," said Catlow. "Right now let them do what they came here to do. Let them and the damned cannibals kill one another for a while. If we want to kill these lawmen, we can do it anytime." He grinned in the darkness. "And we will, I'm sure. But right now, let's just see what goes on here the next few days with them out to take down the Smith brothers and whatever else might come of it. Meanwhile, tell the two Swedes I'll see them now."

"Now?" said Fairday. "Tonight, you're saying?"

Catlow gave him a look. "Yes, that's

87

exactly what I'm saying."

Moments later, although it was the middle of the night, Russell Fairday walked into the dimly lit cantina, whispered to the two Swedish businessmen, then turned and left to go carry their large trunk to their room at the Eagle Nest Hotel next door to the cantina. Later, when the two Swedes were alone in their room, awaiting Catlow, they looked all around to make sure no one heard. One spoke to the other in English too good to be mistaken.

"Let's conclude our business with this pizzle of a frontier outlaw and get out of this godless land of lunatics!" he whispered.

The other only smiled demurely. He seated himself in a wooden chair and rested one hand on the large travel trunk sitting on the floor beside him.

When a knock came at the door, the one standing stepped over, opened it and stood to the side. Russell Fairday walked in first, a sawed-off double-barrel shotgun in hand. He looked around and seemed satisfied. Nathan Catlow followed. He stood silently looking at the large trunk and the man seated beside it.

"God kväll, min vän," said the seated man. He smiled as he stood and smoothed down

the front on his shirt. "In my country that means 'Good evening, friend,' " he said.

Catlow glanced from one man to the other, cool, comfortable. *"Och till er båda också,"* he replied in Swedish, a language he had hardly spoken since childhood. "In your country, that means 'And to you both as well.' "

The man near the door was taken aback by Catlow's speaking their language, but not so the one standing beside the tall trunk. He had learned that Nathan Catlow spoke Swedish. It was precisely what he needed to hear before any transaction took place.

The other man smiled with relief and started to say something more in Swedish.

"Hold it!" Catlow raised a hand to stop him. "Did we come here to talk Swede at one another, or do you have something for me?" He nodded at the tall trunk.

The seated man smiled again. "Aw, how I admire a man who gets down to business," he said, beaming at Catlow.

"Then let's try doing that," said Catlow.

"Yes, of course," said the man.

He stepped to the side, took out a brass key and unlocked the iron lock plate at the center of the trunk lid. He opened the lid a few inches, then stepped away and gestured, beckoning Catlow to come take a look.

Catlow and Fairday gave each other a guarded look.

"Stop wasting my time," Catlow demanded.

He walked over to where the other man stood in front of an oak closet door. He moved the man aside and swung open the door. On the closet floor sat a large canvas case with a lock at its center. Embroidered on its sides was a flock of wild geese flying over a snowy field.

Catlow brought the case over and dropped it on the wooden chair beside the trunk.

"Show me something that'll make me smile," he said to the man beside the trunk.

With Fairday holding the shotgun ready, Catlow put his hand around the butt of his Colt. The Swedes took note of it.

The one at the trunk hurriedly took out another key, unlocked the large bag and spread the top open. Catlow peered down at the bound stacks of U.S. currency.

"And there we have it," Catlow said. He raised his eyes and let his hand ease down from his Colt. "Get comfortable," he said. "You have to count it."

The Swedish men looked at each other. One said, "But we —"

Catlow laughed a little, cutting him off.

"I'm razzing you," he said. "I know it's all there. We pizzles of frontier outlaws trust you fellas." He grinned. "We want to do more business with you. You think?"

On the wooden boardwalk in front of the Eagles Nest Hotel, Pearl Whitcomb stood with a foot raised onto a chair and took a draw on a complimentary thin black cigar from the cantina. The drinking crowd, if you could call the cantina's dozen or so drifters a drinking crowd, had broken away one and two at a time and gone off to where drinkers go for the night.

Moments earlier she'd watched the silhouettes of three riders come out onto the street from a dark alleyway. While she smoked, two more came riding slowly up the street from east of town, the direction from which the coach had arrived. *Interesting.*

She watched a little longer and saw one more silhouette ride out of the alley. *What do we have here?* she asked herself.

She took another long draw on the cigar and watched closely. When a man came out of the cantina, sidled up to her and took her loosely by her arm, she almost jumped out of her shoes.

"Damn it!" she said before she could stop herself from swearing.

"Is this chair taken?" a deep drunken voice asked, ending with a lighthearted laugh.

Now this idiot! she thought. She quickly adjusted her foot on the chair and let out a puff.

"Yes, it is taken," she said coldly. "Can't you see my foot's on it?"

"I can sit right there with your foot still on it," he said. "I've always had an eye for comely female feet and footwear."

"Yeah?" Pearl bristled. She took a deep, hard draw and, holding up the cigar, said through a cloud of smoke, "What if I twist this around in your face, put your eye out for good?"

"I'm just trying to make talk here," the man said. "Take it easy. I've been drinking some all night. I thought you might be one of the cantina doves, but even if you ain't, I like your company."

Pearl took a breath and calmed herself. She'd not seen any additional silhouettes ride onto the otherwise empty street. She turned and seated the drunk in the chair. For anybody watching, he provided a good reason for her to be out here. Two men looked toward her in the flickering torch-light as they pulled a buggy to a hitch rail a block away.

"I've got only a dollar left," the drunk said, already sounding like he was drifting off.

"Don't worry about the money," she cooed as she snapped the dollar bill from his fingers. "You just relax. I'll do the rest."

He sprawled farther down in the chair with a whiskey-lit smile on his face.

"You just close your sleepy eyes and picture me beside you." She let him see her unbutton her dress and hold the top open. "I'll be right here, naked as a water pixie."

The drunk snorted and giggled, grabbing his crotch, trying to keep his eyes open. But he couldn't. In less than a minute, he was out cold. Pearl looked all around the dark empty street, rebuttoned her dress and hurried around the cantina into the long back alley that ran the length of the town.

Dan'l Thorn left his whiskey and half of a clay mug of beer on the bar and walked out without a word to anybody. After a few minutes, Roman Lee wondered what was taking the tall lawman so long out back.

All right, that's his business, Roman Lee told himself, a little tipsy from tossing back mescal shots and washing them down with foamy mugs of beer.

He waited a little longer, but finally he got

restless. He finished a beer, thought, *To hell with it,* and walked out back himself. Looking down along the edge of the men's drainage ditch, he saw no sign of Thorn. He did see what he decided were probably Thorn's boot prints overlapping with countless others. A few yards down the path, those clearer, fresher boot prints veered away from the ditch and led in the direction of the livery barn.

Getting interesting.

Roman Lee continued in the darkness, stooping every few yards and touching his fingers to the prints to help make sure he was still on the right track. The prints went past the rear of the hotel, the building next door to it and a freight office where the commercial street stopped. An empty lot of dirt and knee-high cacti stood between the businesses and the livery barn.

All right. Thorn had gone into the barn, Roman Lee was sure. At the sound of the barn door opening, he crouched and saw the ranger and Thorn ride out at a gallop. In a moment a liveryman closed the door behind them, and the two rode off on a trail leading out of town.

Roman Lee stood and dusted his knees as he stared out at the darkness that had swallowed the two of them. He wondered where they were headed and what they were up to that didn't include him.

Don't take it personal. They're lawmen, he reasoned. They had worked together in the past. *Anyway, it's their business,* he told himself.

He started to turn back toward the cantina, but the smell of the men's ditch was so bad, he turned, walked out to the street and back, the two torches guiding him into their circle of light.

He looked down at the snoring drunk who lay sprawled in the chair outside the cantina. A thin cigar stub lay crushed on the boardwalk beside him. From inside the cantina, he heard neither music nor women's laughter. The rest of the night would consist of nothing but the mindless babbling of tired drunks.

"What the hell do you want to do, Roman Lee?" he mumbled to himself under his breath.

He stopped outside the arched doorway and looked in. Rady Stolz and two Cowboy Gunmen sat at a table, the three swaying almost in unison.

Yeah, Roman Lee, what?

This time he didn't speak out loud. He looked around the darkened cantina. Rady Stolz had a hand spread and planted firmly on the tabletop, as if to keep himself from flying off the side of the earth.

If you leave now, what about Stolz? Roman asked himself.

Those Cowboy pals will take care of him, he replied to himself.

Anyway, Stolz could take care of himself. Roman Lee had seen earlier on the trail that Stolz was no easy kill. If he had been, the blunderbuss that Thorn had busted him upside his head with would have killed him hours ago as quick as a bullet in his skull.

"No matter," he mumbled. He stepped back from the arched doorway. *A man's first job is to keep himself alive. If he can't do that, the rest won't matter.*

Anyway, he was getting his horse and riding out. He'd let the cool night clear his head and see what was going on.

Adios, Stolz. He turned and walked back toward the livery barn.

The first sign of daylight streaked low, purple and blue along the Mexican hill as the ranger and Thorn stepped down from their saddles to stretch their backs and give their horses a short rest from scouting the area. A clean, clear brook trickled past them and they let the horses drink their fill. The men laid their near empty canteens down in the water and filled them while they waited, watching and gauging the slowly rising dawn.

When they'd met at the livery barn last night as planned, they'd seen that the big coach was still sitting in a corral where the pair of drivers had left it. Wheel tracks, both old and faded, recent and clear, ran out of the corral in every direction toward the stone streets and toward the trails out of town.

"I knew in my bones something wasn't right the minute we saw that broken-down coach on the trail," said Thorn. "Nobody in their right mind would take a big, heavy rig like that on these high trails. Breaking a hub sleeve is the least of what could have happened. They would have gotten robbed or killed, had we not come along when we did."

"Maybe, maybe not," Sam replied.

"What does that mean, 'Maybe, maybe not'?" Thorn asked.

"Nothing," said Sam, putting his remark away. "We both had a hunch something was amiss. Turns out, we were both right. The freight wagon we found back by the corral was obviously there for the stolen gold. We should have seen it but we didn't. The big rig was nothing but a ruse." He looked all around the rugged hillsides. "If there's more to it, we'll figure it out as we go."

"All right," said Thorn. "Far as I'm concerned, I'm ready to shoot the Smith brothers and go on about our business. Only fun I've enjoyed this whole trip was busting Rady Stolz upside his head."

The ranger only nodded. He walked along the water's edge in the hazy gray morning light. Along with wet hoofprints, he saw where the wide wheels of a freight wagon had stayed on the trail all the way from the corral, after other wheel marks had gone off in other directions.

Yep . . . he was now certain those tracks belonged to the same freight wagon they had found in front of the corral.

The wagon drivers had watered their horses here. He stooped and touched his fingers to water still lying in the wagon tracks, water that had dripped from their horses' wet muzzles when they moved along.

Close, very close, he told himself, walking on.

A few steps farther, he stepped away from the water's edge onto the trail. Now that dawn began to claim the light of day, he saw that the tracks the freight wagon had left behind continued a few yards, then turned upward onto a narrow trail and disappeared out of sight into rock, brushwood and bracken.

"You going to come get your mount, or am I required to start bringing him to you?"

Without reply the ranger walked back and took Doc's reins from Thorn, who had picked them up and held them while Sam scouted the rough terrain.

"Looks like our wagon has headed up on a rocky path," he said, nodding across the trail ahead. "We'll be catching up to them real soon."

"I believe we will," said Thorn. "Judging from the depth of their tracks, they're packing a heavy load. They'll be lucky if their horses don't pull up lame."

"Yep," said Sam. He stepped up in his saddle and laid his rifle across his lap. "The way it's breaking daylight this quick, if we're not careful, we'll run right over them."

"Then let's get to it," Thorn said. "If we don't get to have breakfast this morning, neither do they."

Riding on from the creek as dawn blossomed into daylight around them, Thorn and Burrack turned their horses up onto the steep path climbing the hillside. They followed the rocky path in the direction the heavy wagon tracks led them. Less than half an hour later, they caught the aroma of fresh coffee wafting over a rise in front of them and stopped near the edge of a cliff.

Tying their horses to a downed pinyon, the two eased forward in a crouch, rifles in hand. They peeped down unseen, hidden by a tall stand of wild grass.

In a clearing enclosed by pinyon and juniper sixty feet below, Sam and Thorn recognized the two drivers from the big rig they'd defended and escorted into Perrito. One of the drivers was bent down beside a small fire, pouring coffee. Slices of side pork sizzled in a skillet. The other driver stood looking down on a lower trail, a rifle in his hands.

"I'll be damned to hell!" Thorn said quietly, angrily.

"I wouldn't bet against it," Sam replied flatly.

As they watched, three more men walked over from where the wagon sat parked at the edge of the clearing, three horses resting in harness. The ranger took out his telescope from inside his duster and used it to gaze down on the three men as they walked to the fire.

"Yep, these are some of our bandidos," he said. "The whole bunch is working together."

He scanned the telescope over to the wagon bed and looked at the large travel bag sitting there, a rope tied around it to keep it in place on its rocky ride. From this overhead angle, he saw that the wagon bed appeared shallower than any he'd seen. Did the wagon have a false bottom in it? He believed it did, but he'd have to get a closer look to be certain.

"They have played us like a couple of damn fiddles," Thorn said. "I think we ought to ride down there, shoot the bunch of them, eat their breakfast and go back to Perrito. Get back some of the sleep this has cost us."

Sam lowered the telescope and slipped it back inside his duster.

"They played us for sure, Dan'l," he said. "I'm betting there was more in that big rig than a few dollars and some earthly goods. There's more at stake here than that."

"What do you mean, Ranger?" Thorn said.

"A while back, the biggest bank in Mexico City was robbed in the middle of the night."

"I heard about it," said Thorn. "The thieves blew out the safe and stole over half a million dollars in cash and gold coins that came all the way from the U.S, mint in Denver City."

"That's right," said Sam. "Nobody has seen a trace of that money, except for some spilled coins they left behind."

"Are you saying all this is tied to that big robbery in some way?" Thorn said.

"Well," said Sam, "the Cowboy Gunmen have their brand on everything that goes on between here and Arizona. I'm wondering if we didn't just help escort some of their stolen loot up to Perrito for them."

"I don't know," said Thorn. "That's a lot to take in on an empty stomach."

"Your letter does say we'll be working together to break up any factions of the Cowboy Gang and any other gangs we come across?" the ranger said.

"Yes, it does," said Thorn.

"Then let's treat it like it's the Cowboy Gang," Sam said, "until something tells us otherwise. We can always pull back and ride away from it. We've got cannibals to find, and we've got my list to work on."

"You're right, Ranger. Let's check everything out good before we stick out our horns and commence shooting."

■ ■ ■ ■

PART 2

■ ■ ■ ■

Part 2

CHAPTER 7

Before daylight, Nathan Catlow had taken the last long drink of whiskey from a tall wooden cup and sat for a moment, remembering the events of the past couple of days in Esplanade. He had thought of how well everything had gone off until someone tinkered with the explosive device and blew up the bank manager, leaving him smoking like a chunk of burned cinder. Other than that, it was a bank job he could be proud of.

Now he took off a boot and let it fall to the floor. He decided to wait a minute before reaching for his other boot, feeling suddenly drained, weary to his bones.

What the hell? he thought.

He felt around on the nightstand beside the bed for the wooden whiskey cup — couldn't find it. It didn't matter, he decided; it was empty anyway. Back to the robbery. He recounted the whole job to himself.

After all, it had been his idea. He'd set it up. He smiled.

There was no robbery the night the bank's safe had blown open. There were no broken locks, no jimmied doors or windows, no timeline for how quick to get the gold and cash out and hauled away. In fact, there was no large amount of gold or cash there. Only a little of each, only enough to make it look as if there really had been a robbery. There had actually been no robbery that night. It had all been staged.

For three weeks the real robbery had been taking place gradually, a little at time, under the supervision of his now deceased partner, the bank manager. By the time the staged robbery took place, the gold and the cash had been siphoned out and packed up in a warehouse where it was purchased by an unscrupulous consortium of Dutch businessmen and sent on its way across the ocean.

Clean as a whistle. He'd drink to that. Except as he looked across his room, bleary-eyed, to a partially full bottle on the dresser, he wasn't sure he could make it there and back. He leaned down to take off his other boot, but he never got the boot off and he never made it back upright. He rolled forward off the side of his bed, landed hard on his forehead, stalled there for a moment, then toppled over on his side, out cold.

In a hallway off the rear of Catlow's bedroom, where guards were often posted to watch and listen to whatever went on beyond the oak door, his street guard, Russell Fairday, held an ear trumpet pressed against the door and listened intently. An hour earlier he'd gone downstairs, had the desk clerk pour him a cup of whiskey and brought it back with him. Couldn't have been gone more than ten minutes.

Dozing with the ear trumpet to his ear and pressed against the door, he'd heard no sound until there came the hard thump of Catlow's head smacking the wooden floor.

"Oh, man!"

Fairday jumped up from his chair, dropped the ear trumpet and swung open the door into Catlow's room with his Colt drawn. Catlow lay in a ball on his side, struggling to raise himself, but finding no purchase.

Fairday holstered his Colt and pulled Catlow to his feet, one foot bare, the other in a high boot. Catlow stood unsteadily, trying to squint his eyes into focus.

"What the hell happened?" he asked, letting Fairday help him get seated on the side of the bed.

"I don't know, boss," said Fairday. "I think I heard you fall. I came right in, an' there you lay. Your head is bleeding!"

"Then get a towel, damn it!" said Catlow.

"Coming up, boss."

Fairday hurried out to a wardrobe in the hall. As Fairday looked for a towel, Catlow managed to pull himself up and stagger over to the closet, where the large carry bag of gold had been sitting since the two Swedes had left.

Gone!

Catlow looked around wildly as if the bag might reappear if he looked hard enough. He kept having to blink his eyes to keep them open. *What is this?* He looked at the bottle of whiskey on the dresser. *Have I been drugged like some ranch hand on his first trip to town?*

"Fairday!" he shouted.

Fairday came running. "What is it, boss?"

He pressed the towel into Catlow's hand. Catlow tried to shove it away, but then he changed his mind, snatched it from Fairday and held it to his bleeding forehead.

"Who's been in the room?" he said.

"Just you and me and, earlier, the two Swedes. I've been sitting out there listening in case they come back and decided to do some thieving."

Catlow grabbed the bottle from the dresser. Poured a drop on his palm and rubbed his palms together vigorously, then sniffed his palm closely. *There it is.* Even under the strong smell of whiskey, he found the unappealing aroma of bittersweet laudanum. He looked at Fairday as he touched his palm to the tip of his tongue.

"Somebody slipped me dope," he said. He stared hard at Fairday as he picked up the cork from atop the dresser, corked the bottle and tapped his palm on it firmly.

"Boss, it weren't me! I don't want you thinking I had anything to do with this —"

"Shut up," said Catlow. "If I thought you did it, you'd be dead before you hit the floor."

Fairday looked oddly relieved. He could see that the powerful drug still had a grip on Catlow. But Catlow knew how to handle it. He knew he'd have to force himself to keep going.

"Here's what I want you to do," he said. "First thing, tell the clerk downstairs to boil some coffee strong enough to float a pistol. If he's got any of the syrup that makes people throw up, get some of it. It's called ipecac. Then go to the livery. Wake the hostler, tell him to ready my horse and yours. Tell him to ready six more horses and stand them by the racks for the men going with us. They'll sort their saddle and such when they get there. Check and see if the big rig is still sitting there by the barn. Gather those six men, quiet-like. Don't make a big thing of this. Just get them back here ready to ride. Bring the new man, Roman Lee."

"Boss, these men will be too drunk to count their own peckers with both hands."

"I don't want them counting their own peckers, Fairday!" Catlow shouted. "If they can't sit in a saddle, we'll leave them lying on the barn floor."

"Yes, sir! It's all coming, boss," Fairday said, and sped out the door.

While he waited for Fairday to return, Catlow held his face over a large china washbowl and poured a pitcher of tepid water over his head. He set the pitcher down and dipped water up from the bowl and repeatedly splashed it in his face. It helped some but not enough. Every time his eyes managed to slip shut on him, he would once again start to drift away.

When Fairday came back, he brought with him a Cowboy Gunman named Foster Whill, who carried his saddle and bridle over his shoulder and a tied-down bedroll under his arm. The two stared at Catlow, who was once again sitting asway on the side of the bed with his eyes half closed.

"Boss," said Fairday. "Wake up, boss! The coffeepot will be right up, an' so will that medicine you want. I brought Foster Whill. He ain't been drinking none tonight."

Catlow forced himself to open his bleary eyes. He looked up at Whill standing over him.

"Yep, that's me," said the red-bearded gunman. "Sober as a judge for tonight only. Tomorrow I'll be drunker than a skunk. So let's get this thing moving. I've got a big Spencer rifle that will knock the ass end plumb off of a flying duck."

"That's what we want here," said Catlow, sounding thick tongued. He forced himself up onto his feet to keep from dozing off again. "What about the stuff I wanted you to get from the clerk?"

"It's coming, boss," Fairday repeated. "The clerk says be careful with it. It'll toss your stomach up for you, but it can hurt you if you take too much. The clerk says it'll make you puke up your boot soles if you ain't careful."

Without responding to the warning, Catlow slipped a big knife, sheath and all, down the center of his back behind his belt.

"What about the rig?" he asked, sounding

111

better the longer he worked at clearing his head.

"The rig is there, boss," said Fairday, "but somebody opened the compartment in its bed and gone through it. It's empty."

"Damn it!" The news, although bad, helped to clear Catlow's head. "All right, nothing we can do but ride down the snakes who did this and kill them."

He dropped back down on the edge of the bed, picked up his boot and put it on. He stamped it into place, then picked up his gun belt from the bedstead and swung it around his waist.

"Let's go catch up to these sumbitches before daylight," he said. "I'm ready to do some serious killing."

Fairday and Whill gave each other a dubious look, knowing it would be next to impossible to catch up before dawn, even though the tracks said there was a freight wagon involved.

"Okay," said Catlow. "Maybe we can't travel that far by daylight, but we can sure as hell get as far as Caballo Creek. Everybody leaving from here has to stop at the creek and water their horses."

CHAPTER 8

"Hold on here one damned minute! I can't believe this!" said Thorn, turning the telescope all around clumsily in his hands. "This blasted thing has quit working!"

Shaking his head, Sam watched him turn the telescope back and forth in confusion.

"You've got it backward," he said to Thorn. He reached out to take the telescope, which Thorn didn't want to relinquish at first.

"I know how a damn army telescope works!" he said. But he let go when the ranger yanked on it.

"Then you know that this way is backward," Sam said quietly. He turned the telescope around and laid it precisely into Thorn's waiting hands, pointing it forward. "Remember, look through the small end; the large end stays out front."

"I was just holding it backward to figure out why it was blurry!"

"I understand" was all Sam said in response.

Thorn grumbled, raised the telescope to his right eye and looked down through it.

"Just like I thought!" he said. "See the woman down there?"

"I see her," Sam said. "She wasn't there a few minutes ago."

"It's Pearl Whitcomb," said Thorn. "She must be a part of this bunch too. What do you think?"

"Her hands are tied," Sam said. "If she's one of them, why do you suppose they've got her tied up?"

"No, they haven't tied her," Thorn said. "I can see better through this lens."

"Maybe she tied herself," Sam said, looking down. "Either way, somebody tied her. I can see it without the lens. Her hands are tied in front of her. A prisoner's lead rope is hanging to the ground behind her. No, wait," he added. "A man standing behind her is holding it."

Thorn gave him an exasperated look. "How the hell can you tell her hands are tied? I can't see her hands from here with or without a telescope!"

"I can see she's tied by how she's standing," Sam said. He reached for the telescope. "People stand different when their

114

hands are tied."

"I know that," Thorn said. He put the telescope in Sam's hand. "It's just not something I was thinking about at the moment. Now that you mention it, yes, I do know that people stand altogether different when their hands are tied. So there."

"I understand," Sam said quietly. "Let's get on down there. You can ask her why she's tied and who tied her." He collapsed the telescope and put it inside his duster. "If we don't hurry, we might be having to ask Catlow and his men."

With her foot, Pearl Whitcomb had rolled a wet log as close as she could get it to the campfire. She sat on it with her tied hands clutching a coarse wool blanket to her breasts. The side of her head felt swollen and raw where one of the men had back-handed her over an hour ago. *What low, rotten bastards you are,* she said to them but only in her mind.

She'd had to beg them for the blanket after losing her coat fighting them when they'd found her snooping around near their horses before daylight. She was still shivering cold, but she dared not say or do anything now that might cost her the wool blanket or earn her another sharp blow

115

across her face. She stared around the fire from one face to the next. *These filthy, lousy, no-good —*

"Show us your legs up to your knees," said an old man the others called Junior. He sat at the fire, turning sizzling slices of pork in a skillet with a two-pronged meat fork. "This is some mighty tasty young pig here. We see some knees, you'll get some of it." His request ended in a watery cackle as he waggled a floppy slice of frying meat on the long fork.

"Damn it, give the woman some food, Junior!" said one of the men.

"She'll get something when I get something," the old man said. "Not a minute before!"

"Here's something you'll get, you old reprobate," the man said. "Give her some food or I will stick your face down in the fire and stand on the back of your head!"

He started rising to his feet. Because he was a man whose threats should not be taken lightly, Junior's old eyes widened in terror.

"I'm only joking, Ollie!" he said quickly. "Can't a man say something joking without getting jumped on and burned alive?"

"Not in your case, Junior," Ollie Prew said. "Every morning I look at you, I can't help wanting to bury your face in a fire and stand on your head! Today . . . well, today I think is the day I'm going to have to do it!"

He spread his big arms wide, like an enraged grizzly, and took a step toward Junior. The old man let out a rough scream and jumped to his feet, still gripping the meat fork.

Abruptly, Prew stopped, frozen in place. As a bullet entered his back, a thick ribbon of blood spiraled out of the center of his chest, transformed itself into a heavy red spray and showered everything around the campfire. The fire sizzled. Pearl's face was badly splattered, as was the old man's. Ollie Prew fell dead across the fire.

In a panic, old Junior stabbed the meat fork deep into one of the dead man's wide-open eyes, then turned and ran, a scream hanging like a blaring siren in his wake. As soon as the rifle shot had exploded from the edge of the clearing, Pearl had shoved herself backward off the wet log and hugged up against it for cover. Her blood-splattered face pressed into the sour earth.

"Good shooting," the ranger said aloud to himself, knowing Thorn was too far away to hear him. As soon as he'd fired, Sam galloped out of the tree line. He led beside him a horse he'd just grabbed from the rope line of saddled horses the men had tied off near the big wagon.

The idea was that Thorn would keep everybody rattled and pinned down while Sam untied the woman and got her into a saddle and the two of them cut out.

So far, so good.

Not only had he stolen a horse for the woman to escape on, but he'd even managed to get a look inside the freight wagon. It did indeed have a false bottom. The secret space hidden from sight carried many large bags of coins. A quick slash with his boot knife revealed the coins as brand-new, bearing the stamp of the Denver City mint. Another slash freed the horses from the rope line and sent them scattering, putting distance between themselves and the loud gunfire.

Time to go!

Sam had considered taking the large carry bag with him, but decided the weight of it was too much. The bag with its wild geese embroidery would have to wait. If he could get himself and the woman out of here alive, that was enough for now. He did see three gold coins lying stuck under the edge of the carry bag, and he pulled those loose and took them.

Proof the gold was here and is still here!

In the next moment he was riding across the clearing like the wind, Doc's hooves pounding fast and determined beneath him. The horse beside him kept up, the sound of gunfire and its reins in Burrack's hand keeping the animal pushing hard.

From the ground against the wet log, Pearl saw the ranger and the second horse coming her way. The bandidos firing at Thorn showed little interest in the ranger racing diagonally across the clearing, not firing a single shot in his direction. These men were focused sharply on the shooter in the opposite direction. He had killed three of them and seemed fully intent on and capable of killing more. Owing to the shooter's deadly accuracy, the bandidos poured their fire at him.

"Hurry! Let's go!" Sam called out, swinging the spare horse around to where she lay. He jumped down from his saddle. With the knife from his boot well, he sliced the ropes from her wrists and tossed them aside.

Wasting no time, Pearl reached up, grabbed her saddle horn and felt Sam give her a firm upward push into the saddle. Sam handed her the reins and threw the blanket from the ground over her lap. She straightened herself quickly and batted her heels to the horse's sides as Sam slapped the horse on its rump. He turned and jumped up into Doc's saddle and put him forward in a full run.

"They're getting away!" Sam heard someone behind them shout as the two dashed wildly across the clearing.

Yet as two gunmen fired at Sam and Pearl, Thorn's rifle, like some dark vengeful thing, seemed even more intent on stopping the gunmen. One fell dead. The other hugged the ground, dirt kicking up around his ears.

"Are you all right?" Sam asked the woman.

The two of them slid the horses to a halt, spinning them around to look back toward the ongoing sound of gunfire.

"I'll do," Pearl said, catching her breath.

"Good," Sam said. "Get down and take cover."

Out of the clearing now and inside the shelter of the pinyon timber, Sam drew his Winchester from his saddle boot and gave Doc a slap on his rump, sending him deeper into the forest undergrowth. The big stallion seemed to know what was expected of him.

"Give me a gun, Ranger. I can shoot!" Pearl said, rubbing her wrists where she'd been tied.

Sam jerked open a saddlebag, pulled up a spare Colt .45 and handed it to her.

"It's carrying all six rounds," he said. "You probably won't need more, but if you do, there're more in there." He nodded at the saddlebags. "Soon as we draw their fire away from Thorn, we're gone. There're Cowboy Gunmen breathing up our shirts by now. This gunfire is only going to stir them up more."

They tied her horse in the shelter of the standing pinyon and hurried to the edge of the clearing. They began to fire on the bandidos. With his boot knife, Sam cut a hole in the middle of her blanket and helped her pull it over her head, poncho style. With the ranger and Pearl shooting at the gunmen's left flank, and Thorn's deadly rifle fire hammering straight on in front of them, the gunmen started to see the value of their position become questionable at best. One and two at a time, they left their cover and ran toward the horses and the big wagon.

"Our horses are gone!" some of them shouted, running back into sight, at which point Thorn picked one of them off in a full run, then another.

But then the firing from the gunmen waned almost to a halt. Sam held up a hand, telling Pearl Whitcomb to hold her fire. She gave him a sharp questioning look.

"We're not hitting anything," he said to her. "We're only wasting our bullets."

"What's happened to your partner, Dan'l Thorn?" she asked, slumping on the ground against a tree, letting the warm Colt rest on her lap.

"I don't know," said Sam, "but we're going to find out."

"Easy does it, Ranger," they both heard Thorn say. "I'm just changing positions, is all."

He walked his stallion, Cochise, out of the heavier undergrowth and stopped close to them. "Miss Pearl," he said, touching his hat brim.

Pearl nodded in reply.

"If either of you is wondering why I shot that first jake," Thorn said, "it's because I saw he was about to ruin breakfast for everybody."

"So you solved that by shooting him into the fire," the ranger said.

"I had him falling some to the left, not forward the way he did." He shrugged. "Anyway, breakfast is off now. I came over here to tell you, we've got Catlow and some of his men riding this way. I saw them crossing a lower trail. I make them to be a couple of miles back, give or take."

"When were you going to tell us?" Sam asked, keeping cool about it.

"Just now," Thorn said calmly. "You've left these jakes stranded on foot, and I'm speculating Nathan Catlow and the rest of the Arizona Cowboys are more than a little aggravated over their gold getting stolen. Question now is, do we want to stay here, keep our heads down and watch a good fight, or mosey on, see what we can see of it until we get out of sight?"

"I'm for going on," Sam said. "I've seen gunfights. Missing one won't upset my day."

"That's about how I feel," said Thorn. They both looked at the woman. "What say you, Miss Pearl?" Thorn asked. "Should we go or stay right here and watch the fireworks?"

The woman looked haggard, exhausted and beaten. She shook her head, careful of her swollen face.

"To hell with the gunfight," she said. "What about all the gold on the wagon and in the carry bag? Are you saying leave all that gold behind?"

"Yes," Sam said flatly. He stepped over, unhitched her horse and led it back. "What are you doing out here anyway?" he asked Pearl. "Stealing gold with these bandidos?"

"No, I'm not," said Pearl. "But I do have

an interest in the gold. I've been trying to chase it down ever since it was stolen from the big bank in Esplanade."

Thorn gave her a curious look and said, "You're a Pinkerton?"

"No," she said. "I'm not. But I am working for an investigation agency. My own." She paused to let it sink in. "I worked for the Butterfield Agency until it changed hands. Then I started my own business. Whitcomb Detective Services."

"We knew there was something about you," Thorn said. "We couldn't put it together —"

In the distance rifle fire resounded from over the rise, along the trail that had brought them here.

"Uh-oh," Thorn said. "It appears our Arizona Cowboys have arrived." With one hand he levered a round into his rifle chamber. "Shall I show them in?"

Both men looked at Pearl questioningly.

"I'm not leaving without that wagon," she said determinedly.

"We understand," Thorn said.

He took a short step forward, snatched the Colt from her hand and pitched it to the ranger. Sam caught it and checked it quickly. It was down to one bullet. He

124

shoved the big Colt into his belt for the time being.

"We've got no time to discuss it just now," Sam said.

Over the rise more gunfire resounded a little closer. He scooped Pearl up and tossed her onto the saddle. The horse stomped the ground restlessly, and Thorn held tight to its reins.

"Okay, okay! I'll go," she said. "I'm not a fool! I don't want to get myself killed. But we can discuss the taking of the gold later, can't we? I mean, over a cup of coffee, maybe? It's not Catlow's gold. Right?"

"Sure thing, Miss Pearl. You can bet we'll talk about it," said Thorn with a dark chuckle. "We can hardly wait!"

CHAPTER 9

After over an hour of hard fighting, Nathan Catlow's men shot their way in and surrounded the forest clearing. Sam, Thorn and Pearl Whitcomb heard the fighting intensify from miles across the hills as they put as much distance between themselves and his Cowboy Gunmen as possible. Catlow had to stay back from the fighting, hanging against a tree, his stomach cramping fiercely, his projectile vomiting raising sour stares from the men, including all those who'd caught up to him and the six who'd ridden out with him early that morning.

"What do you suppose it is?" one asked. "If it's that green-possum mountain fever going around, he'll likely die of it."

"Hell, it's nothing like that," Fairday rebutted. "Some sumbitch poisoned his whiskey with Dr. Steadfast Laudanum."

"Damn!" the other man replied. "It sounds like he's poisoned hisself. I've drunk a whole bottle of Doc Steadfast over a night of mescal and *cocaína*. Never had so much as an ill-mannered belch."

From out of sight came a wet billowing roar from Catlow.

Fairday and the others winced. The sound of gunfire exploded ahead of them from the clearing in the pinyon forest.

"It ain't the Doc Steadfast Laudanum that's got him pinned to a tree. It's some medicine called ipecac. The hotel night clerk gave it to him to slow down the laudanum."

"Hmmm." The other man shook his head. "I'll wager that's one dead hotel clerk soon to come."

"Cat asked for it by name!" said Fairday. "I reckon he knew what he was doing. Never thought of it as being something likely to kill him!"

The man lowered his voice. "I hope your nose is clean in all this, Fairday."

"I've looked out for Cat like he's kin," Fairday replied.

Loose talk of the medicine and his part in Catlow taking it made Fairday nervous. Out of sight, Catlow let go of an awful upsurging heave.

"All right, that's enough talking," Fairday said. "Get up there with all your brothers to the bone and get that damn gold back! That would do a lot to make Cat feel better."

Another heave came from the direction of their boss and the men broke away.

"Great saints above," one man said over his shoulder as they went, "I'd sooner get shot at by bandidos than have to listen to this mess."

When the men were out of sight, Catlow eased forward and stood beside Fairday. He looked weak, with one hand pressed to his sick stomach and the other carrying a canteen he used to wash his mouth out after each violent round of vomiting.

"How's it looking up there?" he asked Fairday, trying to control his shaky voice.

Fairday had noticed his boss's mind had grown clearer since the laudanum had loosened its grip on him. Had the ipecac medicine helped? He had no idea, and he wasn't about to mention it.

"Turns out, these bandidos are fighters, boss," said Fairday. "There're more of them than we thought. They must have had others waiting for them out here, just in case they needed help."

"Oh, they'll need even more help," Catlow said, "when we get through with them. . . ."

He turned and hurried over to the edge of a stand of young juniper. He spewed.

"Aw, man!" said Fairday. He walked away, closer to the sound of gunfire, which he realized had diminished over the past few minutes.

"Mr. Fairday, I have a message!" a young Cowboy Gunman called out.

"Over here, amigo." Fairday beckoned the young man closer. "What is the message? And don't call me Mr. Fairday."

"Yes, sir, Russell . . . ?"

"Don't call me Russell either!" said Fairday.

"Sir . . . Mr. . . . I mean —"

"Just give me the message!" said Fairday. "We'll figure names out later."

"The bandidos have pulled out, but the wagon is gone too!" the young man said, avoiding any names.

"Damn it all!" shouted Fairday. "How long?"

He grabbed his horse and Catlow's by their reins. Catlow heard him cussing and came running from his tree.

"Could have been anytime since we arrived here!" the young man said. "What should I tell the men?"

"Tell them to get on the wagon's tracks and stay on them," Catlow shouted as he ran up. "You go with them!" He grabbed

129

his horse's reins from Fairday. "We'll catch up!"

"Yes, sir, Mr. . . . I mean, Cat . . . er . . . Catlow . . . I mean, boss," the young man stammered.

"Go, boy! Go!" Catlow shouted to get him moving.

When the young man took off running back toward the clearing, Fairday started to say something, but Catlow hurried back toward his tree, a hand raised in the air to keep things waiting on him.

After a moment of unproductive dry heaving, Catlow turned and came back from the tree.

"All right," he said, reaching Fairday and their waiting horses, "let's get 'em. I want the gold back, and I want all of the Lobos dead!"

With some of his former strength, he took the saddle horn with one hand and swung up into his saddle.

"Are you coming?" he said as Fairday stood watching with concern in his eyes. "Or are you waiting for a written invitation?"

"I'm right with you, boss!" said Fairday, reaching for his horse's reins.

At the spot where the loaded wagon had

sat, three of Catlow's men stood waiting with guns in hand, horses ready to ride. Fairday arrived a full minute before Catlow, who rode along slowly, hanging sideways in the saddle, heaving at the ground.

"What's that all about?" asked one of the three, walking up to Fairday with the cut rope the ranger had left behind.

"He's sick, Freddie," said Fairday. Wanting to change the subject, he asked, "What have you got there?"

"Somebody cut all their horses loose and scattered them out of here," Freddie Mason replied, indicating the sliced end of the rope that had held a line until the ranger slipped in and cut it.

"Yep," said Fairday, "it was cut sure enough. Why would somebody do that?"

He looked around as if his answer lay among the dead scattered on the hillside.

"I don't know," Freddie Mason said. "A friend of theirs, I reckon. The thing is, they didn't cut the wagon horses loose."

Catlow rode up and heard the last few words. "That was big of them," he said with a streak of sarcasm, and took the sliced rope Mason held out to him.

"How're you feeling, boss?" Mason asked while Catlow examined the sharp slice a big knife had made.

"Better, thanks," Catlow said. "Someone among them must've wanted the gold for themselves. Who knows how these frontier bandidos think?" He let Mason have the rope back.

Catlow stepped his horse along the tracks left by the loaded freight wagon. "Look how its headed," he said, pointing off into the pinyon forest, "straight out of the pinyon onto miles of a wide surface of stone and probably all the way down into the valley, then the desert."

"Don't worry, boss," said Freddie Mason. "We'll ride them down. They ain't gettin' away with this."

"What do we have here?" Catlow asked, turning in his saddle to see two of his men shoving a wounded bandido along in front of them. "Wait. I recognize this man. He used to be one of us."

The wounded man's hands were tied and his chest was covered with blood. "Howdy, Nathan Catlow," the prisoner said.

"Devin Terne," said Catlow. He drew his Colt, cocked it and laid it across his lap. "What a sight you are. Is this why you left the Cowboys, to join a low bunch like *Los Lobos*?"

Catlow looked him up and down in disgust and disbelief. The man's clothes were old and ragged. His boots were worn down in the heels. His empty holster looked dried out and ready to come apart at the stitching.

"Don't foul-mouth us too badly, Catlow," the man said. "We did manage to take all that gold you and your bunch worked so hard to steal." He gave a painful-looking grin.

Catlow offered a slight smile himself. "You got me there, Terne," he said. His stomach felt better than it had all night and all day. *Maybe you just need to kill somebody,* he told himself. "Let me ask you something. Which of you band of privy rats poisoned my whiskey?"

Terne looked genuinely surprised. "Poisoned your whiskey?" he said. "Catlow, I'll be honest. Every one of us bandidos is a mama-flogging, snake-head-eating —"

"I know all that," said Catlow. "Who the hell poisoned my whiskey?"

"If I knew, I would kill that sumbitch myself," said Devin Terne. "Poisoning a man's whiskey is something no real man would do to another. What did he poison it with?"

"Dr. Steadfast Laudanum," said Catlow, the thought of it bringing back a terrible sourness in his belly.

"Hell, I drink it in my whiskey all the time when I can get it," Terne said.

"Not this much," said Catlow. "This man who did it knew he was poisoning me, so I figure he softened the taste of it enough so I couldn't recognize it right away. I've been drinking ipecac all night. It's helping but not much."

"Ipecac? My Gawd, man, that stuff is more likely to kill you than laudanum and whiskey!"

"So you deny knowing who did it," said Catlow. He gave Terne a cold, narrow gaze. "How long will it take me, say, with a hot skinning knife to get you to admit who did it?"

"It wouldn't take long before I come up with a name," said Terne, "but I'd be lying, 'cause I don't know nothing about it."

"Build me a fire," Catlow said sidelong to Russell Fairday.

"Coming up, Cat," said Fairday. He swung down from his saddle. "You want these others to get after the wagon whilst you scorch him?"

Catlow considered the question for a second.

"Cut him loose," he shouted. Then he looked down at Terne and said, "You're coming with us. I'm not through with you."

Terne held out his tied wrists. Fairday cut the rope and let it fall. Terne rubbed his wrists and looked into his shirt long enough to see that the bleeding from his chest wound had slowed down considerably. The bullet had hit his upper ribs, veered left and come out under his arm. He sighed and closed his shirt.

"Can I get a horse, somebody?" he said.

CHAPTER 10

Thorn turned in his saddle atop a rise and saw the freight wagon hurrying over a bald stone ridge reaching out from the bottom of the pinyon forest. Four men, two on either side, rode hard to keep up with the team of wagon horses. Seeing Thorn's attention on the wagon and riders, Pearl and the ranger stopped also.

"There're our bandidos," Thorn said, "fixin' to show us how to run a good team of horses right off a slick-top cliff."

"It's the gold! It's the gold!" Pearl shouted.

Before either the ranger or Thorn could stop her, she gigged her horse soundly and headed, full run, down the path that would intersect with the trail the wagon riders were on.

"I'll meet you down there," she shouted back over her shoulder.

The ranger started to call out to her, but

he saw it would do no good.

"There goes a woman truly given to the spirit of the chase," Thorn said.

"She is committed," Sam agreed. "If she catches up to them down there, they'll kill her without even slowing down."

"Yep, that's what I see coming," Thorn said, shaking his head slowly. "You think you're getting to know a woman," he went on. "Then somebody shakes a wagonload of gold at her and she comes apart, raving like a fool."

"Let's go," Sam said quietly. "Let's see if we can keep her alive."

"Good idea, Ranger," Thorn said.

But before either of them could put their horses forward, a heavy barrage of gunfire erupted from lower down, out of sight on the bald ridge.

"Uh-oh," said Thorn, "she hasn't had time to get that far yet."

They put their big stallions forward in a run, going as fast as they dared on trails that steep and treacherous. On the next hill over, the gunfire continued almost nonstop. Both of them knew that the woman would not be part of the gun battle going on. Like as not she had gone and gotten dangerously close, but she would have ducked down and lain low once it started raging full bore.

They were right.

Lower down on the trail, they were close enough to the battle that they could hear bullets striking trees above their heads. They dropped from their saddles and led Doc and Cochise along a shallow ditch running alongside the rocky trail. Guns blazed in the very near distance, too near for comfort. Less than thirty yards along the ditch, Sam spotted a large smear of blood right on the edge of the trail and stepped up in a crouch for a closer look.

"Dan'l, over here," he said.

No sooner had he spoken than he saw a horse's leg sticking up from the ditch on the other side of the trail.

"I'm coming," said Thorn.

"Ranger, is that you?" called a weak voice a few feet from the downed horse.

"Yes, it's me, Pearl," Sam replied in a measured tone.

"And me," Thorn said, arriving beside the ranger, his rifle hanging in his hand.

They stepped in close and saw she had slid under a downed pinyon.

"Th-they shot my horse," she said. "He went down with me and I slid under here. Can you get me out? It's hard to breathe under here."

"We'll get you out," Sam said. "Just hold

on. Breathe as deep as you can."

He looked around at the downed horse to make sure it was dead. A large bullet hole high in its ribs assured him it was. Slipping his big Colt into its holster, he crawled down to the very bottom of the rocky ditch.

Thorn leaned his rifle against the rocks and bowed over the pinyon log. He tested the weight of it.

"Only one lift, Ranger," he said. "Pull fast."

Sam stooped over the woman and got his arms ready to throw around her.

"Go," he said.

As Thorn raised the log a few inches, the ranger gave a fast pull with his arms under the woman's armpits.

"Got her!" he said, and he felt the ground jar when Thorn turned loose of the downed log.

Freed from under the log, the woman took a moment getting onto her knees; then Sam helped her to her feet. When she nearly swooned and fell against him, he scooped her up and carried her up to where Doc and Cochise stood waiting.

"I'm okay — no, really," Pearl said. "You can put me down."

But Sam lifted her up into Doc's saddle anyway. Thorn took the precaution of stepping into his saddle and holding Doc's reins until Sam mounted and set the woman on his lap.

"I'm afraid I've lost the pistol you lent me, Ranger," Pearl said, sounding better but still understandably shaken.

"I've got a feeling we'll find replacements on our way down from here," Sam said.

The gunfire had stopped now, but as strong and steady as it had been, the three of them were certain there would be dead and wounded down along the trail.

Moving down steadily, quietly, they could hear gunfire in the far distance, too far away to be concerned with, unless of course it started getting closer.

Rounding a downhill turn, they came upon a horse standing in the middle of the trail, its rider having fallen dead from his saddle, one booted foot wedged in the stirrup.

"There's your horse, ma'am, right on time," Thorn said to Pearl Whitcomb.

Sam studied the man to determine which side he was on. Seeing no red sash at his waist, Sam took him for a bandido. *One of the ones riding guard on the wagon?* he wondered.

"Do you want the horse?" Sam asked the woman quietly.

"Yes," Pearl said. "He looks a little worse for the wear, but I'm not choosy."

Sam lowered her to the ground. Both he and Thorn kept a close eye on her, concerned she might make another break for it and go after the wagon.

Seeing them sticking so close, Pearl said, "Don't worry. I'm not riding into another gun battle if that's what you're wondering."

No sooner had she spoken than a rifle shot exploded and sent a bullet thumping against a tall pinyon just off the trail.

The three backed away fast, off the opposite side of the trail. Sam jumped down from his saddle, rifle in hand. He gave Thorn a hand sign meaning the other man should cover him, and he ran across the trail and into the woods, where he saw the smoke from the rifle shot still wafting in the air.

"I've got you covered, Ranger," Thorn whispered to himself.

He and the woman had quickly dismounted and watched through the low branches as the ranger moved along the direction of the shot. They waited for what seemed a long time.

Finally, Sam called out to them in a low guarded tone, "Bring the horses. Get on over here. We've got the freight wagon."

The woman and Thorn eased into the

pinyons, leading the three horses behind them. The wagon sat in a tangle of underbrush and saplings beside the corpses of two of the bandido trail guards. One of the wagon horses lay dead in its harness. The other horse stood looking down at its body. The smell of burned powder still hung in the air.

Sam looked around for the man who had fired the shot. He was lying in the rear of the freight wagon, barely breathing, his rifle clasped in his hand. The large carry bag of gold was still tied down to the wagon bed, the embroidered geese flying peacefully across its side.

When Sam closed his hand around the rifle to take it from him, the man didn't resist. "Take it. I'm . . . done for. I wasn't shooting . . . at you," he added. "I was . . . signaling for help. But it's too late."

"Stay quiet," Sam said, hearing what a strain talking was for the other man. "We'll get you some cool water and take a look at your wounds."

"Ah . . . save your trouble . . . your water too," the man said. "I'm dead here." He gave a rattling wet cough. He studied Pearl's face with cloudy eyes. "I know you . . . I think. Don't I?"

"I don't know," she said. "It depends on

where you think you know me from." She gave him a thin smile, then loosened his bandanna and used it to wipe sweat from his forehead.

He managed a low chuckle and nodded at the dead men on the ground. "They're . . . from *Tejas,* like me. Tough as hickory . . . What a time we'd've . . . had with this gold." His eyes clouded even more and fixed far off. "Anyway, I'm . . . Texas Joe Carney. God bless Texas," he whispered quietly.

"And that's that," Thorn said.

In the distance another rifle shot resounded. Cowboy Gunmen finishing off wounded bandidos, Sam figured.

Sam stepped down from the wagon bed and walked up to the remaining wagon horse, then pulled his knife from his boot.

"Wh-what are you doing?" Pearl asked, hurrying along behind him.

"Cutting this one loose," he said.

"You can't do that!" she said.

Sam cut her a look. "Can't leave him harnessed here with his dead pal for the wolves to eat," he said.

"But the wagon," she said. "We need him to pull the wagon!"

Sam and Thorn exchanged glances.

"Pearl, you need to understand," Sam said. "The two of us are down here hunting wanted men for Arizona. Nothing else."

"But this is stolen gold from Esplanade, from the French mining syndicate. We found it! If we take it back, there's a nice fat reward for it!"

"Listen to me, Miss Pearl," Sam said. "We have orders to stay out of matters pertaining to Mexico's laws. Right now all we're here to do is take back a couple of murdering cannibals to face American justice. This was just to satisfy our curiosity."

"No!" said Pearl. "That is too crazy to believe! Catlow and his Arizona Cowboy Gang are coming for it right now — they'll take it, and it will disappear! What kind of justice does that serve for anybody?"

"That's not our call," Thorn cut in. "If Catlow gets it, it's his. We have a job to do. None of that has anything to do with us." He said to the ranger, "Sam, cut the wagon horse loose. When Catlow gets here, he'll have horses to pull the wagon for him."

"*Hola* the wagon," a familiar voice called out from inside the pinyons.

The three looked toward the sound of the voice and saw Roman Lee Ellison and Russell Fairday step into view, their hands chest high, but holding on to rifles.

"Roman Lee," said Sam, "you show up in some of the strangest places." He looked

144

closely at Russell Fairday.

"Howdy, Ranger," said Fairday. "Yes, it's me, Fairday, from Sedona years back. Remember? You kept me from hanging and bought me a train ticket all the way to Kansas City. I've never forgotten it."

Sam took note of the red sash at Fairday's waist.

"I see you didn't quite stick to the straight and narrow like you said you would, Russell."

"That's the truth, Ranger, so help me," Fairday said. "But I'd be lying if I said I don't still think about it now and again —"

"Fairday!" a voice called out from the trail. "It's us over here. Cat is sicker than a dog. We're coming in. Don't nobody shoot!"

"Come on in," said Fairday. "We've got the gold wagon, gold and all!"

"No!" said the woman angrily. "We've got the gold wagon, gold and all."

She tried to lever a round up into the dead man's rifle she'd picked up from the wagon, but Thorn snatched the weapon from her hands and pitched it to the ground.

"Pay this woman no mind, Russell Fairday," he said. "All this fresh Denver City minted coin has set her heart aflutter — her trigger finger too, I'm afraid," he added, giving Pearl a hard look.

"Fairday," a voice called out from the trail, "is everything all right in there? Cat wants us to bring him in."

Bring him in . . . ? Sam looked at Thorn, who looked equally surprised.

"What's wrong with him?" Thorn asked Roman Lee.

"Sick at his stomach, I heard," said Roman Lee under his breath. "I don't mean a regular bellyache," he added. "I mean, dog-kicking sick. Can't keep nothing down."

As Sam listened to Roman Lee and Thorn talk, his eyes went to a large number of hoofprints coming and going from the rear of the wagon, almost undetectable beneath a layer of pinyon needles carpeting the ground.

"Here he comes now," Fairday said to Roman Lee. "At least he's walking on his own. A while ago he couldn't even get up by himself."

Off to the side where there were fewer pinyon needles covering the ground, Sam saw the hoofprints become clearer: headed uphill, out of sight over a rise. Then he spotted a gold coin glistening through the pinyon carpeting. He casually moved closer and covered it with his boot. *What is all this?* He glanced at Pearl Whitcomb; she seemed greatly interested in what Fairday was saying to Roman Lee about his boss.

"I'm all right," Catlow said, arriving at the wagon and leaning against it. "Some low-down snake overloaded my whiskey with laudanum. But I'm feeling better now!" he said with a wide, false smile. He patted the wagon. "Especially now that we have this sweet thing back!"

"Let's hear it for Cat!" Fairday said, shaking a celebratory fist. "Hurrah! Hurrah!"

The other men joined in by the second *hurrah*.

Catlow took the praise in stride, knowing he'd had nothing to do with recovering the wagon. He looked at Thorn, then at Sam, then at the woman.

"You three decided to cut yourself in on our gold, huh?" he said. "I figure you'll understand why we're going to shoot you and leave you dead right here in the dirt —"

"They had nothing to do with any of this, boss," Roman Lee cut in.

A tense silence fell over the group. Catlow looked at Roman Lee with dark-circled eyes.

"Roman Lee Ellison," said Catlow, "you don't say much, but when you do, you sure know how to make me want to cut your throat."

"I'm telling the truth," said Roman Lee.

"Fairday and I were listening to them from inside the pinyons." He gestured toward Sam and Thorn. "These two were talking about how they wanted nothing to do with keeping the gold."

Catlow turned to Fairday.

"It's true, boss," Fairday said. "Roman Lee and I both heard them talking. They had no idea we were there, but we got here as soon as we heard Texas Joe's rifle shot. We heard it all."

"What about this one?" Catlow asked, nodding at Pearl.

"She was all for keeping the gold, boss, I'm sorry to say," Fairday replied.

"Well, then, I'm sorry to say she's dead," said Catlow before he raised a big Colt from his holster and cocked it.

Sam clasped his hand around the butt of his holstered Colt, and Thorn gripped his rifle with both hands. The Cowboy Gunmen stood ready to draw.

"Well, well," said Catlow, "looks like a lot of blood is going to be spilled over this gold —"

"There's no gold here," the ranger said quietly yet confidently.

Thorn looked at him in total surprise.

"No gold here?" Catlow repeated.

"My mistake," said Sam. "Whoever stole

it did leave one coin. They must've dropped it when they unloaded the wagon floor. It's under my boot." He took a short step backward and scraped a boot across the pinyon needles, revealing the coin underneath.

"Maybe somebody should check it out," he said.

CHAPTER 11

While Catlow's men cut the carry bag loose from the wagon floor, the ranger stood in the same spot as if guarding the gold coin lying uncovered at his feet. A couple of men went up the hillside, following the many hoofprints that had emerged from under the pinyon needles. When the men in the wagon pitched the heavy bag back to Nathan Catlow, he looked at the ranger.

"Before I open this bag, I'm taking your gun from you, Ranger," he said.

"That's the only way you'll get it, Catlow," Sam replied calmly, his big Colt hanging down his thigh, cocked.

He had managed to raise the big Colt slowly, as naturally as he would have to check and see if it was loaded. Nobody had taken notice of it at first, except Roman Lee and Thorn, both of whom had seen Sam slip his gun into play that way many times before. Roman Lee carried a big round bul-

150

let scar on his chest from the first time he'd seen Sam do it.

Once the ranger's big Colt was drawn, people began to see what he'd done, but it was too late. He had the drop on them. He saw that Catlow was thinking the situation over, with the ranger standing less than six feet in front of him, gun cocked and ready. Catlow gave him a look that said, *Okay, keep the gun. . . .* Close by, Thorn gave a thin knowing smile. Roman Lee looked indifferent. He hadn't seen a thing, yet he had taken a slow half step back out of the way.

Catlow unlocked the carry bag with a key from inside his shirt and kept his gaze on Sam as he spread the top open. He looked down into the bag, then looked back up, his eyes full of rage.

"Rocks!" he growled. "It's loaded with lousy rocks!"

He glared at the ranger, turned the bag on its side and poured rocks onto the ground. Sam stood ready for whatever came next, glad to have drawn the big Colt while he'd had the chance. At the top of the rise, a man waved his hands back and forth above his head.

"Nothing up here, boss," he called down loudly. "Just an empty bag!"

Catlow stayed silent for a moment, breathing in and out, deep, measured breaths. In a deliberately calm, un-rattled voice he asked Sam, "When did you know, Ranger, and how did you know it?"

"A piece of it at a time came to me as soon as we got here," he said. "Only four riding guards and two drivers? On top of this much gold? With an army of Cowboy Gunmen close on their trail?" He shook his head. "That's hard to believe, Cat," he said, taking the liberty of using the other man's nickname just to see if he could.

Catlow caught himself about to throw up again, but he stopped himself, something he hadn't been able to do all day or last night. He seemed surprised and held a hand to his chest until the sensation passed. Then he sighed and crawled into the wagon bed.

"But I've seen outlaws play things down this way to keep people from being too interested," he said.

"But not this time," the ranger replied, "not with this much riding on the line."

"Damn it, you're right, Ranger," said Catlow. "I can say this poison has had me by the flaps all day and night, but I still should not have been caught unawares on this. Now we've got to pull up and get on their trail. No ragged bunch of bandidos is going to do us this way."

He tried to rise up from the wagon bed, but as if out of nowhere, Pearl swooped in and with one hand pressed him down.

"No, no," she said. "I told you to lie still and that's what you're going to do! This will only work if you listen to me and do as I tell you." She raised a gourd dipper she held carefully in her other hand. "Here, I just made this. You have to drink it before it settles."

"Just like before?" Catlow asked.

"Exactly," she replied, holding the gourd down to him. "It's the very same as the first one. You need to drink it all down while it's fizzing."

Pearl gave the ranger a look as Catlow drank the concoction she'd made up from root scrapings and wild herbs.

"There," she said, taking back the empty gourd. "How much did the first dose help you?"

"A lot, Miss Pearl," Catlow said. "I felt myself getting ready to vomit but stopped myself."

She patted his shoulder. "That's great," she said. "We've got you headed in the right direction. Let's keep it up."

Catlow nodded. "I don't know where you learned all this, but I'm sure glad you were here," he said.

"I told you, Nathan," she said in a sweet tone, "I was a nurse supervisor in U. S. Grant's army. We treated every kind of minor illness, wound or dark malady you can imagine, much of it with herbs and roots right there at hand."

"Amazing," Catlow said. "Lucky for me you were here. I might have been dead by now otherwise."

"You may have indeed," said Pearl.

When Pearl stepped away, Catlow turned to the ranger.

"I'm going to find whoever did this to me and kill that person deader than hell," he said. "Meanwhile, I'm sending some men ahead to find these poltroons and get the gold back before they scatter and it's lost forever. I know you and Thorn are some sort of badge toters. But damn it, this is Ol' Mex. Can the two of you ride along? I'll pay well for helping find these bandido bastards."

"Can't do it," Sam said. "We're hunting those cannibals, the Smith brothers."

"But we're all headed the same direction," said Catlow. "We might find these jakes before you have to turn off on the trail to the cannibals."

"What about Pearl Whitcomb?" Sam asked.

154

"She stays with me. At least for now," said Catlow. "We'll be no more than a day or half a day behind. She'll have to understand I'm not letting that much gold get any farther from me than I have to. The way she seems to love gold, I think she'll understand. Don't you?"

"You're probably right about that," said Sam. "We'll ride along with you until we have to turn off. As to paying us, I won't speak for Thorn, but I can't accept any pay."

"Because the money is stolen?" Catlow asked.

Sam said, "I've worked this side of the border enough to know the situation here with the French, the Germans, the Irish. Law here hangs on by a thread. My job is to see to it that string doesn't break. I can't do that if I'm working on more than one payroll. Understand?"

"Not at all." Catlow grinned. "But I won't offer you pay again. You've got my word. I'm obliged you'll be riding along with me until I'm feeling better, or until you reach your turn."

"If Thorn and I are going on ahead for you, we need to be leaving now. With this much, I figure whoever has possession of the gold needs to keep it all together. If you or somebody doesn't hold tight rein around it, it'll soon break off into small amounts and disappear."

"Ever think about being an outlaw, Ranger?" Catlow asked, only half joking. "Sounds like you could be as good at it as you are at being a lawman."

"No," Sam said, "I'm good at being a lawman because I believe in the law, and I believe in what I'm doing, upholding it. But I wouldn't feel that way about being an outlaw. No offense intended," he added.

"None taken, Ranger," said Catlow. He motioned Fairday over and said, "Tell the woman we're hitting the trail and taking her and her friends here with us. And tell Roman Lee Ellison I want him riding with the ranger and Thorn, scouting ahead of us until we catch these bandido bastards."

As soon as the ranger walked away, Fairday said, "You dropped this, boss." He handed Catlow the folded piece of paper Bidden Matelin had given him before he'd killed the jeweler in his own rancho.

"*Gracias,* Fairday," said Catlow. He glanced at the three names written on the paper, refolded it and slipped it inside his shirt into a hideaway pocket.

Adios, Matelin, you dead, greedy bastard, he thought.

He still remembered the names clear

156

enough without the piece of paper, but he liked being reminded of them every time he changed trousers. Those three men had to die.

Bertram Leonard, the leader of the Lobos, pitched the heavy bag of gold down to one of his men's waiting arms. He watched as the man walked three steps and pitched it into the iron-wheeled French military-style cargo wagon, where it landed among the other bags.

"Is that about all of it, brother George?" he asked, swinging down from his saddle. "Packing gold around is wearing me out."

"Me too," said his younger brother. "I like spending it, not handling it."

"How many bags now?" Bertram asked.

"Dang it, Bert, I ain't kept count." George laughed. "You're supposed to be the leader of this ragged-assed bunch of deserters. You tell me!"

"That one makes forty-three," Bertram said without hesitation. "We've got three bags still coming. Forty-six in all."

"See?" said George. "You knew it all along. You was just jingling our bells!" He laughed again.

The rough-looking gunmen sitting around in the rocks and dirt beside their horses laughed with him.

"Here come your brothers Henri and Newlin right now," said one of the gunmen, standing and dusting off the seat of his threadbare Mexican cavalry trousers.

All eyes turned to look down on the two riders racing across a stretch of sand-swept desert flatlands. One led the saddled horse of one their fallen bandidos. They rode a trail winding through rock, dry cutbanks and sparse cacti eighty feet below.

"Don't drop them bags, brothers!" Bert said under his breath, squinting against the afternoon sunlight. "Who's that dogging their tail?" he asked anyone listening.

A gunman named Paco Cord stood up, pulled open a telescope and raised it to his eye. "Apache, I make it," he said after a moment.

"Be sure," said Bert.

Paco lowered the lens, spit on the front end of it and wiped it on his shirt. "Yep, Apache," he said after another look. "A half dozen of the old White Creek bunch."

"Let's see if my brothers are smart enough to get rid of them," said Bert.

"Want us to ready our rifles in case they're not?" Paco said.

"A couple of you get ready," Bert said, "but stand by. No need to shoot just yet.

Let's not interfere unless we have to."

He knew that the Apache were near starving, and so were their horses. Neither the warriors nor their animals had the strength for a long-running fight.

"What the hell's this? Your brothers are slowing down," said one of the men.

"What?"

Bert hurried over to the telescope Paco held out to him, and raised it to his eye. Through the circle of vision, he saw the horses slow down just a little in a roiling blow of dust. Without completely stopping, his younger brother Newlin leveled a big Remington six-shooter at the riderless horse a few feet steps behind him. He let go of its reins and fired a bullet into its forehead.

The horse went down immediately, rolling away, limp, its reins flying wildly, then settling around it.

The two brothers booted their horses back into a run, but not as hard as before.

Through the lens, Bert looked back at the Apache. When the warriors arrived at the downed horse, his brothers were long gone. The Apache dismounted and gathered around the dead horse on the sand like hungry wolves. Two of them took out big knives and fell upon the animal with haste.

"Good move," Bert said under his breath

to his brothers, seeing them far ahead and veering toward the trail that would lead them up to the designated meeting spot.

"Clear thinking on your brother's part. We would have spent the night fighting if they had led them Apache to us," said Paco, who'd come to retrieve his telescope.

"Yeah," said Bert, "better to give them a dead man's horse than any of our gold."

"Your brothers will be a half hour or more getting up here," said Paco. "You want some jerked goat?"

"Who did the jerking?" Bert asked.

"Some of the women in Perrito," said Paco. "They're good at it. I've got a chunk in my saddlebags. I'll bring you some."

"Yeah, okay," said Bert. "Look at this."

He gestured down to the desert floor where the Apache had already butchered out the horse's hindquarters. A few women and small children had arrived as if they'd risen from the desert sand. The women had brought butchering knives of their own and gone to work on the quickly diminishing carcass.

"Poor sumbitches," said Paco. He waited for a second, then turned. "I'll get that goat meat," he said.

Purple dark had filled the sky and mantled

the western horizon with a thin line of failing red sunlight. When Newlin and Henri Leonard rode in, each with a bag of gold on his lap, the other men gathered around them, took the bags and tossed them on the cargo wagon.

"What is that smell?" Henri Leonard asked, breathing deep and taking in the aroma of the horsemeat sizzling on the desert below. "If ol' Bill was alive and knew his horse smelled that good, he'd've killed and et it himself."

The two brothers dropped down from their saddles and let one of the other men lead their horses away.

They took canteens that were offered and drank until they'd soothed their parched throats. Bert came and stuck slices of jerked goat meat in their hands. As his brothers ate, Bert gestured Paco away, back to the saddles and blankets strewn on the ground.

"All right," he asked his brothers, "how many men did we lose to this Cowboy Gunmen sumbitches?"

"I make it a dozen," Newlin said solemnly.

Bert looked at Henri.

"Yeah, that sounds right to me," Henri said. "Damned shame. They were all good men. But I reckon it's the business we're in. Ain't that right, Bert?"

"Yeah," said Bert, "I reckon it is." He walked away, chewing on jerked goat.

"What's got him down in the mouth?" Newlin asked Paco, who stood at a small smokeless campfire drinking a cup of hot coffee.

"I reckon it bothers him to lose men like it does any good leader. I'd be leery of riding with anybody it didn't bother. He's standing up here smelling one of his best men's horses roasting over a fire. Likely wishing he had a big slice of it on his knife blade for himself." He shook his head. "It would bother me, for damn sure."

"All right," said Newlin. "I reckon it would bother me too."

He handed Paco the canteen and walked away, catching up with Bert at the wagon. They looked down at the Apache campfire glowing on the desert floor.

"What's the plan?" Newlin asked. "Are we selling this gold at a discount or keeping it ourselves to let it cool off awhile?"

"We need to let things lie as they are for now," said Bert. "Let Catlow and his men go loco trying to find all this gold. Meanwhile, we're going to a hiding place I know about above here." He nodded toward a long hill line west of them.

"Anyplace I ever heard of?" Newlin asked,

gazing off with him.

"Yeah," said Bert, "you've heard of it. But I doubt you've ever been there."

CHAPTER 12

Thorn and the ranger set their horses on a cliff fifty feet above a sandy stone trail. The narrow trail reached into the lower rock hills below them and meandered back in the direction of Perrito. Catlow, Pearl and the Cowboy Gunmen Gang were a half day behind them, just like Catlow had said they'd likely be.

Through his telescope, the ranger looked down and spotted the large burned circle the Apache campfire had left in its wake. A scattering of horse bones lay in the sand surrounding it. In the night, winds across the desert floor had swept through and covered the tracks of the Apache, their horses, the dogs and the coyotes that followed.

"Don't see our cannibals wandering around down there, do you?" Thorn asked.

Sam ignored his joking. "If they're still holed up a couple of days' ride out of Perrito, we're still close," the ranger said. "Wouldn't you agree?"

He lowered the telescope, collapsed it between his hands and put it away. He nodded at the rocky trail he'd spotted below.

Thorn dropped his joking attitude.

"I agree," he said. "So it's not like you've put them out of your mind with all this stolen gold and such?"

"No," Sam said, "I've been thinking about them all along. If I was a cannibal, and ever' so often got the urge for human flesh and blood —"

"Let's don't do this, Ranger," Thorn said. "This is dark, ghastly stuff!"

"But hear me out," Sam said. "When I got that urge, I'd be drawn to places where I could find what I'm craving, wouldn't I?"

Thorn sighed and looked off across the endless desert. "Yes, you would, I suppose," he said.

"I wouldn't want the body of someone who died from disease or anyone who'd been dead for more than a little while."

"Right," Thorn said, tight-lipped.

"So look at all the fighting and dying we've seen since we've been out here. It's been like a battlefield."

Thorn took an interest. "Yes, it has! Fresh meat, only hours old." He looked the ranger up and down. "You've been thinking all this?"

"Say a man has a lifelong craving for strawberries," the ranger continued. "Would it make sense that he'd want to be as close as he could to a plentiful source of strawberries?"

"This is getting worse," said Thorn. "But I see where you're headed. While we're searching for these cannibals, they could be looking around at the dead, the fresh kills we're leaving behind for them." He paused and actually glanced around. "They could be anywhere!"

"I've heard all sorts of stories about things that happened during the civil conflict," Sam said, "where some soldiers arrested folk and often shot them for trying to steal bodies right off the battlefields."

"I thought that was cadaver snatchers getting bodies for doctors to practice on," Thorn said.

"I'm thinking it could be both," the ranger said quietly.

"What are you two talking about?" Roman Lee called out, riding out of the sage and sprigs of wild grass behind them.

"What the hell do you mean, sneaking up on a person like that?" Thorn shouted. "Scaring the bejesus out of a fella!"

He'd almost gone for his Colt. But he caught himself and took his hand away from the gun.

"I don't mean anything, Dan'l," said Roman Lee. "I rode up through the sage, hearing about cadaver snatchers and practicing something on dead bodies —"

"It's nothing, Roman Lee! Just nothing," Thorn said.

Sam looked away, keeping Thorn from seeing him muffle a laugh.

Thorn settled down and took a couple of breaths. "We were just talking about the Smith brother cannibals we're looking for," he said to the young gunman.

"Oh, those two," Roman Lee said.

"Yes, those two," said Thorn.

The ranger turned back to face them. "I figure we've likely ridden a good twenty miles out of Perrito," he said. "What do you think, Roman Lee?"

"I agree," Roman Lee replied. "The main trail swings around wide and skirts a lot of Perrito. The little trail down there was a game trail. It's longer. But it goes past most everybody's places. Yeah, from here back to town is a day. From here out's another day."

Sam and Thorn both nodded.

"What's the next town that way?" Sam asked Roman Lee.

"That would be Gato Saltando," Roman Lee said.

"Jumping Cat," Thorn translated with a chuff, shaking his head a little. "Right here on this spot, we are halfway twixt Little Dog and Jumping Cat?"

"That's about right," said Roman Lee, "if memory serves."

"We could split up here," the ranger said. "One of us goes on farther, scouting around for anything we can find on the Smiths. One goes the other way, back to Perrito."

"Who goes which way?" Thorn asked.

"Pick which way suits you," Sam replied.

"Catlow and you get along better. Meet him at Gato Saltando. I'll go back. I'll ask everbody about the Smiths between here and Perrito," Thorn said.

"Where will I be going?" Roman Lee asked. "I know the area pretty well in either direction."

"With Thorn," Sam said before Thorn could answer. "If I hurry, I'll have time to make a couple of laps around the hillsides before I meet up with Catlow and his men."

"Good idea," said Roman Lee. "Catlow keeps asking me about Pearl Whitcomb."

"What do you tell him?" Thorn asked.

"I tell him I don't know her," said the young gunman.

"What do you tell him about us," Thorn asked, "the ranger and me?"

"I told him the ranger shot me, sent me to Yuma," said Roman Lee. "I ran into the two of you lately in Bad River, and we've gotten along without any problems. You don't ask me about my business, and I don't ask about yours."

"Sounds good," said Sam. "What does he think about the woman?"

Thorn cut in. "I bet he thinks she taught Jesus how to play the banjo," he said.

"Not quite," said Roman Lee, "but close. He thinks she saved his life, knowing what to do for the poisoned whiskey somebody slipped him." He looked at the ranger and asked, "What do you think of that whole poison situation, Ranger?"

"Haven't thought about it much," Sam said.

He had an opinion he'd been working on, but he wasn't ready to share it. Not yet anyway.

Seeing that the ranger wasn't going to offer any more on the matter, Roman Lee and Thorn started to back their horses from the edge and turn them. The ranger had started to do the same until he stopped and looked off in the direction of Perrito.

"Here comes Catlow now," Sam said,

169

spotting Catlow and his men coming toward them on the trail below. He came out with his telescope and focused it on the riders.

Catlow and the woman rode in the wagon, Catlow leaning back against some thick pillows. The woman sat beside him, holding a canteen up to his lips. Three men rode along behind the wagon, and yet another man was behind them, carrying a shotgun across his lap. Fairday sat in the driver's seat. Mounted guards on horseback stayed close to the wagon, three on either side.

"Are you two ready to backtrack, scout the terrain back into Perrito?"

"Yeah, we're both ready, Ranger," said Thorn.

"Then get out of here," Sam said. "Find out anything you can about the Smiths. Come tell me about it in two days in Gato Saltando."

Sam tapped his heels to the big stallion's sides, and Doc loped off to the thin trail leading down through the rock and sage to meet Catlow's gang on the desert floor.

"*Buenos días,* Ranger," Catlow said as Sam rode up, half circled the wagon and noted that the hands of the three riders behind the wagon were tied. Their horses were led by short ropes tied to the wagon. Sam didn't try hiding his look of interest and concern.

"Oh, them?" said Catlow, before Sam asked. "They're bandidos, war prisoners from yesterday's fighting." He gave the three a hard stare. "They're soon to be dead bandidos. I'm getting ready to enjoy some target practice with them." He smiled. "You're just in time to join us."

Keep out of it, Sam reminded himself. *Here's how they do it in Mexico.*

"No, thanks," he said. "My shooting's good."

Catlow beckoned him closer to himself and the woman. Just between the three of them, Catlow whispered, "I'm cutting them loose. I just want them to sweat awhile, thinking about it."

The woman looked pleased. She silently mouthed the words *Thank you* to Catlow.

"I understand," Sam replied.

He rode Doc at a walk to the front of the wagon and touched his hat brim courteously to Pearl Whitcomb.

"You appear to have your patient on the mend this morning," he said to her.

"I've never been better!" Catlow cut in. He sat up straighter. "This little lady has been an angel sent to save me."

Pearl only smiled. She still sat close beside

171

him, very near, the canteen in her hand. Catlow reached over and patted her leg above the knee, surprising the ranger. Pearl still only smiled. She made no effort to move his hand or to slip her thigh from under it.

"It might surprise you to know, Ranger, I've asked Miss Pearl to stay right here with me. Enjoy this beautiful countryside."

Sam glanced around the bleak and barren desert hills and flatlands, a place some said looked like the doorway to hell on a slow day. He wasn't going to say anything. Pearl had shown herself to be her own woman.

"I realize I'm well enough on my own now," Catlow continued, "but I think I'd like to keep her around. Call her my good-luck charm." He squeezed her thigh. "Now what have you got for me, Ranger?"

"I found where they gathered with the gold and reloaded it to a wagon," said Sam. "Up there." He nodded up at the spot from where he, Thorn and Roman Lee had been watching them come into sight. "They loaded the bags of gold and left in the night, headed northwest."

"And now you're cutting away from here for Gato Saltando?" Catlow asked.

"I'm scouting from here into Gato Saltando. Then back. If I see anybody along

172

the way, I'll let you know."

Catlow rose a little and pointed toward the burned-campfire spot.

"What was that about?" he asked.

"I didn't see them, but it's a good bet it was Apache. Looks like they butchered and roasted a horse out there."

"Why do you say a horse?" Catlow asked.

"When I rode through, I saw scrapes of horse bone and a few strands of mane and tail hair. It was a small band. They had their women and their young with them."

"No tricks though?" said Catlow. "No bandidos posing as Apache?"

"No," said Sam. "I would have spotted any tricks. I didn't see anything like that. The bandidos had things well planned to get away this clean and fast."

"I've got men up ahead, searching on the other side of Gato Saltando," Catlow said. "Obliged for your and Thorn's help between here and there. Wouldn't mind seeing you again when your business around there is taken care of. I like your tracking."

"*Gracias,*" said the ranger. "It might be you will see us again, Thorn and I."

He looked at Pearl and touched his hat brim again. There was nothing in her eyes that showed any fear or apprehension. No get-me-the-hell-out-of-here look.

"Miss Pearl," he said quietly.

"Ranger," she replied with a smile.

She appeared pleased that he wasn't saying anything to butt into whatever she was up to. And she was up to something; he was certain of it.

"When you see Roman Lee, send him back to us, Ranger," Catlow called as Sam and Doc turned and rode away.

Gato Saltando, Mexico

The town of Jumping Cat was larger than the ranger had expected it to be. But he'd started realizing what to expect on his way in as he passed row upon row of abandoned French mines in the near distance. From the main trail, fifty yards out, the stretch of boarded-up mine entrances wavered and glistened in the noonday sun.

Some entrances had been turned into working doorways. People — *residents,* Sam decided — stood under awnings they had installed. One wooden front had been turned into a painted welcome sign that read in wavering Spanish: BIENVENIDO TO GATO SALTANDO. Then in wavering English beside it: DRINK WHISKEY AT PEDRO'S CANTINA. Women stood in the awning shade and waved. Some beckoned Sam to

174

ride up a thin stone pathway leading to them.

He rode on.

Along an ancient stone-tiled street, he saw another sign advertising Pedro's Cantina this one's letters not wavering in the heat of the day.

Stepping down from his saddle, Sam gave a small silver coin to a tough-looking young girl who came from the town well carrying a small pail of water with a gourd dipper in it. Sam took a drink from the dipper and thanked the girl. He gestured the pail toward Doc, who stood at a post with an iron ring on it, watching with his ears perked. The girl set the pail down and kept a foot on its edge for balance. Sam hitched a slack rein to the iron ring on the post, leaving Doc room for drinking his water.

"Gracias," the girl said, and stepped under the awning in front of Pedro's Cantina.

Before Sam could walk into the shade, two men wearing red Cowboy sashes loose around their necks stepped out, blocking the open doorway. Sam looked them up and down, not recognizing either of them, but he recalled that Catlow had men scouting out past Gato Saltando, looking for the vanished gold wagon.

The men stopped and stood rigid in front

of the ranger.

"You're standing where we're walking," one said to Sam. His voice was a little whiskey-slurred.

All right, they're drunk, Sam told himself. He started to take a step to the side.

"Pardon me, gentlemen," he said.

But the two didn't walk on. They stood firm.

"Gentlemen?" one sneered. "Watch your language."

Sam started to move away. But before he could, one reached out and pointed at Sam's badge, nearly jabbing his chest.

"Well, look at this," he said. "We've got us a ranger. All the way down here in Ol' Mex!"

"What happened, Ranger?" the other one asked. "Did you make a wrong turn? What are you doing here?"

The two half circled him.

Sam watched them move into fighting position. They made no sense, their questions. What was he doing here? Didn't they know Catlow had gotten him, Thorn and Roman Lee, one of their own, to join in looking for the gold?

Before he could say anything, he heard Thorn call out in a booming voice behind him.

"Look here, Roman Lee!" he said. The

two of them had stepped out of an alley together. "We can't leave him alone five minutes without him starting trouble with somebody!"

"A damn shame," said Roman Lee. "He can't seem to stop himself."

He sidestepped away from Thorn and lifted his black-handled Colt from its holster, slow and easy-like, still practicing how to do it with no cause for alarm, the way the ranger did. The way the ranger had done it when he'd shot Roman Lee over two years earlier!

The two drunken gunmen looked back and forth between Thorn and Roman Lee.

"Who are these two drunken jackasses we're fixing to kill here, Ranger?" Thorn asked.

"I don't know who they are, Dan'l," said Sam. "I don't think they know either. They're both carrying Cowboy sashes, but I don't think they're Cowboys. You know them, Roman Lee?"

"Never seen them before in my life," Roman Lee replied.

He'd done it! He'd gotten the Colt out of its holster without anyone seeming to notice. Real good! He held the gun down his thigh, cocked, ready.

The two fake Cowboy Gunmen looked at

the red sash around Roman Lee's waist, its tails hanging down his side. Their sashes still hung around their necks.

"Sonsabitches!" one of them shouted, knowing it had all gone too far to stop now. Every one of them would either live or die on this spot today.

Both gunmen drew at once, fast but not fast enough. Their guns were still coming up from the holsters when three bullets hit them and took them to the ground. One fell dead, raising a large puff of street dust. The other one struggled, trying to get back up onto his feet, his gun still in hand.

"Where do you think you're going, huh, hero?" said Thorn. He stepped over calmly. "You going somewhere, are you?"

The man had balanced himself up on one arm. With a sweep of his boot, Thorn took the other man's arm out from under him and watched him hit the ground. Thorn stepped back and started replacing his spent round. The man struggled, then collapsed dead on his face.

Sam walked over beside Roman Lee.

"Never seen them before?" he said.

"That's right, never," said Roman Lee.

On the street, the townsfolk of Gato Saltando drew in closer around the three of them. A dog slipped from under a short boardwalk, ran over, lapped its tongue through the fresh blood on the tiled street, then turned and raced away.

A man in a too tight black suit walked toward the scene with a look of authority about him.

CHAPTER 13

The townsfolk who'd gathered at the sight of the dead men on the stone street tiles began drifting away as the town councilman in the black suit arrived and started asking questions. As soon as he saw that the two dead men wore red sashes around their necks that matched the one Roman Lee wore around his waist, his questions turned less probing.

Recognizing the ranger's badge, the councilman narrowed his questions even further until he finally tipped his hat, wished the three Americans a good day and left.

Roman Lee smiled as the town official walked away.

"He never once said anything about these two and me wearing Cowboy sashes," he said.

"I think he was fixin' to," Thorn chuckled, "but the sight of the ranger's shiny badge stopped him cold."

The three turned as one when a young man led three horses from the shade of the same alleyway Thorn and Roman Lee had come out of. He also wore a red Cowboy sash around his waist. Seeing the three standing there, he tried to turn away quickly, but he was too late.

"Hey! Hold on there, hero!" said Thorn, stepping over quickly and grabbing the horses' reins, causing all three to stop.

The man jerked to a sudden halt with three sets of reins in his hand.

"Allow me to venture a quick guess," Thorn said, his hand slickly lifting the man's pistol from its holster, cocking it and tapping its barrel on the man's chest. "One of these horses is yours, and the other two belonged to your friends lying there?"

Sam and Roman Lee stepped in closer. The man looked from one to the next, then down at his own gun barrel standing against his belly.

"I'm Shelby Burnes — from right here! I almost don't even know these two," he said in a shaky voice. "We just drunk some together. I was bringing their horses when I saw what was going on. I pulled back until the councilman shut up and left."

"Where'd the three of you get the red sashes?" Roman Lee asked.

"What, this?" Burnes said, in feigned innocence. "They gave it to me, must've been a spare! I believe they belonged to that Arizona Cowboy Gunmen bunch!" His words got quicker as he spoke and saw three expressions disbelieving every word he said. "See now, the thing is —"

"You three are phonies, impersonators," Roman Lee said, having to cut him off. "If any of you were Cowboy Gunmen, I would know you. But I don't. Now explain it before we send you rolling off with your pals there."

Two townsmen had arrived with a mule cart, into which they lifted the dead.

"Okay, they told me they're bandidos. That's a gang widely known to be from over near —"

"We know who they are and where they're from," the ranger cut in. "Why are they posing as Cowboy Gunmen?"

Thorn lowered the man's gun from his belly.

Burnes lowered his voice. "Maybe you three haven't heard," he said. "The bandidos gang stole a load of gold from the Cowboy Gang and are hiding it somewhere around here. We figured if we posed as Cowboy Gunmen and got our hands on a bandido who was in on the robbery, we

could scare him into taking us to the gold."
He tried a sly grin. "Not bad, huh?"

Thorn looked away and shook his head.

"Listen close, hero," he said, looking back
at the man. "If we see you again, we're going to kill you for being too stupid to live."

"But why?" Burnes asked, feeling a little
emboldened now that his gun was not stuck
in his belly. "It's a pretty good plan. What's
wrong with it?"

"Shut up about it," said Thorn. He took a
deep breath. "What do you know about the
Smith brothers?"

"You mean the flesh eaters?" the man said.
"I know they were some terrible sonsabitches. Folks who live near them cut out
long ago. Now a lot of folks think they're
dead. But they still give wide berth around
the Smith place up on Old Curly. Afraid of
flesh-eating ghosts if you can make any
sense of that."

"Old Curly?" Thorn asked, avoiding the
topic of flesh-eating ghosts.

"Yep, it's on a high ridgeline that way."
He pointed northwest, where layers of hill
lines appeared to overlap upward until
cloud cover took them over. "I can tell yas
how to get there, step by step."

"What're the odds of this?" Thorn asked,
looking at Roman Lee and the ranger.

He turned back to the man. "I've got a better idea," he said. "You're going to ride with us, show us the way. We'll even pay you for it once we see you're not lying."

"All right."

"That's good, Shelby," said Thorn. "How far are we talking about from here?"

"Three hours or so," Shelby replied. "What time we spend here talking about it, we could be on our way up there and back."

"All right," said Thorn. "But if it turns out you're lying to us, Shelby, we'll leave you lying dead up on Old Curly."

Perrito, Old Mexico

Catlow and Pearl Whitcomb sat on the wagon seat with a large canvas canopy raised against the blazing midafternoon sun. Catlow gazed out across the rolling desert floor with a pair of binoculars he carried in a leather case on the seat beside him. Beside the binoculars case lay his big Colt in its holster, his gun belt wrapped around it.

A tall chestnut bay stood saddled and bridled behind the wagon, its reins tied to a rear hitch ring. Pearl looked back affectionately at the handsome animal.

"No one has ever given me a horse! I think I can easily get used to living this way, Nathan Catlow," she said. She reached up and brushed her fingertips along the billowing canvas overhead.

"I hope you can, Pearl, my darling," Catlow said, still watching the desert floor. "A horse is only one thing I want to give you. It would be a shame to possess all the gold I've hidden here and there with no one like you to lavish it on."

"Oh, my!" Pearl said, fanning herself with her hand. "It takes my breath, hearing you say things like that!"

Catlow smiled behind the binoculars.

"That's why I say such things," he said. He lowered the binoculars. "It pleases me to take your breath and to make your eyes sparkle like gold."

"Oh, you." She leaned over and kissed his cheek.

"After what you did, I owe you so much," he said softly, touching his fingertip to her chin. "I hardly know where to start."

"If I may say so," she said, "I would love to see all of this gold I've heard so much about, although I heard the Lobos have stolen it all?"

"Nonsense." Catlow chuckled. "They took some, one little shipment. Not all. There aren't enough bandidos alive to take all the gold I've got hidden." He tapped the tip of her nose affectionately. "When would you like to see it?"

"Oh, my! I wasn't prepared for this!" she said. She composed herself. "No hurry," she added offhandedly. "Just someday?"

"How about tomorrow?" Catlow asked.

"So soon?" Pearl said. "Is it far from here?"

"Not so far," said Catlow. "But there and back is a full day, especially if we need to stop once or twice to, let's say, spend some time together?"

"Yes, certainly," Pearl said. "We must never neglect our time together."

"Okay, here they come!" Catlow said, looking out on the desert floor again.

Only now the three men he'd earlier called war prisoners were riding in. Without the binoculars on them, they were no more than black spots on the sand. In the magnifying lens, he saw them clearly, their hands still tied, mounted riflemen guarding them, front, back and sides.

They sat watching in silence as the group of men rode closer. When the men stopped ten feet from them, one of the prisoners called out to Catlow.

"Boss, remember me, Jim Hebert? I worked for you. You don't have to do this. I've never said anything about anything

we've done. You'll never have to worry about
—"

A shot exploded. Pearl managed not to scream, but she threw her hands over her ears and gasped. She turned her wide eyes toward Catlow as he recocked his big Colt and took aim. The mounted guards pulled their horses away from the two remaining prisoners.

"Adios, Lobos!" Catlow shouted.

Even with their hands tied, the two prisoners tried to boot their horses away from the sudden death facing them. The one Catlow had shot had fallen and was trying to crawl away, a bloody exit hole in his back.

With the gunshot ringing sharp and loud in her ears, Pearl heard Catlow's muffled laugh.

Gunfire exploded again. One of the fleeing men fell sideways from his saddle. The other lay low on his horse's back and raced away. The guards backed their horses farther away as Catlow drew a rifle from under the wagon seat. He raised the rifle's long-distance sight, adjusted it and raised the butt to his shoulder.

Catlow squeezed the trigger and watched the last of the three prisoners fall from his horse's back.

One guard jumped down from his saddle

and walked over to the first man Catlow had shot, who was still crawling across the sand, leaving a dark red trail of blood behind him.

"You need to hurry up and die, Hebert," the guard said. "No need for you dragging this thing out."

"You go . . . to hell," said the crawling man. "You know . . . this ain't right. . . . We've been . . . good hands . . . for the Cowboy Gang!"

"Sometimes good ain't good enough. But whatever Cat says is right, is right," the gunman replied.

He pointed his gun down, fired two shots into the back of the man's head and turned and walked away.

"Oh, my God!" Pearl said, her hands still clasped on her ears from the surprise and the impact of the first gunshot.

Catlow chuckled as he thumbed fresh loads into his smoking Colt. A big bird of prey turned a low-scanning circle in the sky overhead. Catlow closed his gun, raised it, aimed and cocked it at the big carrion hunter. He followed it across the sky, and when his aim came around far enough that the gun was pointed at Pearl's face, he held it there for a moment.

Pearl gazed at him in return, trying not to

give in to her fear.

Catlow lowered the gun and uncocked it with a sudden sharp click.

"I have to say, you handled that pretty well, Pearl," he said. "Your days on the battlefield prepared you well for this sort of thing?"

"Yes, they did," she said.

She wouldn't mention that for a second she thought he was going to kill her. This was not the man she thought she knew only yesterday.

Looking at her closely, Catlow said, "I can see something is troubling you. Do you want to tell me what it is?"

"Yes, I will tell you," Pearl said. "I heard you tell the ranger you were holding those three men prisoner only to make them sweat a little. That you would then be turning them loose."

"I said that?" Catlow gave a little puzzled smile. "To the ranger?" He paused, then said, "Oh, well. They robbed me and my Cowboys. They were bandidos. Who knows what else they might have done if I didn't kill them? I had a right to kill them. So now I have. Out here it's kill or be killed every day under the sun. The ranger knows that."

"I understand," she said.

All the way back into town, she sat quietly

beside him, staring straight ahead. He said he would show her the gold tomorrow. That they would make a day of it. All right, she would just have to put up with him.

Ride it out, she told herself. Nothing as important as a wagonload of high-grade Denver City minted gold ever came easily. She'd never thought it would. But every move she'd made so far had brought her hands closer to it. She couldn't back out now. Not now when she could all but feel the hard, silk touch of it jingling down, pouring through her fingers.

Okay! Who has the most gold? Which should I rob? she asked herself almost playfully. *The Cowboy Gang or Los Lobos?*

It really didn't matter to her. She had now become close friends of both sides. She had helped the bandidos steal the gold. She was sleeping with Cowboy leader Nathan Catlow himself. Either side had plenty. With a little work, maybe she could rob them both.

■ ■ ■ ■

PART 3

■ ■ ■ ■

PAID 3

CHAPTER 14

The riders topped a narrow, overgrown game trail one at a time. First came Shelby Burnes leading a spare horse he had brought along to carry supplies. Seconds behind him, Dan'l Thorn rode up, his rifle across his lap. Right behind Thorn, the ranger rode up, his telescope standing in the lapel pocket of his riding duster. He held his Winchester in his left hand, his reins in his right.

Somewhere on the sand-and-rock shelves angled like stairsteps down to a forested valley on a wide creek below was Roman Lee Ellison. He'd gone on ahead of the others to scout the wild remote terrain.

Sidestepping his animal enough for the ranger to stop beside him, Thorn looked across the land below them right to left.

"Nobody's trekked through here on shod horses for a mighty long time," Thorn commented.

In the dust at their feet, layer over layer of unshod horse prints, elk prints, coyote and wolf prints ran in every direction.

"Let's keep moving," Sam said.

He'd looked around and realized how skylighted they were up here. Anybody who saw them would realize they were likely on some sort of business. Cannibals or no, this desolate land struck him as a place to get through and keep going. Anyone up here wouldn't want their whereabouts known.

So be it, Sam thought.

"Stories like the one about the Smiths get started, it gives some folks the willies for a long time," Thorn said. He smiled. "But us hard-to-the-bone lawmen, we never get the willies, do we?"

Sam only looked at him sidelong as if answering such a mindless question would likely encourage more of the same.

"You fellas coming?" Shelby Burnes asked, setting his horse less than thirty feet down from them on the next stone ledge, the lead rope to the supply horse in hand.

The thin game trail appeared to connect ledge after ledge to the valley floor.

"Don't make me go and leave you," Burnes said.

"The farther we've gone, the cockier he's gotten," Thorn said. He raised his voice and

194

called out to Burnes. "When you feel jumpy, jump, Shelby!" he said. "I've got my rifle sight ready to tickle your backbone, any offhand move you make!"

A silence came and went.

"I'm sorry, Lawman Thorn," said Shelby Burnes. "I reckon I don't know none of you well enough yet to make jokes."

Thorn looked at the ranger, grinned widely, then said down to Burnes, "Damned right, you don't, Shelby! Now stop fooling around and tell us what we're looking at down there!" He feigned explosive rage. "Are those the valley and the creek you talked about or not?"

"Yes, sirs, both of you, they are!" he replied in a nervous voice.

"All right," said Thorn. "What're the names of the valley and the creek?"

"I don't know the creek's rightful name, but growing up near here, we always called it Hanging Man Creek."

"And the valley?" Thorn asked.

"Well . . . Cannibal Valley, we always called it."

"They always called it Cannibal Valley," Thorn repeated cheerily as if Sam would not otherwise have heard.

"Thanks," Sam said flatly.

He put Doc forward and down the game

trail. Thorn fell in behind him on Cochise.

The two rode onto the lower ledge where Shelby Burnes had stepped down from his horse and stood holding his horse's reins and the supply horse's lead rope in hand.

In a lowered voice, as if to keep from being overheard, he said, "I don't know what's happened to your Cowboy Gunman friend," he said. "Hasn't been a peep out of him."

He nodded at hoofprints in the dirt — the only shod prints they'd seen all day. "Here's his horse," he added. The prints led farther down the game trail. "Want me to call out for him?"

"No!" the ranger said sharply. "Keep quiet."

The ranger and Thorn studied the downward path winding toward the rushing creek below.

"I did see a glint of a canteen or rifle barrel or something now and again," said Burnes. "But now I don't even see that anymore."

Sam stood close to Thorn and spoke almost in a whisper. "I'm going down a ledge or two. Stay here. Give me five minutes. If you haven't heard from me by then, come on down."

"Be careful now, both of you." Burnes sounded rattled.

"We'll all three be careful, Shelby," Thorn said to Burnes. "If I go down because my ranger friend hasn't answered, I'll have you right beside me."

"Sure," said Burnes, now visibly shaken. "I wouldn't have it any other way."

Back in the saddle, Sam rode to the next ledge down, where Burnes had last seen any sign of Roman Lee Ellison. He looked all around, quietly, meticulously. Roman Lee's horse stood patiently reined to a pinyon sapling. The sight of the horse there alone hit the ranger like a punch in the gut. He walked over and laid a hand on the horse's neck. The poor creature had been left standing in the hot afternoon sun, which Roman Lee would have never done if he'd had even the slimmest of choices.

Sam looked at the sky. The heat of the horse's flesh under his hand told him the horse had been there half an hour or longer. He untied the reins and led the horse two feet over to the shade and retied it. Then he took down Roman's canteen and gave the horse a drink of tepid water from his sombrero.

He walked to the stone edge and picked up Roman Lee's rifle, which had been laid out of the sun in the shade of a spindly cactus. He felt the barrel and stock and found it still warm, too warm to have been in the shade for long.

He looked toward the next ledge up, where Thorn and Burnes waited. The rifle had lain glinting in the sunlight until the sun had moved on. That was when Burnes had stopped seeing it.

Sam carried the rifle to Roman Lee's horse and shoved it down into the saddle boot.

There's your horse. There's your rifle. Where are you, Roman Lee?

When Thorn and Shelby Burnes came down and joined the ranger on the next ledge, they found him sitting on a rock near the front edge of the cliff, gazing down. His sombrero lay at his feet. A long coil of rope lay splayed out in the dirt beside him, one of its ends tied around a large juniper. His stallion, Doc, and Roman Lee's horse, Randy, were standing in the shade nearby. Sam nodded in acknowledgment, then gazed back down.

"Ranger?" Thorn said quietly. "You didn't come back. What's going on? What's got you looking down there?"

"Roman Lee's down there," Sam said without looking at him.

"Down there?" Thorn asked.

He rushed forward and looked down, but even squinting, he saw little. He turned to the ranger, who was already holding out the telescope. He raised it to his eye and muttered as he scanned the creek's edge.

"Where at down there?" Thorn asked.

"That big split boulder," Sam said. "Follow the blood."

"Oh, no!"

Sam could tell by Thorn's voice that he'd spotted Roman Lee bobbing in the surging water in the fissure between the split rocks.

"What happened to him, Ranger?" Thorn asked. "Did he slip and fall? Trip over something? What the hell happened here?

Shelby Burnes stood off to the side, not certain where he might stand in all of this.

The ranger stood up and untied the rope he had left looped around his waist. He pitched it on the ground.

Burnes awkwardly picked it up and started coiling it. He spoke in a meek tone. "Can anybody drink some coffee, if I boil some?"

The ranger and Thorn both nodded without saying a word. Sam walked closer to the edge and looked down and all around the rugged land.

"I saw something was wrong," Sam said. "I swung myself out on the rope and looked all up and down this hillside. I saw no marks to show he struck the rocks as he fell, no blood or anything else. And we heard no shouting, nothing."

Thorn gave it thought. After a moment he looked back down at the creek. Overhead two large scavengers circled and soared.

"Sonsabitches!" he growled skyward, then recomposed himself and said, "You think he was pushed, don't you, Ranger? Come on, say it if you think it. Was he pushed?"

"I don't know, Dan'l," said Sam, feeling himself getting a little testy. "I do know that if we want to find out anything else about it, we'd better get down there quick before those buzzards come soaring in."

The ranger walked over to Shelby Burnes, who stood waiting beside his two horses.

"What's the quickest way down this hillside?" he asked. "We want to get our friend out of the creek and get him into the ground."

"I know," said Burnes. "You don't want these devil birds pecking his eyes out."

"You're right," said Sam. "Tell us how to go."

"It'll be easier by half if I lead you down," said Burnes.

"All right," said Sam, "start leading."

"I will, I will!" said Burnes, seeing that the ranger and Thorn were both morose and edgy over losing their friend Roman Lee Ellison. "I need to tell you this path we're taking down can be awfully rough on horses. You'll be walking them as much as riding them."

"What are you implying, Shelby?" Thorn asked, striding up to the two of them. "Are you saying we should leave our horses here and one of us stay with them?"

"There're worse ideas," said Burnes. "By the time we get down there, it'll be getting dark —"

"We're taking the horses with us," said Sam, cutting him off.

"I understand," said Burnes.

Offering no more on the matter, he led his two horses to a thin game path hidden by saplings and wild grass. Sam and Thorn gathered Doc and Cochise and walked onto the path, one in front of Burnes, one behind. Sam led Roman Lee's horse on a length of rope.

The first thirty yards down, they led their animals through overgrowth, vine and brush entanglement, through breakaway walking stones and loose dirt and gravel.

"Santa Madre!" Thorn said in a raised voice, straightening Cochise and pulling him forward just as one of his rear hooves scraped down off the edge of the steep path.

Sam and Doc stood a few feet behind Burnes, waiting to cross the same dangerous section, Sam helping Roman Lee's horse.

"If I lose my stallion down this hillside because of you," Thorn said, "it's a sure bet you're going down behind him."

"I told you how it is," Burnes spit back at him. "If you want to blame somebody, blame yourself. You couldn't stand the thought of buzzards eating your friend down there."

Seeing Thorn get a certain killing look in his eyes that he'd seen many times before, the ranger cut in.

"Burnes!" he said. "Does it get better or worse from here?"

"It gets better right along here, then worse, then better again." He gave a dark little chuckle.

Sam heard Thorn's Colt cock and swung a hard gaze toward him.

"Put it out of your mind, Dan'l!" he said. "A gunshot could send all of us and half this hillside straight down."

Burnes's dark cackle stopped. Thorn uncocked his Colt and lifted his hand from its butt.

Burnes took on a more serious tone. "It'll be easier for a while. The next spot this bad is a long way down. Then it's done."

"All right, both of you settle down," Sam said. "We made this trip down for Roman Lee's sake, at risk to life, limb and horses. Let's keep moving before we burn up all the daylight."

They moved on in silence. At places where the thin path had washed away, they led the horses up a few feet and crossed a spot no less hazardous yet with some offer of footing. At other places they squeezed along the face of land-stuck boulders so tight that the horse's sides wore streaks of wet dirt, shade moss and stone scrapings.

Finally, as the sun leaned further west and long shadows filled rock crevasses and intersecting trails, the dirty, sweaty party of man and horse stood worn and haggard on the rocky bank of Hanging Man Creek.

"It's a real rusher, ol' Hanging Man," said Burnes above the powerful sound of water over rock.

Thorn and Sam just looked at each other.

"It'll be dark soon," said Sam. "Let's get Roman Lee and go."

Only twenty yards upstream, the ranger was not surprised to find the two large boulders he'd seen Roman Lee lying between. That was how well he'd kept them on course.

"I ever lose a silver dollar in a cyclone, I hope you're there to help me find it," said Thorn in a worn-out voice.

Sam took off his sombrero and looked up the side of the boulders. It was a climb of no more than fifteen feet, with handholds and footing. Sam studied the boulder sides and took the rope that Burnes had coiled earlier.

"Are you going to be able to lift Roman by yourself?" Thorn asked.

"I don't even know yet if I can get the rope around him," the ranger said. "We'll see."

"I'm here. If you need me, holler," Thorn said.

Sam looped the rope over his shoulder, stood Doc firmly in place and climbed up. Standing atop the saddle, he stepped over against the big boulder and started climbing.

Above the spray of the rushing water, the surface on the two split boulders was dry and radiated heat from the long hot Mexican day. Walking to the front edge of the boulder, Sam eyed a large pool of dried blood. Farther ahead he saw more dried blood near where he'd spotted Roman Lee's body down between the split boulders bobbing in the surging water. He regretted going closer, knowing what he would find.

Here goes, he told himself, preparing.

Minutes passed. On the creek bank, Burnes had sat down on a rock. Thorn stood with an arm over Cochise's saddle, chewing a bite of an apple he'd taken from his duster pocket.

"Is it taking him a long time?" Burnes asked.

"Yep, it is," said Thorn. "A little longer, I'm sending you up to see what's going on."

"I ain't going," said Burnes, raising his voice. "I'll watch the horses."

"You're going!" said Thorn a little louder yet. "I don't trust you with the horses. So you're going!"

A small pebble dropped onto Thorn's duster sleeve. He turned his eyes to it, then raised them and saw the ranger standing atop the boulder.

Cupping his hands around his mouth, he called down, "Neither of you is going! Roman Lee is gone."

"He's gone?" said Thorn. "What the hell do you mean, he's gone?"

Instead of replying right away, Sam looked down at the footholds on the boulder. Without waiting, he turned, stooped and slid the first couple of feet on his stomach. He found purchase with the toe of his boot and moved down, successfully finding a handhold that eased him down farther, then another. When he was less than ten feet from Doc, he pushed himself out slightly and dropped the last few feet into his saddle. He gave Doc a rub, even though the stallion stood steady, barely flinching.

"I mean, Roman Lee's body is not there, Dan'l."

"He's not there?" Thorn echoed.

"Look at me, Dan'l," the ranger said, with no patience to start over. "Roman Lee is gone —"

"Okay, I get it!" said Thorn testily. He started to ask, *"Gone where?"* but caught himself in time and said instead, "What do you suppose happened to him?"

"I'm working on it," Sam said.

CHAPTER 15

When Pearl and Catlow arrived back at his hotel room, she had already started planning her getaway. Shooting those three men down like animals, men who had worked for him in the past and had now changed sides to the bandidos? What absurdity, what childishness! It was time to start making her move. Not that she couldn't handle Catlow. She could, for certain. But for how long?

She had found herself entangled with bullying men in the past, never realizing it until it was too late, never considering how dangerous these men could be until she found herself running from them, changing her looks, her name, whatever it took.

She stopped herself and took a composing breath. That was over. It was always much easier to climb into bed with men like Nathan Catlow or Bertram Leonard than it was to get away from them later. Well, those men would never foil her plans again. She was on top now. She could think of nothing, *nothing* she wouldn't do to stay there.

Pearl Whitcomb, Private Investigator. She smiled to herself. From her personal bag, she took out a very small bottle of clear liquid and poured half of it into a glass of bourbon she had set aside for Catlow. She capped the little bottle and hid it under her dress. Tonight, when the bourbon and its special potion had done its job — either killed him or left him in a permanent drooling stupor — she would slip out and go see a man who'd befriended her at Perrito Cantina. He was a friend of the bandidos. Maybe he was one himself. Either way, he would see to it she made it safely out of here, away from Perrito, away from Nathan Catlow, to Bertram Leonard and his Lobos' secret encampment.

In the middle of her thoughts, the door flew open and Catlow walked in boldly. "Knock, knock, I'm here," he said, sounding edgy.

He was already exhibiting a brusqueness fueled by bourbon, *cocaína* and a dark, insidious suspicion she'd had something to do with him vomiting his guts everywhere in the first place. Yes, she had saved him, he thought. But had she saved him only from what she herself had put in motion?

"Well, well, you certainly are here," she said, giving him her smile of glowing admiration. "I was just now thinking about you, hoping you would show up. I can't stand being alone when I could be getting my hands on a big strong man who's running loose."

She wasn't going to bring up how terrible he had acted earlier out on the sand flats. Instead, she crossed her legs toward him, both of them bare from the knee down and the top leg rocking back and forth languidly.

He leered, stepping forward. "What're the chances we go to bed early and stay up late?" he asked.

She laughed as if she had never heard that old stringer. "Very good chances," she said.

He looked around. "May I have a drink?" he asked.

"Of course, you certainly may." She gestured toward the glass of bourbon sitting on the small table beside him. "I made it for you." She smiled as he picked it up and swirled the glass.

"Ah, yes! Tell me, dearest Pearl," he said, "did a lot of love go into pouring this for me?"

"Oh, yes, I put a tremendous amount of love in each and every drop."

She watched him throw back the double shot in one gulp and let out a satisfying whiskey hiss. He wiped a hand over his mouth. As he unbuckled his gun belt, he set the empty glass down with his other hand, then lowered himself down on the edge of the bed and let his gun belt fall behind him. He lifted a boot for her to pull off.

She smiled winsomely, stepping forward.

Although Catlow was still awake, she knew he would be drifting off any minute. Looking up at her lying atop him, Catlow gave her a weak little smile and spoke in a low voice.

"I have a confession to make, Pearl," he said. "The way I was acting today? It's because I honestly thought you poisoned me."

"Why on earth would you think such a thing, Nathan?" she asked. "Isn't there anyone you trust?"

"No," he said quietly, "and there hasn't been for a long time. I'm afraid this rotten life I live beat all the trust out of me many years ago."

She brushed a hand across his forehead.

"How terrible that must be," she said sympathetically. "Did you mean it when you said tomorrow you'll show me where your gold is hidden?"

"No," he said sadly. "That was a lie. I won't show you because I don't know where the Ciudad Esplanade gold is. I have lots of gold stashed across Mexico and on the other side of the border, but as far as the big haul I made in Ciudad Esplanade, the gold I know you want to see, the bandidos stole it the other night. I have no idea where any of it is. Will you forgive me? Can we start over? I'm so sorry I doubted you. I know now that you wouldn't do something as terrible as poison me to get on my good side by saving my life. I have been a fool."

"Oh, my," said Pearl. "Yes, I forgive you."

She pushed herself up from the bed, straightened her dress and stood looking down at him. She rolled him off of the gun belt and picked it up, snapped it and tossed it up on her shoulder.

Catlow rolled back over and looked at her curiously. "What are you doing?"

Pearl smiled. She took a large sombrero from the bedpost and adjusted it on her head.

"I'm taking your gun, Nathan." She crossed the room, picked up a leather fold-over bag of gold coins and hefted it to judge its worth. "And your money."

She picked up her poncho serape, which she'd hung over a tall chairback, and tossed it over her other shoulder, then stepped into her large Mexican boots.

"You're not leaving?" he exclaimed. Seeing she meant it, he shouted, "But why?"

He tried to roll up out of bed but his arms and legs wouldn't cooperate. He flopped like a large helpless fish, and Pearl stifled a laugh against the back of her hand.

"You poor, dumb bastard." She shook her head. "I just poisoned you again. That's twice I got you." She started for the door.

"I'm poisoned? Again?" he said.

"Yes," she said, "I paid the room clerk to send me up more of the same, only stronger."

"Am I going to die?"

"I sure hope so," she said. "You're fading pretty fast."

"Don't leave me!" he said. "Stay with me! Cure me again! I'll get you gold. All the gold you'll ever want!"

She stopped at the door and looked back at him.

"Naw, I don't think so," she said. "I'm going to where I know the Esplanade gold is. So adios, Catlow. I'm sorry you have nothing else to offer me. I really do love the horse. *Gracias!*" She touched the brim of the large sombrero and departed.

As she left, Catlow rolled onto his back.

He stared vacantly at the ceiling and let out a long sigh. *Adios, crazy bitch.*

In Perrito Cantina, the Texan known only as LaPiers stood at the far end of the dark, lantern-lit bar, his hand up the dress of one Rita Dallis, seated atop the bar in front of him, her knees clasping his sides. A wooden bottle of mescal stood by his other hand.

"Señor LaPiers," said Pedro, speaking softly as if not wanting to awaken the four card players at a front corner table.

"*Sí,*" said LaPiers under his breath, Rita Dallis's mouth on the side of his neck.

"The *loca* American woman is back," said Pedro. "She wants to see you."

"Oh," said LaPiers. "But young Rita here wants to see me too."

Pedro held out a gold coin in the palm of his hand and grinned. "The *loca Americana,* she gave me this just to tell you she's here."

"Really?" LaPiers looked at the shiny new coin. "The *loca Americana,* eh?" He grinned, thinking about her.

"*Sí,* she wants to see you bad, I think," Pedro whispered, leaning in closer.

"So does Rita, I think," said LaPiers.

"*Sí,* but this *Americana* always brings money to give you," Pedro said. "Rita wants only to take money from you."

"Good point." LaPiers pulled Rita's face back from his throat and looked down at her in the flickering glow of the lantern. "Okay, Rita, time to go," he said. "Business is business."

He lifted Rita down from the bar. She smoothed down her dress and quickly disappeared out the rear door. LaPiers took the bottle, its cork and the unused wooden cup from the bar top and walked over to the table where the woman sat.

Sombrero, gun belt and all, LaPiers told himself.

"Didn't think I'd ever see you again, Miss Beverly," he said, sitting down across from her.

She glared at him an angry twenty seconds. "I'm *Pearl,* you mindless jackass," she hissed.

"Whoa! Miss Pearl, I am nothing, nothing but sorry." He shook his head. "I've had so much on my mind lately, I don't know —"

"Listen to me, you idiot! You buffoon, you joker!" she snapped at him.

He'd never seen a woman so upset over her name being mistaken.

"Bertram Leonard told me that if I needed help, money, anything, to find you and you would contact him for me! Do you remember that?"

"Yes, I do remember, Miss Pearl," LaPiers said. "And I'd like to call you, Pearl, if I may be so bold . . ."

"Of course you may, *Hudson,*" she said, getting back at him.

LaPiers looked embarrassed.

"All right, Miss Pearl," he said, ignoring the Hudson remark, "I will see to it that Bertram Leonard hears you want to talk to him."

"No," said Pearl, leaning closer, a fist closed tight on the tabletop. "I don't need to just talk to him. I need to see him."

"Okay, I've got it," LaPiers said. He gave her the expectant look of someone wanting money.

"No!" she said. "You're taking me to see him tonight! I will make it worth your time and trouble, but we're going tonight. Right now! Do you understand?"

LaPiers caught a glimpse of Rita Dallis coming back in through the rear door.

"There is only one thing I am going to be doing tonight, Miss Pearl," LaPiers said, "and you ain't invited."

The sound of a gun hammer cocking under the table drew his attention.

"Get off your ass! You're taking me to Bertram Leonard."

"Easy, Miss Pearl," LaPiers said, his hand

raised in a show of peace. "We're going." He stood slowly. "You don't want to shoot a gun in a place like this. Innocent people can get hurt."

She didn't reply other than to raise Catlow's Colt from under the table and motion it toward the front door.

"It is a long ride," he said over his shoulder as they went out to the horses at the hitch rail. He walked over to a black-and-white paint horse and unhitched its reins. "I say that just so you know what to expect out there. This Mexican desert where we will be traveling is not a friendly place to either humankind or beast."

"Save your bull-dabble spiel for the sightseers," she said. "I've already heard it."

She uncocked the Colt, stuck it in the holster on the gun belt hanging down her shoulder. She motioned for him to get into his saddle. When he did, she mounted the chestnut bay Catlow had given her, which she'd not yet named.

"Miss Pearl, that is a fine-looking animal you've got between your knees. I hope it has been well-fed and watered sometime today."

"It has," she said.

"The reason I say this is because we don't

appear to be taking any food or water with us —"

"Are you hungry, LaPiers?" she asked impatiently.

"No —"

"Thirsty?" she queried.

"Well, no." He chuckled a little.

"Then let's go, damn it to bloody hell!" she demanded.

"Yes, ma'am."

Oh, man! The mouth on this crazy American bitch.

As they backed their horses away from the hitch rail, she said firmly, "You need to know that whatever behavior I see out of you, good or bad, will be reported to Bertram first thing. You will find that he and I are very close. *Very close!*" she repeated for emphasis.

It was nearing dawn when, after an almost silent nightlong trek, LaPiers led Pearl Whitcomb inside a guarded adobe-style fortress. Ancient remnants of a long-abandoned adobe city inside the wall appeared to be clinging to an eroding mountain of limestone and black lava stone. From a catwalk above their heads, an armed guard called down to LaPiers as the two rode inside toward dim candlelight.

"What brings you out here this time of morning, LaPiers?"

The tired, hungry LaPiers gestured sidelong at the woman as if that answered any further questions the guards might have. The two heard restrained laughter from along the catwalk as they rode on.

"Wait here, Miss Pearl," LaPiers said as they veered toward a vacant hitch rail.

Pearl set obediently still in her saddle until a door opened for LaPiers and he stepped inside and closed it behind him. She listened intently for a moment, hearing quiet male voices. Finally, having heard enough, she slipped down from her saddle and marched to the unlocked door like a woman on a mission. Without knocking, she swung the heavy door wide open.

"Hold it, ma'am," said LaPiers. "I told you to wait outside."

He stepped forward as if he would stop her, but instead, Bertram Leonard stopped him with a raised hand.

"It's all right, LaPiers. I'll see her."

LaPiers stood firm for a moment, thinking of how Pearl had acted all the way there. But when he looked at Bertram Leonard, he saw that whatever Bertram had to say to her was more important.

"I'll be right outside if you need me,

boss," he said.

He looked Pearl up and down on his way out the door.

"Can I pour you a drink, Pearl?" said Bertram, sounding pleasant enough for a man who'd been awakened too early from a sound sleep.

"I never drink before breakfast," she said. "I came here to get my share of the gold, which you said would be here for me when I needed it. Remember?"

"Yes, I do remember," said Bertram. "Things were moving pretty fast at that time. Maybe we need to start all over."

"Start over? Over on what?"

"We never got to how much your share would be for poisoning Nathan Catlow, then curing him to gain his confidence." He smiled. "I have to say that was well worth it, even though I don't see what it got us."

"It got you and your men the chance to steal all the gold while he was distracted, heaving his guts out!" Pearl retorted.

"I have to admit, it was enjoyable." Bertram Leonard chuckled under his breath. "But come on, how much do you figure you have coming for that? He didn't even die."

"Not that minute," said Pearl, "but he started getting a little tough with me yesterday, so I poisoned him again — this time with a more powerful mixture."

"That's great," said Bertram. "So this time he's dead for sure?"

"If he wasn't dead when I left, he's there by now." Pearl smiled on her own behalf.

"That's wonderful, Pearl!" He spread his arms. "Come here. Let me hold you against me."

"First," she said, "how much is my share? I want a lot of it in Denver City gold-struck coin and a lot more of it in good ol' U.S. cash!"

Bertram Leonard gave her a troubled look. "Yes," he said, "I think we have to have a serious talk about this."

CHAPTER 16

The ranger, Thorn and Shelby Burnes camped for the night under a deep overhang above the banks of Hanging Man Creek. Before midnight the sky turned black and thick and a heavy rain descended on them. It poured straight down, strong and relentless. The horses gathered close to one another in the pitch-darkness of the overhang. The three men sat wrapped in their dusters around a low fire and listened to the pounding rain on the world of rock surrounding them.

Thorn nodded at the rainstorm. "There go any tracks or signs we might have found," he said.

"This is always a busy creek," Burnes put in. "It surges a lot. Might well be the water took an upsurge from some rain higher up last night and washed him away."

The creek surges a lot? What does that mean? Sam asked himself.

x

221

Sam and Thorn cut a glance at Burnes, then back to the fire. His words, right or wrong, carried a suggestion that they leave Roman Lee's body and never know where it went or what happened to it.

The ranger stirred a dry branch around in the bed of glowing coals. "We're not giving up, Burnes," he said. "How much farther to the Smith brothers' place?"

"Their place?" said Burnes. "As far as boundary line and land title, we're likely on it. Down water another hundred yards or so, there're a path and a runoff branch that lead right to their cabin door."

"So we would have had to climb down here anyway?" Thorn said.

"Yes," said Burnes. "And when we saw your friend lying down here ready to be supper to anything that crawls or flies, you wanted to get to him. So we did, or we tried to."

The ranger leaned back against his saddle on the dry ground. "As soon as this rain lets up, we'll go on to the Smiths' cabin. Maybe we'll run into Roman Lee's body on the way."

"Some wishful thinking," Thorn said under his breath.

He leaned back, dropping his Stetson over his face. Burnes did the same, with a feeling that one or both of those two would know about any move he might make in the night.

In the early hours of a dark dawn, the rain stopped as quickly as it had started. A trickle of water had found its way down the hillside, found the overhang and meandered across it. It ran against and under one of Thorn's feet, waking him.

"Aw, damn it!" he cursed, sitting upright from against his saddle. "I hate wearing a wet sock!"

"I'm glad you let us know that, Dan'l," said the ranger. "I've always wondered."

He had almost grabbed his Colt from the rise of his saddle.

"My apology for waking you," Thorn said in a gruff tone.

He pulled off the offending wet sock, squeezed it and dropped it beside the smoldering coals of last night's fire.

"That's all right. I was awake," said Sam. "I woke up when the rain stopped."

"So did I," Shelby Burnes said meekly. He rose to his feet, picking up the cold coffeepot on his way. "I expect we've got time to get some coffee in our bellies?" he asked, reaching for his boots.

"Yes, obliged," Sam said.

As Burnes stamped his boots into place and headed out from under the overhang,

Sam walked into the silvery gray mist and looked down. He and Thorn watched as a shadowy image of Burnes made its way in and out of the mist until he reached the creek's edge.

"I've got this, Ranger," Thorn said. "I'll have this jake covered until we know what became of Roman Lee. I liked the fella."

"We both did," Sam said. "Had he spent a little more time around us, he might have given up his outlaw ways."

"Yeah," Thorn said with a faint smile, "or we might have taken them up. I hate to think these flesh-eating Smiths might have slipped in and gotten him from between the boulders."

"Don't think about it," Sam said. He paused for a moment of consideration, then added, "It's bad enough to think wild critters are eating one of us. It's worse thinking one of our own kind is doing it."

The two continued watching in silence as Shelby Burnes started back through the mist, onto the rugged path, up toward the shrouded overhang. Only a single beam of sunlight shone through the mist and stood slantwise on the limestone-and-lava hillside.

"It's clearing up now," Thorn observed, looking toward the strip of sunlight.

Sam turned and started toward the horses

when the sound of a rifle shot exploded from somewhere along the creek bank below. He spun around in time to see Shelby Burnes tumbling down the rocky hillside. A large splotch of blood covered the rocks where he'd just been walking. The bouncing coffeepot rattled down the hillside behind him, slinging water.

The ranger saw Thorn's Colt already up and cocked, his eyes searching the breaking mist surrounding them. Sam raced to their saddles and bedrolls by the fire. He pulled both of their rifles from their saddle boots and hurried back to Thorn. He pitched Thorn's rifle to him, and they stood crouched on either side of the overhang's opening.

"Any chance he's alive?" Sam asked, speaking low.

"I saw it hit him," said Thorn. "If he's alive, it's a damn miracle. Loudest rifle I've heard in years."

They scanned the hillside as they spoke.

"We need to find out," Sam said.

"If you say so," Thorn said. "I'm more interested in who made that incredible shot."

"One of the Smith brothers?" Sam asked.

"I have no idea," Thorn said. "If it is, I haven't heard another sound out of them.

They're watching, waiting for one of us to show our topknots."

"We can't stay here long," Sam said.

Thorn replied, "But we can wait until the sun's out good and clear, see if they're still there or not."

"I'm going to see if Burnes has managed to still be alive. Cover me."

"Why, hell yes, I'll cover you!" Thorn said cynically. "My job is to give you my expert trailman's opinion, then watch you do as you damn well please."

"Obliged," Sam replied as sincerely as he could make the word sound.

With a cryptic trace of a grin, Thorn shook his head and wiped his thumb along the rifle's front sight.

"See if you can bring back our coffeepot. Fill it first if you get a chance."

Four wounded and badly beaten members of the Arizona Cowboy Gunmen Gang sat in a row of old yet solidly built wooden chairs that sat facing an unlit fireplace. Their hands were well bound behind them with strips of rawhide. On a tin stove in the corner of the adobe-and-stone shack, the smell of fresh wild pork strips sizzled in a large iron skillet.

One of the men, in better condition than

the others, pleaded in a barely audible voice to be taken outside to relieve himself.

"Please, somebody . . . ," he said. "I have got to go really bad."

"Then go," said a huge armed guard who sat facing them, a shotgun on his lap. "Do like the other jake did." He nodded at an empty chair with a large sodden circle on the floor beneath it. "Let flow when ready." He cackled with laughter.

"That's not the kind of relief I need," the prisoner said. "I need to go really bad before I —"

"For God sakes!" said the man doing the cooking. "Take him out so's he can go. I'm not cooking if we have to sit here eating in somebody's stink."

Two other men stood up, one walking to the door, the other over to the man in the chair. He pulled the prisoner to his feet.

"I saw what happened to the man who let himself go in the chair," said the one at the door, looking at the dark spot under the chair. "I don't mind killing a sumbitch, especially one of these damned Cowboy Gunmen. But I can't see torturing a man this way."

"Take him outside and shut up about it!" the huge man with the shotgun said. "You're bellyaching more than these three. Ain't that right?" he said to the three prisoners sitting slumped in their chairs.

Not one replied.

"Hell," the shotgun holder said, "march these three outside too. Let them all go in the woods." He turned to the prisoners and said, "What about it, Cowboy Gunmen? Who needs to relieve themselves?"

Two of the prisoners nodded their bloody, unsteady heads. The third one didn't move a muscle. He sat as silent and unmoving as he had all morning.

The two men looked at the man with the shotgun. He saw the third man's head move just enough to show he was alive.

"Take them out," said the shotgun holder. "Looks like this Cowboy Gunman is looking down, searching for the road to hell." He gave a wide terrible grin. "I'll see to it he gets there."

In the wooden chair the remaining prisoner sat as silent as stone, not a muscle moving, not a nerve twitching. Yet behind him he busily plucked at the rawhide knot with his thumbnail and fingers, blood from his fingertips softening and stretching the wet rawhide as he worked. And now at last, he had it. He slipped the knot loose and felt it fall onto the chair seat. He was free. . . .

Just in time.

"Hey, you, Cowboy Gunman!" said the man with the shotgun, standing up from his chair, leaning in for a closer look. "Are you dead yet?" he asked.

When he got no answer, saw no movement, no breathing, nothing, he said, "Yep, you've run out your string."

He intended to pull the man from his chair and drop him on the floor as final proof of his death. But when he raised the man and turned him loose, the man spun around full circle in a flash and brought up the chair by its back.

The frightened man let out a scream as he saw the heavy wooden chair coming around fast in a wide circle. He even forgot to raise his shotgun before the heavy chair broke into pieces across his chest, his face, his shoulder, his side ribs and flew into splinters and larger pieces in the air.

The man at the stove went for his gun, but both his hands were so greasy, it slid from them and hit the floor. He grabbed for a hatchet; that slipped away too. The prisoner now held the huge man's single-barrel shotgun. Knowing it had only one shot in it, he flipped it around in his hands and punched the man in his face with the butt plate.

Seeing the cook stagger backward but still

going again for the gun he had dropped on the floor, the prisoner grabbed the hot skillet by the handle and busted the cook on the side of his face with a full swing.

Sizzling pork flew in a spray of hot grease. The prisoner stooped and grabbed the cook's dropped gun, rubbed it quickly on the bib of his Townsend denim overalls and turned it toward the huge man, who had stumbled to his feet. He heard the gunmen outside shouting, running back to the shack.

Instead of breaking every chair in the place over the huge man, he cocked the greasy gun three times, putting each bullet into the man's wide chest. He looked at the pistol, a big black-handled Colt, as he shoved it into his overalls. On his way out the back door, shotgun in hand, he picked up the hatchet the cook had also dropped and kept moving.

Looking in every direction out the back door, he saw no sign of the other gunmen or prisoners, but he heard the front door open and close and the sound of boots inside now on the part of the floor that was made of wide, seasoned pinyon boards.

"Man! What a mess!" one man shouted.

"Look at Hank and Utterly!" another man shouted. "They are messed up!"

"Go get the son of a bitch before he turns

the other three loose!"

"There they go already," shouted a gun-man, looking out a dirty window.

The three other prisoners were running, helping one another along, getting out of sight. Behind them the fourth prisoner ran along barefoot in his ragged Townsend overalls, the shotgun in his hand, the black handle of the big greasy Colt sticking out of his overalls' side pocket.

Hearing what sounded like a full-scale gun battle erupting from the direction the ranger had taken, Thorn listened as long as he could stand it. If the ranger was in trouble down there — and Thorn felt that in all likelihood, he was — Thorn needed to get the horses and ride down there to him.

The ranger had no trouble finding the spring running down alongside the path leading through the woodland to the Smith brothers' cabin. He'd noted a lot of hoof-prints and boot prints going back and forth along the thin, partly overgrown path to and from what Shelby Burnes said was the Smith brothers' place.

The cannibal brothers, Sam reminded him-self.

When the shooting started higher up, he

stepped off the path and continued on, hoping to make himself less of a target for any gunman looking down on him from farther up the gentle roll of hillside that was so unusual in this Mexican high-desert terrain. He had to be careful of any sounds coming up behind him. Knowing that Thorn would have heard the shooting too, Sam was certain he would soon come riding up any minute.

When he heard unsteady shoeless feet running slowly down the slope of hillside toward him, Sam went down deeper into a level of thick, tall undergrowth where he lay still and quiet, watching, waiting.

Gunshots rang out. Bullets struck trees, tore through foliage and whistled past them overhead.

"Keep moving," said the man carrying the shotgun. His face was beaten and cut and swollen. He limped and held one arm against his side, protecting his side or his arm or both. "If they catch up to us, they'll kill us." His voice was impaired by the condition of his beaten face.

"Leave me here!" another voice said, near sobbing. "I can't make it."

"Yes, you can," said the man with the shotgun. He leaned and pulled the man over his shoulder. "Hang on, I've got you." He managed to hold on to the shotgun.

Sam saw other armed bandidos running at the fleeing men, still firing, topping a low rise fifty yards away. He ran out to the man in the overalls, his rifle in one hand, his other hand raised in a show of peace. The other two prisoners had vanished into the thick foliage, with no offer of help.

"Come with me," Sam said. "There're horses coming for us."

He could tell the man hadn't clearly heard him, yet he came with the ranger all the same, Sam helping him along with the weight of the other man on his shoulders.

The men topped the low rise just as Sam caught a glimpse of Thorn riding up the path on Cochise, with the other horses on a lead rope beside them. Thorn sat with the lead rope under him on the saddle and fired round after deadly round from his rifle, sending the few men who had charged so boldly, running over one another now, making their retreat.

Sam pulled the wounded man from the other man's shoulder and laid him on the ground beside him.

"Take care of him!" Sam said, and he joined Thorn, who had shooed the horses deeper into the cover of foliage and thick vines.

The two fired shot after shot in the direction of the Lobos who had fled out of sight. After a heavy fusillade of bullets, Sam and Thorn both ceased firing, realizing the men they were shooting at had taken to the ground and wouldn't come out until more bandidos joined them.

"Oh, no!" the man in Townsend overalls said in his swollen distorted voice. "This man is dead."

The man lay stonelike, his eyes wide open, two bullet holes in his side.

The man in overalls shook his bowed head and shouted at the distant unseen bandidos, "You rotten sonsabitches!" He drew the black-handled Colt from his overalls and started to fire.

"Hold it," said Sam. "Don't waste your bullets —"

The man lowered the gun and sat holding it in his lap. Sam and Thorn looked at each other, astounded, then back at the gun.

Sam reached over and picked it up carefully. At first the man didn't want to give it up, but then he somehow decided it was all right. Sam turned the gun in his hands and held it for Thorn to see.

Anger flared in Thorn's eyes. "Where did you get this gun?" he asked, somewhere between a query and a demand. His hand tightened around his gun butt.

"I've had that Colt since I was a kid, mister," the young man said, his split, swollen lips making it hard for him to talk.

The two lawmen had to let the other man's words sink in. Then it struck them.

"Holy saints!" Thorn whispered, amazed.

Holding the black-handled Colt, the ranger looked at the injured man intently and questioningly until at length he saw behind the black swollen eyes and badly beaten face and recognition came to him.

After a long moment, he asked quietly, "Roman Lee, is that you?"

CHAPTER 17

The three fought the Lobos for over an hour, each hurried attack with fewer gunmen than the one preceding it. It became clear to the ranger and Thorn that Roman Lee remembered them, was aware of who he was, where he was and what had happened to him. At first, he flinched if one of them approached him too quickly or spoke to him too suddenly. They understood.

"He's had the living hell beat out of him," Thorn said during a lull in the fighting.

Roman Lee had to concentrate as he listened to them, but he was getting better. Large knots on his head and face appeared to have already gone down a little, or at least Thorn and the ranger liked to believe so. Thorn handed Roman Lee an open canteen. They watched him pour water into his cupped hand and carefully wash his face a little at a time.

"Nothing like a good ol' gun battle to get

the blood flowing back in the right direction," Thorn said, loading his rifle beneath a cloud of thick gun smoke. He handed Roman Lee a clean bandanna to dry his battered face.

"Listen to that," the ranger said, looking to their right when he heard the distant sound of hooves galloping down a trail not far from them.

"Horses!" said Thorn.

"They're pulling out," the ranger said.

"Maybe they had to be somewhere first thing?" said Thorn with a faint grin.

Roman Lee watched them, listening, making his addled brain pay attention as he strove to get back to being himself.

The ranger looked at him. "Do you feel like riding up there with us, take a look around?" he asked.

"You mean, look around for the Smith brothers?" Roman Lee asked.

"That's right, the Smith brothers," the ranger said, glad to hear that the brutal beating might have been starting to wear off a little.

Roman Lee looked around, confused, but only a little. "Where's my horse?" he asked.

"He's over there," said Thorn, nodding toward where the five horses stood.

"What's your horse's name?" the ranger asked.

Roman cocked his head curiously. "It's Randy," he said.

Sam and Thorn both looked relieved.

"Yes, it is Randy," Sam said. "And Randy is right there with the rest of them. We wasn't going to get rid of him right away."

"Obliged," said Roman Lee. "Where's the man Burnes, who was traveling with you?" he asked.

"With us, Roman Lee," said Thorn. "He was traveling with *us*. The three of us were traveling together, remember?"

"Yeah, that's right. I remember now," said Roman Lee.

The ranger and Thorn watched him struggle to his feet and dust the seat of his overalls. He stuck the black-handled Colt into his side pocket.

Seeing the two taking note of his overalls and bare feet, he said, "I hope one of us killed the man who stuck me in this confounded getup."

"If we didn't kill him, somebody will soon enough," said Thorn. "Nobody gets by with treating a person this bad for long."

"Took my clothes and boots and stuck me in this," Roman Lee said. "No wonder I've got only half my senses."

After gathering the horses, the three rode along up the narrow path that Roman Lee and the other prisoners had been marched up like steer. They counted six dead bandidos strewn here and there on their way to the wide-open door of the Smith brothers' cabin. A wild desert hare streaked out the rear door and disappeared into a nearby patch of brush and foliage.

"How are you feeling now, Roman Lee?" Sam asked as they stepped down from their saddles and hitched the horses at a wood-pole hitch rail.

"I'm good, Ranger," said Roman Lee. "I just wish I could recollect it all together the way it happened."

"It'll all come back to you, Roman Lee," Thorn said. "Give it time."

Walking inside the Smith brothers' cabin, the three looked around at the mess left by Roman Lee when he had made his getaway. Knowing the bandidos would be back any minute, they wasted no time and pushed the broken chair, the iron skillet and the strips of fried pork aside. They walked into the other room and inspected it for any sign of the Smith brothers having lived there recently. They saw nothing of any value to their search for the infamous brothers.

Sam noted a large rusty iron crank and

what appeared to be the rusting steel helm of a cargo boat leaning against the wall. He stooped and looked closer at the two items. They were dry, yet he saw the plank floor beneath them was rust stained and water circled from the items, which had been placed there wet and allowed to dry.

Many times? How many? he asked himself. What were they? Was this equipment of some sort that the bandidos had used recently? Or something from the Smith brothers' time here in years past?

He called Thorn and Roman Lee over for their opinion. When they said they had no idea, Sam told them what he thought.

"You're right," Thorn said to the ranger. "It looks like the helm of a boat." He picked up the heavy iron object and held it as he would a boat helm. "Too heavy though," he said. "A boat helm is made of wood or the ones I've seen have been."

While Thorn held it, Sam eyed the middle at a two-inch round opening made to slide onto a shaft of some sort. An iron lug would have held it in place.

"Interesting," the ranger said as Thorn set it down.

"What did you decide?" Thorn asked.

"I'm working on it," the ranger replied.

"Good luck," Thorn said.

"It looks like a dam wheel and a gate key," said Roman Lee, studying the two items.

"I've never seen a damn wheel or a damn key that looked like either one of them," Thorn put in with a little laugh.

"I'm not saying a damn-with-an-n wheel or key," said Roman Lee, sounding more like himself. "I've seen river dams set up with this kind of equipment. If people want to let more water through a dam, they unlock the gate with this long key."

He pointed at the long rusty crank-looking apparatus, then at the rusty iron wheel. "Turn this wheel," he said, "and it opens and closes underwater gates. People adjust the water flow the way they want it, then lock it down and take this wheel off. Keeps anybody from monkeying with it."

The ranger and Thorn stood looking at Roman Lee for a moment, thinking about what he'd said.

"I'm going to take your word for it, Roman Lee," said Thorn. "I'm glad to see you're getting better."

"I've seen what you're talking about, Roman Lee," the ranger said. "The one I saw was on a river and was a lot bigger, but it looked the same. It took two workers to turn it. They turned the gate wheel and the river level went down. And they locked it there."

He looked in the direction of Hanging Man Creek. Roman Lee and Thorn looked with him.

"This is not cattle country or crop country," Thorn mused quietly. "What the hell? There's nothing important enough going on here to make anybody want to dam Hanging Man Creek, is there?"

He gave the ranger a curious look.

"I don't know," Sam replied. "Like I said, I'm working on it."

LaPiers rode beside Pearl Whitcomb as close as she would allow. Before leaving the Lobos' stronghold, Bertram Leonard had made it clear to him that if the woman were to, say, fall off a cliff or get eaten by a bear, it would be a shame, but not surprising there on the untamed Mexican frontier.

Twice, along the trail, LaPiers had tried to talk to the woman to let her know how dangerous it could be to issue mindless threats or curse and condemn a man as well respected as Leonard was now that he'd taken all of the gold from a group like the Arizona Cowboy Gang.

Leonard had even made it clear to him that should something terrible happen to Pearl, and the money — six thousand ninety dollars, shut-up money he'd given her —

were to disappear, nobody was going to inquire too deeply as to its whereabouts.

True, LaPiers had killed people before, some for free and some for money. True also, he had never killed anyone for an amount as large as six thousand ninety dollars. But that figure struck him as probably an amount Bertram Leonard just happened to have on hand when Pearl had shown up making demands. Without propositioning LaPiers in so many words, Leonard made it understood that LaPiers could kill the woman and keep the six thousand ninety dollars.

All right, he would try one more time to talk to her. He saw her point after she'd done what she had to grab all the gold, and now she was being brushed aside with an amount that sounded like no more than Leonard's pocket money.

In the pale rosy dawn, he sidled a little closer.

"I can't blame you for being mad at Bertram," he ventured. "If I was you, I'd be —"

"Move over, LaPiers!" she snapped, her voice sounding so full of venom, LaPiers's horse sidestepped away without its rider tugging on the reins.

"Easy, boy," he said to the horse.

"Begging your pardon, ma'am," he said, keeping his distance. "I only want to say, I see how you've been treated. If I could, I would go up-country with you and see what can be done to right this situation."

"Oh, would you?" she asked, a bitter ring to her voice.

"Yes, Miss Pearl," he said, "I truly would, and I truly mean it."

"So," she said, "you really did move in close to talk. Not to look for a chance to shove me over this edge and ride down and take the money off my body — all six thousand ninety dollars of it?"

Seeing that she held the amount in as much contempt as he did gave him heart.

"That is a cheap, cheesy figure if I might say so," he said. He relaxed just a little. "It's unforgivable. I'll be honest. There's nobody whose head I would not chop off for that amount. But not this time. I mean it. He just humped you bad in front of strangers. If you see a way I can help you seek retribution, I am your man." He paused, looking her up and down, then said, "There, that pretty much sums things up. My hand of friendship is open to you."

"For a price, of course," she grumbled.

"Yes, for a price, I don't mind saying," he replied. He gestured a hand around at the

244

grainy dawn. "Who else is out here making such an offer?"

She stared straight ahead.

Russell Fairday knocked lightly on Catlow's bedroom door, then let himself in before he heard a response. Carrying a tray with a covered breakfast on it, a pot of steaming coffee and a large cigar lying beside a cup turned upside down on a saucer, he walked to a bedside table, gave it a quarter turn with his boot and set the tray on it.

He walked to a half bottle of bourbon standing on the small bar, poured three fingers of bourbon into a glass and carried the glass back to sit beside the coffeepot.

"Aw, thank you, Fairday," said Catlow.

He reached past the coffeepot, picked up the glass of bourbon and drank it down. He let out a hiss, belched and set the glass down. "Should I have asked if Pearl Whitcomb has been near that bottle before I took a drink from it?"

Fairday looked startled for a second.

"That's a joke," said Catlow. He sipped his hot coffee, smiled above the cup and said, "What a night I had last night, eh?"

"Boy, I'll say so, boss," Fairday replied. "When I heard you in here, for a minute, I thought the woman genuinely had poisoned you. Again!"

"No! No. Once was enough for me, Fairday," said Catlow. "If I ever allow myself to fall for something like that again, I deserve it."

Catlow set his coffee down and laid his hands on either side of the covered breakfast plate. "Now, then," he said, "any report for me?"

Fairday stood with his hands folded in front of him. "Well, sir," he said, "she left here and went like a dart straight to the cantina. She rousted LaPiers out of there and the two of them hightailed it up to the Lobos' secret hideout."

"So do we now know exactly where that stronghold is?" Catlow asked.

"Oh, yes, we had a couple of our scouts follow her. So we know now for sure." He smiled. "If we forget, LaPiers knows."

"Sumbitch knew all long," Catlow said. "She just set a fire under his butt. She's impressive as hell." He chuckled. "I'm going to miss her." He paused, then added, "For an hour or two."

"Yes, sir, boss," said Fairday.

"She's the first investigator I ever pulled skin with." He sipped coffee and looked off as if briefly reminiscing.

"Okay, Fairday," Catlow said, snapping

back to himself, "what else have I got going on today?"

"Our three Cowboy Gang leaders are here, boss. They went on up to Gato Saltando, said they had hotel rooms reserved. Said they would see you when you get up there."

"They're scared we'll kill them in their sleep," Catlow said.

"With their armed guards right beside them?" said Fairday.

Catlow shrugged. "If they're scared, they're scared," he said. "Let me eat my breakfast. We'll talk more later on the trail."

back to himself, "who else have I ever run across?"

"I have decided to leave, teacher," he told Pedro. They had taught him every-

CHAPTER 18

The town of Gato Saltando was abuzz with the arrival of heavily armed men in the middle of the night, eight of them. They soon appeared to have taken over the running of the Gato Saltando Hotel and Pedro's Cantina next door, and of drinking and eating establishments open late farther up the stone-tiled street and of anything else that attracted them.

Six of them were steely-eyed bodyguards; the other two were those being guarded. The two being guarded were powerful top leaders of the Arizona Cowboy Gang. North was an older man whose years in the business world had awarded him several banks, which he now contracted out to other people and companies to run for him. He owned hundreds, perhaps thousands, of acres of prime American grainland. He'd killed three men in his life: two with a revolver; one with his bare hands. Wilson

Wright's story was similar to North's, except no one ever quite knew how he'd made his fortune or, for the past two decades, how he'd kept it. There were only sketchy details of how many men he might have killed, who they were or why he'd killed them.

The two of them sat at a table set up for them in the small lobby of the hotel, drinking whiskey, smoking cigars.

"How much trouble is Nathan Catlow capable of giving us?" Wilson asked.

"Not much as far as I'm concerned," North replied. "I do wish we had removed him back when this business started with the bank explosion. He probably thinks we had something to do with the timing being off."

North shook his head. "Yeah, that was when he started suspicioning that we were out to get him. Damned shame."

"I hate to say it, but that's when we should have had him shot," Wilson said, "and saved us all a lot of trouble."

North said, "Trulock is still talking like he wants to do the killing himself. I'm tempted to let him go on and do it."

"Good grief," said Wilson, "what are we, some kind of criminals?"

North only stared at him until they both

caught the irony of Wilson's remark and laughed.

"Hell, you know what I mean," Wilson said.

"I know," said North.

He looked around. Four of the six guards sat at a long table against the wall. The other two stood close by with rifles held at port arms.

"What's the matter?" one of the standing guards asked.

"Nothing," said North. "Where's Trulock?"

"Said he was hungry," one guard said. "He wouldn't let anybody go with him."

"Go check on him, Charlie," said North to one of the seated guards.

"I will," said Charlie Tree. "If he sees me, he'll piss a squealing worm."

"Don't let him see you, Charlie," said North straight-faced. "We don't want squealing worms all over the place."

Charlie Tree — half Southern Cheyenne, tall and whip-handle thin — rose and left. A long knife in a hand-tooled scabbard sat on his left side.

"I expect we'll be seeing Daniel Thorn and Ranger Burrack most anytime now," said Wright. "I heard they've both been sniffing around up here. Probably waiting for somebody to give them a payday."

A payday? North knew better, but he let Wright's comment pass. He'd never heard of the ranger taking a bribe from anybody. Thorn had always carried a rumor of being on the take, but North had knowledge of it firsthand. *Loose talk,* he decided.

Wright scooted his chair closer to the table and leaned forward some. "Have you thought any more on what we've talked about — about bringing the Lobos and our Cowboy Gang together?"

"Yes, some," said North.

He took his time, took a cigar from his shirt pocket, bit off the tip and spit it on the stone-tile floor. He waved away a guard who started to strike a match for him. Instead, he struck a match for himself with his thumbnail. Puffing the big cigar to life, he blew out a stream of gray smoke.

"Meanwhile," he continued, "I'm prepared to have both gangs kill hell out of one another up here if we don't get our gold back."

"I'm with you on all that," said Wright.

He drew out a cigar of his own, bit off the tip, spit it away and puffed the cigar up on a flaming match that the same accommodating guard held out to its tip.

■ ■ ■ ■

The ranger, Thorn and the healing Roman Lee Ellison had dragged Shelby Burnes's body down among some larger, heavier rocks on the steep hillside, covered him with both rocks and dirt against the elements and left his crude grave site unmarked.

"It always feels strange, planting a man with no marker saying who he is or what put him here," said Roman Lee. He stood graveside with his hat in his hand. "Not that it really matters, I suppose."

"The only things interested are wolves, vultures and land rats," Thorn had said. "None of them read anyway."

The ranger had stood quietly opposite Roman Lee. He'd looked up a short distance to where dark blood still streaked and stained the limestone facing of the hillside. In a slow, lifting morning mist, sunlight had crept through and shone onto the stone facing not more than ten feet wide. Burnes walked into that slanted ray of light, carrying a coffeepot, taking what, two steps, three at the most?

Sam looked down at the pile of stones. *Who could have made a shot like that?* He could clearly recall the sound of the rifle.

Something big, powerful . . . His eyes scanned along the limestone facing. *Large caliber, Civil War? Maybe a lucky shot? Could be.* But somehow he doubted it.

They walked back to where they had tied the horses. In moments they were at the Smiths' cabin, not on the same narrow trail they had first used. This time they had ridden farther up creek from the overhang where they had previously taken shelter from the rain. They'd soon found an overgrown game trail. They'd followed it up as far as they could. Where the path had run out, they circled high above the cabin and watched from brush cover, making sure there were no gunmen there before riding down any closer.

When they'd convinced themselves the place was empty, they made camp some thirty yards behind the cabin. They chose a spot out of sight from every direction. Buried in a stand of maturing juniper and pinyon, the camp could be spotted only from atop a high, rough-faced cliff looking down on a turn in the banks of Hanging Man Creek.

While Thorn watched the cabin and the trail below it through the ranger's telescope, the ranger rode down to the vacant cabin and brought back with him what they now referred to as the dam key and the dam wheel.

"This place won't sit empty long," the ranger said, tying the wheel down with rope on a spare blanket behind his saddle horn. "Today might be the only chance we get to search the place good."

"Search for what?" said Thorn, tying down the iron key behind his saddle.

"I don't know," Sam replied.

"It would help us to know," said Thorn.

"I can't say what," said Sam, "but I can say where. We're looking for something along the creek, something with a place for a wheel to attach to it."

"Like a water valve," Roman Lee put in.

"All right, a water valve," said Thorn. "Let's get started." That was as much as they knew — for now anyway.

Seeing the ranger turn Doc in the upstream direction of the path, Thorn asked, "Why this way?"

Even as he asked, they rode along at a walk, three abreast for now, until the path narrowed.

"Something Burnes said about when the creek surges it washes a lot of things away," he said. "The body that was thrown in to make us believe it was Roman Lee was lying in water between two boulders. When the creek surged, it washed the body away."

"So?" said Thorn.

"Why does the creek surge?" Sam asked. "When there's a lot of rain, a creek will surge, but not very often and not for very long. Especially after a long dry spell."

"So Burnes wasn't wrong?" Thorn asked.

"He made it sound like it was something that happened often," Sam said. "But why would it?"

"You should have asked him while you had the chance," Thorn said. He looked at Roman Lee and asked, "Why somebody else's body, Roman Lee? Why didn't they throw you in?"

Roman Lee said, "All I can figure is they're bandidos. Knowing I'm a Red Sash Cowboy, seeing me riding with you two, they wanted to hear from me what the two of you might know about the goings-on up here with the gold." He let out a tight breath. "I managed to get away from them before they went to work on me."

"Lucky for you," Thorn added. "Since you didn't know anything to tell them about us or the gold or anything else, they would have killed you for sure. Only slow and really bad-like."

"We're in a tough spot here between two gangs and a mountain of gold," said the ranger. "It's going to start getting tougher all the time. We need to find out if the Smiths are dead or alive. If they're alive, we gotta grab them and take them in."

"And if they're dead," Thorn said, "show proof of it. Take something back to prove it. Settle things one way or the other and get out of here," he added.

They both looked at Roman Lee.

"You're welcome to leave with us when we get our knees in the wind," Thorn said. He looked at the ranger.

"You sure are welcome, Roman Lee," said Sam. "We've gotten kind of used to having you around."

Thorn gave a thin smile. "Yeah. You're a fair shot, and you don't eat too much," he said. "You can stick around."

"Obliged to both of you," Roman Lee said.

They rode on, only a few yards from and parallel to Hanging Man Creek. When they passed the place where the two split boulders stood half in, half out of the creek, Roman Lee looked at it in passing as if he had no recollection of what had happened to him there.

"Roman Lee," said Thorn, "if you ever felt like telling us what happened to you, we'd be interested in hearing about it."

"There's nothing to remember," said Roman Lee. "I was standing there on a ledge above the creek. Something hit me from behind, knocked me cold. The next thing I remember, I opened my eyes, and I was tied down over a horse's back."

"And that's all you remember?" Thorn said.

"I wish I could tell you more," said Roman Lee, "but right now that's all I've got. Yesterday I couldn't remember any of it. Every hour, I gain a little more —"

"Hold it!" the ranger said to the two of them. "Do you hear that?"

He held himself still in his saddle, trying to make out a muffled, barely audible sound of metal on metal, a hollow thump that seemed to come from the earth itself. Neither Roman Lee nor Thorn heard it at first, yet the horses grew restless and stepped back and forth nervously. Doc scraped a front hoof on the ground.

Swinging down from his saddle, Sam drew his rifle from its boot and tied Doc's reins to a young juniper.

"I hear it now," Thorn said quietly. He also stepped down and reined Cochise to the same tree.

"So do I," Roman Lee said.

"Where the hell is it coming from?" said Thorn.

"What the blazes is it?" Roman Lee asked. "Wait for me," he said quickly.

He reined his horse, Randy, with the other horses and the men walked a few feet away. Still hearing the sound, the three of them each looked and listened in different directions, unable to pinpoint the sound's origin.

It stopped as quickly as it had started. It stopped cold, the creek bank seeming to have coughed it up, swallowed it and gulped it back down. Silence loomed. Instead of trying to search for the sound, the ranger kept his eyes and senses fixed on the spot where he thought he'd last heard it.

"Got it!" he whispered.

Without moving his eyes or using his other senses, Sam started walking straight ahead. He stepped into the shallow rushing water, crossed it and walked up a two-foot-high cutbank. Where the cutbank stopped, a high cluster of large stones the size of houses lay tumbled and piled a long way up a tall, sloping hillside.

He stopped at a two-foot-wide crevice and slowly pulled aside a sumac bush that covered the opening in the stones. Across the creek, Thorn and Roman Lee stood tense, rifles ready, prepared for anything.

They saw Sam stoop slightly and examine the ground.

"What's he doing?" Roman Lee asked.

"He's found something," said Thorn, "a sign or something."

Sam straightened up and flashed a hand signal.

"He's found footprints!" said Thorn.

"Paw prints? Hoofprints?" said Roman Lee.

"No! It's footprints," Thorn said. "Uh-oh, somebody's in there."

They watched Sam disappear into the dark crevice, his rifle barrel guiding him.

Thorn glanced at the horses, then turned and stepped forward, saying, "Let's get over there."

As soon as they took a step, a long yell rolled and resounded from inside the crevice, but it ended suddenly as the familiar thump of a rifle butt on a human head caused the two men to stop midcreek. They watched a limp figure half stumble, half soar out of the crevice and land, knocked cold, at the water's edge.

Roman Lee and Thorn hurried to the downed man and dragged him backward onto the gravelly creek bank. The cool rushing water started to revive the man immediately. His mouth hung wide open; his eyes rolled, unfocused. Roman Lee stooped and rolled the other man's thickly bearded face back and forth.

"Hey, wake up. You're all right. Wake up."

Roman Lee slapped him, not hard, but enough to help him get his thoughts restarted. After what Roman Lee had gone through himself, he seemed to know what he was trying to do.

Thorn and Roman Lee dragged the man a little farther up from the water's edge, raised him and leaned him against a rock. Out of the crevice flew a pair of handcuffs, which landed beside the addled man.

"Put these on him." Sam said, emerging from the stones with a lantern raised in his left hand.

Roman Lee clicked the cuffs on the man's wrists.

"What were you doing in there so long?" Thorn asked.

"You won't believe it until I show you," said the ranger. He pointed at the rushing creek. "I was down there."

Roman Lee and Thorn both stared at him.

"In the creek?" said Thorn. "We didn't see you in there."

"I wasn't in the creek, Dan'l," said the ranger. "I was under it."

CHAPTER 19

The three stood around the long-bearded man in a close half circle as if at any second he might vanish. The ranger did the talking, and he wasted no time, knowing that the longer they spent in the open on those hillsides, the more likely they were to be seen by bandidos coming into the area. Right now something else must have been holding the outlaw gang's attention in Gato Saltando, he thought, but that could change at any time.

"Are you Ludall or Larson Smith?" Sam asked.

"I'm both," the man said in a tight, shrill voice. A flicker of a grin showed itself behind the unkempt beard. The grin went away and the man's eyes turned serious. "That is, one of us is dead. I'm the other."

"Here we go . . . ," said Thorn under his breath.

Sam gave Thorn a no-nonsense look, then

turned back to the bearded man. "What name should I call you?" he asked.

"Well, I —" The man stopped and looked confused at this simplest of questions.

Sam saw that he wasn't used to talking to people. "I'll call you Lude. Is that all right with you?"

The man nodded his head yes but he said, "I'm Lars. Lude is dead."

"All right," the ranger said. He showed the bearded man his badge. "I'm Arizona Ranger Sam Burrack. This is Daniel Thorn. We came here to take you and your brother back to Arizona —"

"He's dead," the man interjected.

"We understand," said Sam, going right on. He motioned toward Roman Lee. "This man is a friend of ours. Have you ever seen him before?"

Roman Lee and Thorn looked surprised by Sam's question, but the bearded man nodded.

"I've seen him," he said. "I watched one of the badmen knock his head off and drag him away."

Sam was starting to realize this was a man who could talk straight, given some guidance.

"Do you know the badmen?" Sam asked.

"They know me," he said, staying on the

conversation. "They're always after me, making sure I stay away from my sanctuary." He saw Sam glance at the crevice in the rocks.

"Not this sanctuary," he said. "They've never found this one. I'm talking about my other one." He gestured downstream. "The one they've taken from us. That's the one where they keep all their gold hidden."

A silence fell over the four and drew tight around them. The bearded man chuckled to himself, childlike.

"All that gold," he said. "The Arizona Cowboy Gang made a killing stealing it from the banks. The Lobos made a killing stealing it from them." He grinned, this time enough to show his teeth. They were small, sharp-looking. Teeth the color of gray iron ore. "Me?" he said. "I'm making a killing all the time just holding on to it."

"Why are you holding on to it?" Sam asked, mostly to keep the man talking.

Lars had started talking after what Sam judged to be a lengthy silence, so Sam wanted to hear everything the man had to say.

"Why?" the man said. "I don't know. Gold has a way of making you hold on to it." He considered for a moment. "Just for meanness maybe? To be contrary?"

He pondered Sam's question further. Then he said, "So that someday, instead of being remembered for all the bad we've done, folks might ask, whatever happened to the Smiths? And somebody will say, 'Didn't you hear? They went to Mexico and made a killing in gold.' " He cackled again.

Sam looked at Thorn and Roman Lee and nodded toward the place inside the rock hillside. Smith, still laughing but more quietly now, rose to his bare feet with Sam's help and stepped up toward the entrance behind the large sumac bush.

"No tricks," Sam warned the handcuffed man, the two of them leading the way.

Thorn and Roman Lee followed behind them, Thorn carrying the glowing lantern.

"No, Ranger," said Smith. "My brother and me are not tricky people. I am not a tricky person."

Thirty feet inside the crevice, the hand-cuffed man unlocked a thick steel door on rollers and shouldered it open. Once they were all inside, Thorn and Roman Lee rolled the door back into place, leaving it open wide enough to slip back through, should the need arise.

Looking up in the flicker of lantern light, they saw the ceiling of the winding, down-

264

sloping stone-and-gravel tunnel. Overhead was an assortment of heavy interlocked boulders that lay half buried in the creek bank above them.

Farther along, the flicker of lantern light showed a ceiling six feet above them reinforced by thick pinyon timbers. Every five feet, wall-support timbers reached up and crossed over their heads. Finally, the traveling lantern threw its circle of light onto an uncovered stone wall.

Lars Smith looked around at the others in the dimness. "This was a wall of an ancient city," he said. "Imagine our surprise finding it here."

"Yeah, imagine," Thorn said to Roman Lee.

"I'm trying to," Roman Lee replied, looking all around.

Stepping through a passageway in the ancient wall, the man showed Sam a larger lantern standing on a rock. Beside the rock, a long cap-and-ball rifle leaned against the wall. At a glance, Sam wondered if it was the rifle that had killed Shelby Burnes. The look in the cuffed man's eyes turned guarded, which said it might have been. Stepping over to the rifle, Sam raised the hammer, took out the firing cap and dropped it in his pocket, then leaned the rifle back where he'd found it.

Lighting the second lantern, they resumed walking, with glowing lanterns to their front and rear, into a large open room surrounded by the same stone wall that wound farther back under the hillside. Here, long wooden tables were piled with gold of all sorts and fashions. Gold goblets, plates, platters — gold chains the size of harbor chains. Ancient golden blocks, too heavy for the big thick tables, were stacked on the floor along the wall.

"Look at all this," Roman Lee said in awe.

"None of this came from the bank job in Esplanade," said Thorn.

"If it did," said Roman Lee, "that bank has been there a lot longer than we thought."

"Easy does it," said Sam. "The gold has nothing to do with us."

"This is only the gold we found when we opened this hillside years ago," Lars informed them. "The gold the bandidos hid is farther downstream. Its value is far greater than this."

Sam put the issue of the gold aside. Here stood one of the men he'd come for. He didn't know if the other Smith brother was dead or not. All he had was this one's word on the matter. He still had a job to finish.

"Anyone live down here — besides you, that is?" he asked, looking around.

"No, only us," said Lars.

Sam looked toward a large door built into the wall, off to the side. A heavy lock hung from its hasp.

"What's in there?" he asked.

"Supplies," Lars said.

"What kind of supplies?"

"Food supplies," said Lars. "It's a cooling cellar where we keep food preserved."

A dubious looked passed among the other three.

"Is somebody in there?" Sam asked.

"No," said Lars. "Not the way you mean."

"There it is," Thorn said quietly, instantly painting a dark picture for everyone.

"Let's take a look," said Sam.

Roman Lee and Thorn took a sidelong step away. Thorn's rifle leveled in his hands. Roman Lee's rifle hung at his side, but his black-handled Colt slipped easily out of his holster, cocked and ready, the way he'd been practicing lately.

Lars hesitated as if thinking hard for something to say.

"You told me you're not a tricky person," Sam said, almost just between the two of them. "I believed you. Don't disappoint me."

Lars let out a tight breath. "First, I want to tell you something," he said to Sam confessionally. "We haven't eaten human flesh in a long time. I hate it. We don't even eat meat of any kind." He shook his head. "I don't!"

Sam said, "Look at me, Lars."

The bearded man turned his eyes to him slowly. Whatever was going on here, Sam knew it was now his job to give witness to it as much as necessary to uphold the law.

He held Smith's gaze. "Is there a dead body in there?" he asked deliberately. If there was, he knew he had to see it.

"No," Lars said stubbornly, almost pouting like a child. "Anyway, I didn't do it. That's the truth!"

"Are you saying your brother, Lude, did it?" Sam asked, gathering as much as he could while he could. He stepped forward and saw that the big lock on the door wasn't engaged.

"I told you my brother is dead," Lars said. "We didn't do it."

Sam raised the lock from the door and handed it over his shoulder to Thorn.

Roman Lee reached forward and pulled Lars Smith back a step. The ranger pulled the big door open, and a draft of air rose from a round pipe in the stone floor. The rising air was cool, but not fresh enough to overcome the smell of death.

"Holy Mother of God!" said Roman Lee, gaping at the dead man hanging from the ceiling, the point of a large meat hook sticking out of his bloodless chest. Upon a closer look at his thick red beard and bushy red hair, Roman Lee said, "I know this man! He's one of the Cowboy Gang! His name is Foster Whill. He was Catlow's best shooter."

Sam had stepped into the cool room, taking in more dead bodies. One was on a wide butcher block farther back. Another body lay on a metal table, limbs separated from the trunk.

"You know you're going back to Arizona with us, Lars," Sam said.

"We'll go right along, Ranger," Lars said. "You'll get no argument out of us. We've had a good long run of it, brother Lars and me, but now the chase is over."

"Wait," said the ranger. "You said you're Lars. Your brother is Lude."

"No, Ranger, you must have misunderstood."

The ranger gave it some thought and asked, "Is there anybody hereabouts who can say which brother you are?"

"No," the man said. "We've lived our lives avoiding people. We haven't made any friends — leastwise, no one who can say for sure what our names are."

"Let it go, Ranger," Thorn said, pulling Sam away from the Smith brother. "We'll take him to Yuma and let them figure it out."

"But all this gold?" Sam said. "We can't just leave it all down here."

"Oh, we can, believe me, Ranger," said Thorn.

"No. We need to get it into the right hands," said the ranger. "See to it the Mexican government takes over the safe-keeping of it. The right word here isn't *stolen* gold, Dan'l. This is the gold of some ancient tribe of people. They're dead, so it belongs to whoever finds it."

"In that case, it belongs to the Smiths," Thorn said. "Do you want to ask Lude there, or Lars, or whoever the hell he is, what he wants us to do with it? If he had his way, we'd be hanging in there on a meat hook beside Catlow's rifleman. Look what he did to Shelby Burnes."

"We don't know that he killed Burnes," Sam said.

"He killed him, Sam. Blew his head like it was a ripe melon. We both know it," Thorn said. "Anyway, what are we bickering about? There's more gold here than him or us either one knows what to do with! Who does it belong to? Nobody, that's who. It belongs to us if we want to claim it. If not, it's gold lyin' around, belongin' to nobody!"

"You're right," said the ranger. "Let's get out of here. Shut this place down. Make sure no one can see we've been here. We'll go somewhere and figure all of this out."

"I'm with you on that, Ranger," said Thorn.

"Get a short length of rope. Tie a lead rope around this man's waist. Make sure he sticks right with us all the way to the horses."

"Good thinking," said Thorn. "I'll walk him out of here myself like he's a yard hound."

CHAPTER 20

Gato Saltando, Mexico

In the early morning, one of the Cowboy Gang guarding the town of Gato Saltando rode onto the tile streets at a hard gallop. He slid his horse to a halt out front of the hotel, jumped down from his saddle and ran inside. Around the long table set up for the gang, bodyguards tensed, ready to come up from their chairs, guns drawn, poised to fire.

At the head of the table, Kelso North sat relaxed in his chair, a cup of coffee raised to his lips.

"Okay, men, stand down. I've got this," he said, confidently. A bone-handled Colt lay across his stomach in a studded slim-jim holster. "What is it, Jenkins?" he asked the out-of-breath guard.

"Catlow and his men riding in on the south trail," Jenkins said. "I make them two miles out. They're coming at a walk though,

272

not a gallop."

"Good work, Jenkins," said North.

He sipped his coffee, set the cup down and nodded at the street out front as he stood up. The men at both tables all stood up as one.

"You heard that, men," said North. "Catlow was supposed to be here tomorrow." He spoke loud enough for everyone to hear. "But instead, he comes in a day sooner just to throw us off."

He looked from face to face, at the rough-hewn gunmen seated at the long table and at the ones at another table set against the wall.

"Why?" he asked. "I'll tell you why. Because that's the kind of sumbitch he is."

As he spoke, the front door of the hotel opened and closed again. This time Wilson Wright hurried inside and leaned back against the door as if to hold trouble at bay.

"Catlow is coming?" he asked, out of breath himself.

"Yes," said North, his voice clear and deliberate, "Catlow is coming."

"I thought he was coming tomorrow!" Wright said.

Three of his bodyguards had caught up to him and arrived out front, wanting to get inside. Wright opened the door and let them in.

"Tomorrow *is* when we expected him," said North. "But he has decided to arrive today, Wilson. So we need to get ready for him." He paused and asked, "Anything else?"

"No."

"Good," said North. "Let's get our gunmen ready. When Catlow and his men get here, we'll settle everything right out there in the street."

Inside the small, crowded lobby, heads nodded in agreement.

"Where's Trulock?" Wilson blurted out.

"I'm right here," said Simon Trulock at the top of the steep, narrow staircase.

He came down one slow step at a time, no bodyguards to his front or rear. He held a cigar close to the lapel of his long double-breasted dress coat. Smoke curled up the back of his hand.

"What can I do for you, Wilson?" he asked calmly with what would, in a pinch, have passed for a smile.

The gunmen, who had not been lacking in confidence to start with, became, upon seeing Trulock, almost excited at the prospect of a coming gun battle. Gunmen, fully armed and ready, gathered in front of the

Gato Saltando Hotel.

Down the street, at the only other hotel in town, a seedy place called the Bella Rosa, Pearl Whitcomb leaned out of the third-floor window.

"You might want to see this, hon," she said to LaPiers, who lay naked on the bed behind her, a dingy towel covering him in the right place.

"What is it?" he asked. "I'm trying to think."

His gun belt, the holster empty, hung from a bedpost. His dusty hat hung over it. The big Colt hung from his finger. He'd cleaned the gun earlier. Now he twirled it some and let it hang there again, liking the clean feel of it.

"Gunmen!" she said. "Arizona Cowboy Gunmen from the looks of them. Maybe we're in line for some good luck today!"

She smiled to herself, watching the gunmen coming and going from the lobby of the Gato Saltando Hotel. The iron hitch rail outside the hotel was full. So was the hitch rail at Pedro's Cantina next door.

"I'll take some good luck if anybody cares to bring me some," said LaPiers. He eyed her leaning at the window. "You look damn good from back here," he said. "What say we play some 'lead a big dog around by its nape'?"

She turned around to face him, her hand high up on her hip. LaPiers tried a wicked smile on her, but it wasn't working.

"What say you get up off your lazy rear end, and we go see what's happening around here?" she said. "Ride out to the cannibal place you told me about."

"I can't right now," LaPiers said. "I'm thinking about something."

"What?" she said flatly.

"About robbing a little bank they've got here."

"Why?" she said, "We've got money enough to keep us going until we get the gold."

"If we get the gold," LaPiers said. "Anyway, I'm not going to be your kept man. I ain't designed that way. Now, if I was carrying that money, it would —"

"Huh-uh," she cut in. "I'm carrying the money! If you want to rob a bank, go ahead. I'm going out to the cannibal place to look around."

"You don't know where it is," he said. "You'll never find it alone!"

"Oh, did I say I would be alone?" Pearl said coolly. "I bet there're Cowboy Gunmen, some secret Lobos, even a freebooter or two who'll show me to the cannibal place! I bet I won't even need a horse to get there and back."

LaPiers cursed and grumbled under his breath. He grabbed his trousers and summer underwear from a chair by the bed and pulled them on angrily.

"This right here," he said, pointing at the floor, "is exactly why I never married."

He stomped around the bed and took down his hat and gun belt and put them on.

"I have a clean bandanna if you need one for the bank," she said.

"Don't worry about the bank," he snapped. "It's not going anywhere. I can rob it anytime."

"So . . . you're going with me?" she said.

"I'd better!" he said. "Somebody needs to." He threw his gun belt around his waist and buckled it, then stepped into his boots and stamped them into place. "When we find this gold, I want it understood from the get-go that half of it's mine.

Half of the gold yours? In a pig's eye, you stupid bastard, she thought.

They left by the hotel's rear door while the gathering of gunmen grew larger and louder at the Gato Saltando Hotel. They had hitched their horses back there earlier, knowing that a lot of Cowboy Gunmen as well as bandidos rode through town almost daily.

Riding down a tight alleyway that offered a narrow passing view of the street out front, Pearl and LaPiers stopped and saw what they both took to be Red Sash Cowboys ride up and form a half circle in the street, enclosing the Gato Saltando Hotel. Yet no sooner had they seen the half circle of Cowboy Gunmen closing in than another half circle of mounted men closed around them.

"That's a gun battle about to happen," LaPiers muttered. "Let's get out of here. We'd be safer at a cannibal banquet than we would be here."

"I saw Catlow out there on the street," said Pearl in a puzzled tone. "I'd swear it's him!"

"Then he's not dead?" said LaPiers.

"If that's him in the street on a horse talking to people, I'll venture a guess and say no, he is not dead."

"So you didn't kill him?"

Pearl looked away and shook her head.

"You mean that after all that happened between the two of you, he's still alive?" Before she could answer, LaPiers said, "You poisoned him twice, and he is still alive?"

He shook his head. "That is just too hard to believe."

"You want to ride back and look?" she offered.

"No," he said, "I want to get the hell out of here and go find that gold."

Roman Lee had ridden out under a full moon, and he came back before dawn to the new camp they'd made the night before. It was well hidden from sight and farther away from the Smith cabin than their old camp, high enough up on a craggy hillside to offer a wider, fuller view of Hanging Man Creek and the trails leading into the valley.

As soon as Roman Lee's boots touched the ground beside his horse, the ranger met him with a tin cup of steaming coffee.

"Obliged," said Roman Lee, taking the cup with his gloved hand. He jutted his chin at Thorn and Smith seated at a small campfire. "Any trouble out of our cannibal?" he asked.

"No," said Sam, "Lars has been no trouble at all."

"If it is Lars," Roman Lee said. "Is it Lars or Lude?"

"He answers to either one. He's not particular," Sam said. "But he is Lars unless proven otherwise. Thorn put that bandanna round his neck in case he started getting loud and crazy, so we could lift it over his mouth, but we haven't had to. What about you? Did you see anything going on out there?"

Roman Lee blew on his coffee. "Nothing's going on," he said. "This area is clear enough to travel. I saw a few bandidos scattered around, a couple here, a couple there, but no numbers worth mentioning."

He sipped his coffee and wiped his mouth on the back of his hand. "It's puzzling," he said. "They've got gold stashed in what this one calls his other sanctuary. You'd think they would have plenty of armed men guarding the spot. I didn't see any one spot more attended than another."

"Maybe they know the gold is safe enough where it is. All a larger presence of gunmen would do is get people wondering why there were so many there. It would be a dead giveaway to anybody searching for it."

"I admit I looked that hillside over real good," said Roman Lee. "Never saw a spot on it that I would have thought might have a large amount of gold hidden on it. If showing a lack of gunmen is their idea of a diversion, they've sold me on it. I would never have thought it."

"Neither would I," Sam said. "The Lobos

have never been fools, and neither have the Arizona Cowboys. We'd do well to keep that in mind."

Thorn rose from beside the fire and joined them. He saw Sam's eyes widen as Lars, sitting alone, picked up a plate from the ground bedside him, held it up to his face with cuffed hands and lapped it like a dog.

"Don't we have a spoon for him to eat with?" Sam asked.

"Yes," said Thorn, "it's lying at his feet. This is his preferred dinner etiquette. He won't use utensils and doesn't like anybody watching him eat. Says it makes him nauseous." He gave a thin smile. "We don't want that, do we?"

The ranger shook his head and turned back to Roman Lee. "Our cannibal told us of a secret door to the other sanctuary that the bandidos don't know about. He's been afraid to risk going there alone."

"You trust him?" Roman Lee asked.

"No," the ranger said flatly. "But we're getting ready to ride there anyway and see if it's true. Do you want to ride with us, or stay here and get some sleep?"

Roman Lee looked around at the secluded campsite.

"I can sleep anytime," he said. "I wouldn't

miss seeing his other sanctuary for any-thing."

After coffee, the three cleared their camp-fire and doused it with their leftover coffee. They gathered their horses and rode across the creek at a low sandy spot on the trail, continuing downstream past the sanctuary they'd found the day before and the trail leading up over the hillside to the Smith cabin. They saw no sign of any people, either bandidos or Cowboy Gunmen.

Eventually Hanging Man Creek dropped down between two taller banks that lay at the bottom of steep stone-layered hillsides.

"Stop here," Smith said all of a sudden.

The ranger looked around at the high stony hills and the rushing creek. *Yes,* he decided then and there, *if I ever need an underground hideaway, this is where I will put it. So far, so good, Smith brothers . . .*

"What do you say, Ranger?" Thorn asked.

He and Roman Lee sat silently in their saddles, the shallow water rushing around the horses' hooves.

"If he says this is the place, this is it," Sam replied.

"Follow me, everybody," Smith said.

He stepped down from the horse and led it forward in the shallows of the creek.

The ranger followed him closely. Behind

the ranger came Thorn, his rifle in hand, and last was Roman Lee. They kept their horses moving along slowly, as quietly as they could, knowing how outnumbered they would be should the bandidos find them this close to the gold.

Twenty yards down the creek, the banks, which were already tall, grew even taller and began to recess farther back behind over-hanging tree roots and vines. Smith led them in behind the roots and vines and deeper under the hillside.

"I read once that there're more poisonous snakes in Mexico than anyplace else in the world," Roman Lee said under his breath.

"Thanks. Glad you told us," Thorn replied.

As the darkness grew blacker, heavier around them, Thorn lit a lantern he had taken earlier from his saddlebags. He held it low on the bankside of him, keeping the light confined to the hillside.

"Right here," Smith said, putting a hand on the rough, root-laden dirt wall twelve feet back under the creek bank.

"What the hell is this?" Thorn whispered, holding the lantern out.

"It's a secret doorway," the brother whispered without turning around. "In case we ever needed to escape."

He leaned forward, pressed his shoulder against the rough dirt bank and roots and pushed hard. The creek bank made a loud screeching sound, and a four-foot-wide portion of it slowly began to open.

The light from Thorn's lantern now revealed the hillside to be a large iron door. They followed Smith through the opening. Roman Lee stopped for a moment and ran his hand over the roots and vines covering the rough face of the door. To his shock, they were held in place by unseen bolts, clasps and fasteners.

"Amazing," he murmured. "No one could ever tell this is built from the creek bank itself."

In the dark under the creek bank, the closed door was next to impossible to distinguish from the rest of the earth, roots and vines. Open, the door showed a path leading twenty feet back into the hillside to a set of steep iron stairs.

Smith lit a large lantern that he took down from a wall peg and handed it to Roman Lee. With Thorn carrying the light in front of them, and Roman Lee carrying the larger light behind them, they climbed the stairs until they came to a small landing and another door. Lars Smith turned to the others.

"Behind this door is the gold the outlaws all want so bad. Be careful in here. Don't touch any levers or handles. This whole level can be dropped into the creek."

His audience listened in some astonishment as he continued.

"We created it to give everything up to the water rushing through a grillwork below," Smith said. "A flushing system? Back there the water was only a few inches deep. Here, we have dug the bed four feet deeper and lined it with stone. It's deeper but the water runs through just as fast. It will carry away anything dropped into it. Whoever comes here to lay claim to the gold will have to be careful they don't wash it all away."

He opened the door and held the lantern close to an iron grille, behind which heaps of gold shone and glittered brightly, casting light on the ceiling above it.

"Holy Mother . . ." Thorn let his words trail off as if having lost them midspeech.

The ranger looked at the gold for just a second, then looked at the handle Smith indicated. He stepped over between him and the handle for good measure and motioned everybody out of the area.

All this time he had thought about the gold only in passing. Now the reality of it — sacks and piles of it — under lantern light that cast its radiant glow in all directions was very close to overwhelming.

He had come here on behalf of the United States government to arrest and bring back wanted men. But now he and Dan'l Thorn had come upon the gold that was being sought by two of the largest outlaw gangs on either side of the southern border. He laid a hand on Thorn's arm.

"Dan'l," he said quietly, "there's something I need you to do."

"I know," Thorn said, equally quiet. "I'll head out as soon as we get out of here."

CHAPTER 21

The ranger and Roman Lee sat on their horses at their new campsite. They'd picked a spot atop a cliff hidden by brush and scrub and veiled by the shadow-dark background of a deep overhang. The cliff provided a good long view of both Hanging Man Creek and the valley surrounding it. They'd watched Thorn until he rode out of sight on a thin trail below.

From this new position they saw two separate groups of Lobos ride from a direction that circled wide to the west, avoiding Gato Saltando. Had anybody other than Thorn gone the way he had, the ranger would have been far more concerned, but he knew as soon as Thorn got wind of these bandidos, he had slipped down from the road, skirted around them in the rock and brush and come back up when he knew they were out of sight.

"I would have gladly gone, had you asked

me," Roman Lee said, studying the ranger's face for worry. "I could have maybe talked my way through the bandidos. I know a few of them."

"I liked Thorn for the job, Roman Lee," Sam said. "You could likely talk your way through the outlaws. But when you got to the Mexican army, could you have handled, say, a captain or a major?"

Roman Lee had no reply. The ranger continued.

"Dan'l Thorn has an introduction letter signed and stamped by a high-ranking official of the Mexican government. It tells who he is and why he's working here below the border. Can you top that?"

"No, I can't," said Roman Lee, realizing it was true and wishing he had not opened his mouth. "I was thinking maybe you didn't trust me."

Gazing down at the dusty trail, Sam thought a few seconds before speaking.

"Roman Lee Ellison," he said finally, "I trust you more than any man I've ever shot in the chest. But this was Thorn's job, and he's got signed papers to help him with it. We came here searching for the Smith brothers and came upon a load of French gold stolen from a Franco-Mexican bank."

Roman Lee shook his head slowly. "Life

was easier to figure out when I was riding high, wide and wild on the outlaw trail."

"Living right requires thinking right, Roman Lee. Once a badge starts carrying a man around, he has no choice but to do what's right in the eyes of the law. I've been tempted all along to ride away from this thing, to let the governments handle it," the ranger added. "But I can't do that. We'll alert the Mexican army, then get out of their way. Take our prisoner and head home."

"Thorn talks like we could keep the gold ourselves."

"I know he does," the ranger said. "He says it, but he doesn't mean a word of it. When it comes down to it, he'll go out of his way to see to it all of the gold gets to its rightful owner, same as I will."

"I don't know if I trust myself enough to think that way, Ranger."

"That's an honest admission," Sam said. "Better than trying to deceive the world and yourself with it. Once you know you can trust yourself, life starts getting easier. Once you start wondering about it, you're off to a good start."

Sam turned and looked behind him at the bearded prisoner sitting on a rock in the shade of the overhang. "He's et nothing all day. I'm going to open him a tin of beans and heat them for him."

"I'll watch the trail a while longer," said Roman Lee. "See what else comes drifting up off the desert."

"If you're thinking about all this, be careful you don't overthink it."

"I will, Ranger. And if you're feeding our cannibal, careful you don't get your hand too close."

On the trail below, Dan'l Thorn saw Pearl Whitcomb and LaPiers riding toward him from around a huge land-stuck boulder the size of a two-story house. Luckily, all three riders checked their animals in time to keep from running headlong into one another. Pulling the horses back, they sized one another up. Recognizing Thorn, Pearl put on her best smiling-small-town-neighbor face.

"Why, Dan'l Thorn, I swear to goodness!" she said. "Imagine running into you out here!"

"Yep, imagine," Thorn said, feeling Cochise step back and forth restlessly underneath him.

He eyed LaPiers, a man he knew by his reputation, all of it bad. LaPiers stared back at him.

"Look, hon, it's Dan'l Thorn!" said Pearl.

"Did I tell you we're friends, Dan'l and I?"

"No," said LaPiers, "but I know him."

"LaPiers," Thorn said, "the man whose other name got away from him somehow. How are you, hero?"

"A whole lot better than you'll ever be, Thorn," LaPiers said with a voice full of contempt. "And don't start that hero stuff on me!" He turned to Pearl. "If Thorn starts calling you hero, like as not he's fixing to shoot you down like some damn mangy dog."

Thorn returned a smile Pearl gave him. He knew she was wondering if he would be mentioning the gold or anything else pertaining to the last time they'd seen each other.

"Mr. Thorn?" Pearl said. "Is that the truth?"

"No, of course not, Pearl." Thorn grinned. "You know how people say crazy stuff, and they always find a few idiots who believe them."

LaPiers smoldered with anger. "Here's something you can believe!" he exclaimed. His hand went to his gun butt. "When met on a trail or an open road, the person approaching on the left is always required — by God, I'm saying always required — to side over to their right and give the other rider the right to proceed!"

"Easy, hero," Thorn chuckled. "Miss Pearl knows she's got the right to proceed anytime we're on the same road." He shifted his gaze back to LaPiers. "Where did you hear something like that anyway?"

"It's the law, Thorn!" said LaPiers. "The law in Philadelphia, Pennsylvania! Lot of other fine damn places too, I'll wager."

"Philadelphia, Pennsylvania?" Thorn chuffed. "Listen, hero, they're always making up laws there for anybody stupid enough to believe them."

"I warned you about that hero malarkey!" LaPiers shouted, red-faced. "Drop out of the saddle. We'll shoot the all-fired hell out of each other right here and now!"

"Listen closer, hero," Thorn said. "There is nothing I would like better than to kill you so quick hell wouldn't have time to change the linen." He paused and looked at Pearl and touched his hat brim. "I am on an urgent errand right now. But it's always a pleasure seeing you, Miss Pearl."

"Something to do with the gold, is it?" she said as he tapped Cochise forward.

Thorn didn't answer.

"I bet it is about the gold," Pearl said looking after Thorn as he and Cochise neared the turn in the trail. She swung a sharp look

292

at LaPiers. "If we're smart, we'll follow him!"

"Follow him hell!" said LaPiers. "I want to straight-out kill him!"

"Why?" Pearl said. "He is such a wonderful man!"

"Oh, he is?" said LaPiers. "Watch what I'll do to this wonderful man of yours!"

He stepped over into the middle of the trail, spread his feet shoulder width and drew his gun and twirled it the same way he had when he said he was going to rob the bank in Gato Saltando.

Bull, Pearl thought. He wasn't going to do anything!

"Hey, wonderful man!" LaPiers shouted, the pistol twirling in a shiny blur. "Come back here, you son of a bitch. I'm going to kill you deader than hell!"

Thorn stopped Cochise and looked back at LaPiers without turning the big stallion around.

"That's right!" said LaPiers. "Deader than hell. Get off that horse and come back here!"

Thorn only waved him away like a pesky fly.

"Did you see that?" LaPiers shouted at Pearl, his voice turning high and shrill. "He's afraid to face me! He's a coward!"

He stopped twirling his gun. Watching Thorn ride Cochise slowly out of sight around the boulder, he dropped his Colt back into his holster. "That's the kind of yellow-bellied dog he is!"

As he ranted and raved, Cochise and Thorn rode back into sight.

"He's come back," said Pearl.

"Ha, I don't think so," said LaPiers. "That's over fifty yards! He's not coming back!"

"No, he is back," said Pearl.

LaPiers looked for himself, puzzled. Why would Thorn ride out of sight, turn around and ride right back? It made no sense!

Atop Cochise, Thorn held his Colt out at arm's length.

LaPiers shouted, "You'd better get on out of here before I —"

The big Colt bucked once in Thorn's hand. LaPiers flew backward a second before the gunshot roared, sounding to him like a round from a field cannon. Pearl saw LaPiers hit the ground in the middle of the trail, a bloody hole in his upper chest. She shrieked, jumped down and ran over to him.

"Adios, hero."

Thorn slipped his Colt back inside its holster and rode on.

■ ■ ■ ■

Inside the lobby of the Gato Saltando Hotel, Nathan Catlow clutched a bottle of whiskey by its neck and drank from it when the mood hit him. He and his men had stood out front in an old-fashioned standoff for close to half an hour. Both sides had issues they needed to settle. Finally, when the Mexican sun got too hot for them, they at least agreed to move their differences inside to a long table in the lobby.

"Where we can continue settling our problems like gentlemen," said Simon Trulock.

"Until I spill the blood of whoever tried getting me hanged by missetting a certain clock, nothing will be settled here, only postponed." Catlow looked around the room slowly, making sure everyone knew what he was talking about without getting more specific.

Simon Trulock took his cigar from his mouth and spoke.

"I have it on good information that the man who was behind that incident — if there was such an incident — has been killed."

"When you say, 'if there was such an

295

incident,' " said Catlow, "it sounds to me like you're flat-out calling me a liar."

They both stood their ground. In truth, while they had given up their guns on entering the lobby, they both had a hideout gun just in case the talk got a little too hot and tight.

"I don't need to call you or any man a liar," Trulock responded. "I say, let a man play out his hand. The truth is always what's left on the table."

"I don't know what the hell that means, and neither do you, Trulock!"

"Catlow," a voice called out loudly, "leave this on the table, you sumbitch!"

Two gunshots rang out. A clerk who had been hiding behind the hotel desk sprang to his feet, let out a scream and ran out the back door as a bullet struck the doorframe above his head.

Two of Trulock's top men grabbed him and pulled him toward the front door. But he shoved them away, pulled a hidden .45 and shot at Catlow. But Catlow was quick enough to jump away from the table and run through a door into a dining room. His men had taken one side of the lobby. Simon Trulock gathered his men on the other side. Some members of both groups spilled out into the street as bullets flew.

Even in the middle of a growing gunfight, Russell Fairday ran from man to man along the street to find out who supported getting rid of Simon Trulock, Wilson Wright and Kelso North and letting Catlow take over the Cowboy Gunmen Gang.

"Catlow is giving five hundred dollars to every man who stays with us and helps get back the gold the bandidos have stolen from us," Fairday said to three gunmen huddled beside the livery barn.

A bullet thumped against the side of the barn and sent out a spray of splinters.

"Count me in," said an older Red Sash Cowboy named Manuel Hickey who'd ridden guerrilla for Bloody Bill Anderson in the civil conflict.

"Okay, Hickey, I've got your name down," said Fairday. "Catlow will be glad to hear it."

"Good. Now where's my five hundred dollars?" Hickey inquired.

Fairday started to try to explain, but Hickey gave him a shove.

"I'm funning with you, Fairday," he said. "Get out of here before you get your top-knot blown off."

"Right you are," said Fairday, moving away quickly.

A shotgun blast sent the lobby's large glass

window flying out of its frame in wild shards both large and small. A professional woman who had spent two days and nights with a Cowboy Gunman on the second floor crashed screaming through a window, naked save for the man's red sash tied loosely around her waist. She leaped from the front balcony as flames flared up behind her, licking from the windows and up the front of the hotel.

"Catch me!" she screamed, jumping toward the waiting arms of several men vying to catch her and break her fall. Yet upon seeing her fly down so fast, at the last second they hesitated and jumped back.

The woman hit the stone tiles with a loud *smack* and lay there a long time before starting to move her arms and legs stiffly and brokenly. The Cowboy Gunman she'd been staying with came running from the hotel with her clothes in one arm, his rifle and bullet bandolier in his other.

"Good Lord, Sally, I thought sure you was dead!" he shouted above the gunfire, the screaming, the rearing and neighing of horses tied to the hitch rails.

"So . . . you brought . . . my clothes?" she said haltingly.

"Yeah, here, put these on," he said in a rush. "We've got a fight commenced. I got to help Catlow!"

He started to turn and run, but on second thought, he spun and kissed her first, brushing aside the mussed hair covering most of her face. Bystanders clapped and cheered. He waved at them and ran toward gunmen gathered at an open wagon in the street.

As the fighting raged, a young man with a sharp butcher knife ran along the hitch rails, cutting in turn every set of reins tied down, thus freeing a wild-eyed, screaming herd of horses into the chaos already on the street. The horses ran in every direction, their reins now too short to be easily grabbed.

A red, white, and green fire apparatus rolled out of a makeshift firehouse. Drums beat loudly. A trumpet blared. Pulled by a large wagon horse and a mule, the colorful apparatus rolled up to the hotel. Firemen stretched a hose from a large water tank on the rig to the door of the hotel while two more men began pumping water.

Amidst the noise and bedlam on the streets, Pearl rode in from the back of town. Beside her she led LaPiers's horse up the same alleyway that had taken them out of Gato Saltando. LaPiers was leaning all the way forward in his saddle, his face crisscrossed with strands of the horse's mane.

"Wipe your face," Pearl said with little

sympathy.

"Oh, God!" LaPiers moaned. "He's kilt me sure enough."

He clutched a hand to his bloody shirt and coughed.

Pearl stopped at the rear door of the doctor's office, rather than use the front door facing the unruly street. She helped LaPiers down from his saddle, looped her arm low around his waist and helped him to the door.

"I've got a man with a bullet wound here," she said.

She started to step forward but an elderly woman with her hair in a tight bun blocked her way.

"Everybody in town has a bullet wound today," the woman said. She looked LaPiers over. She reached behind him and felt his bloody shirt. "The bullet went through. He'll be all right."

"All right, hell!" LaPiers said. "I want to see the doctor!"

"Well, you can't, so shut up," she barked at him. "I'll give you dressings." She looked at Pearl. "If you'll wrap bandage cloth around him to stop the bleeding, he'll be fine. Bring him back in three days after everything settles down here."

The woman left them waiting at the door

and came back with a bundle of bandage cloth, a bottle of alcohol and a roll of surgical tape.

"Now, then," the woman said, "go somewhere nice and quiet and bandage him."

Before Pearl could ask her anything more, the door shut in their faces.

"I'll be damned," Pearl said. "I'm still saddled with your worthless ass."

"What did you want to do, go off and leave me?" LaPiers said.

"Yes," said Pearl. "It's your fault you got yourself shot, not mine! I want to go after the gold! I believe Thorn could have told us something if you two hadn't started arguing about the laws in Philadelphia."

"Go right ahead and leave, then," LaPiers said. "I'll get by."

"No," said Pearl, "you're going with me. Let's get you bandaged up and see this thing through."

Chapter 22

The Lobos had assembled and had been riding military style, in a column of twos, since daylight. They took a trail leading wide around Gato Saltando on their way back to Cannibal Valley, on Hanging Man Creek. It was time to relieve the twenty men they'd left there to guard the place. On their way they would meet with Russell Fairday and see where things stood on bringing the two gangs together as one.

When they heard all the gunfire coming from Gato Saltando, they looked in that direction, but only barely slowed down. No one stopped, not even their trail scout, Evan Niro. He reined his horse around beside Bertram Leonard at the head of the column.

"Looks like Jumping Cat is jumping mighty high today," he said. "I hope Fairday don't get himself shot dead before we talk about joining our forces."

"I hope not too," Bertram said, riding on,

the whole column of horses at a walk. "Why don't you drop over there and get a good look at things? Could be just some drunken vaqueros forgot to go home last night."

"Sure thing, Bertram," said Niro. Turning his horse, he said, "I'll meet you at Hanging Man Creek or along the way there."

As the scout rode away, Bertram's younger brother George rode up to him and said, "What do you suppose all the shooting is about over there, Bertram?"

"Hell, who knows?" Bertram said. "If you're wondering if it's got anything to do with us bringing the two gangs together, put it out of your mind. As long as us ol' bandidos have all the gold, we've still got the upper hand on everything." He grinned. "So don't get nervous on me."

"I won't," George said. "Newt and Henri were talking about it. I decided to come ask you instead of letting it bother me."

"Good decision, George," said Bertram. "Go tell them it'll be the time to start worrying when I say it's the time to start worrying. Until then, everybody take it easy."

George Leonard looked greatly relieved, being one to always follow his brother Bertram's lead on things.

"How is it going to feel," George asked, "being an Arizona Red Sash Cowboy?"

He shook his hand at his thigh as if shaking an imaginary red sash hanging there.

"It'll feel just fine, brother George. First thing, I'm going to order me some of that brand of kiss-my-ass bourbon like Bidden Matelin always kept on hand. I figure if it's good enough for a jeweler, a man steady enough to cut diamonds for a living, it's damn sure good enough for me."

"Me too. Get me some too!" George said, excited at the prospect of drinking bourbon such as an important gang leader like Bidden Matelin would drink.

"You realize Matelin is dead, don't you?" said Bertram.

"Of course I do," said George. "But I like to talk about somebody like they're still alive. I always feel better."

"Suit yourself." Bertram looked over in the direction of the gunfire as they passed it. "Matelin always treated me right. Once we get things worked out between our two outfits, I can't wait to kill Catlow for what he did to him."

"I thought part of us joining the Cowboy Gunmen and the bandidos together is to get rid of all the grudge fights and revenge boiling between us?"

"It is." Bertram smiled. "But still, there's always a little straightening up to be done.

Get everybody feeling peaceful with one another."

"But still, you're going to kill Catlow?" George asked.

"Oh, yes," said Bertram. "If I don't kill him, there ain't a dog in Georgia."

Their laughter was cut short when they caught sight of a woman leading an injured man up onto the trail twenty yards ahead of them.

"What the hell . . . ?" Stopping his horse, Bertram stood in his stirrups as if doing so gained him a better view. "I hope that's not who I think it is."

"Ahoy!" Pearl called out, waving her arms over her head.

"Yep, it's her, damn it," said Bertram. "She must think we're a ship."

"It sounds like it." George chuckled.

Beside Pearl sat LaPiers, wobbling, ready to fall from his saddle.

"Looks like she's about used LaPiers up and is ready to drop him off."

"I don't understand it," said Bertram. "He knew how much money I gave her. All he had to do was kill her, dump her for the wolves and keep the money." He shook his head.

"Here she comes, Bertram," George said. "Want me to make something up, and you ride away real fast?"

"Naw, that won't stop her," Bertram said. "Nothing will stop her but a bullet. I wouldn't even count on that."

He returned Pearl's wave and offered her an artificial smile.

"Well, well," he called out. "If it's not my favorite lady investigator, Pearl . . ." He couldn't remember her last name.

"Whitcomb," she said, her smile gone. "Pearl Whitcomb. You know, the woman you bought off for a measly six thousand and ninety dollars?"

Bertram let it go, and said, "I see you're still with LaPiers. *Hola,* LaPiers. How goes it?"

"I'm shot to death," LaPiers said weakly. "I lost all my blood."

Bertram looked back and forth between them, questioningly.

"No, I didn't shoot him," said Pearl. "That murdering dog Dan'l Thorn shot him. You wouldn't believe what they were arguing over."

"No, I expect I wouldn't," said Bertram. "There was gunfire back in Jumping Cat. Was that where this happened?"

"No, this was much earlier," said Pearl. "I took him to Gato Saltando, but the doctor wouldn't see him. A woman gave me bandages and whatnot, said come back in three days. I haven't bandaged him yet. I need some shade and some water to wash him."

"Looks like you'll need a clean shirt too and some trousers, amigo," Bertram said loudly as if LaPiers was deaf.

"Where were you following Thorn to?" Bertram asked.

"I didn't say I was following him," said Pearl. "Where are you and your men headed?" She looked back along the long column of riders and before he could answer said, "Oh, checking on the gold, I bet. The gold *I* helped you take away from Catlow and his Cowboy Gunmen."

"For which I paid you a handsome amount," Bertram said, not giving way.

"A miserly amount," Pearl corrected him. "I think if you had your way, this poor soul would have slain me and taken even that pitiful amount from me."

Would have slain *her?* Bertram looked at LaPiers. "Did you tell her that, LaPiers?" he asked.

LaPiers shook his bowed and weary head. "Nobody ever has to tell her anything," he said, struggling to speak. "She just knows. . . ."

"Is that why you're out here, Pearl Whitcomb?" Bertram asked pointedly. "You're

307

out to gouge me for more money?"

"No," she said. "We rode through that mess in Gato Saltando and just happened onto you here. We ran into Thorn, riding the other direction. He was in a hurry. Everywhere I look there's something going on. I know it's all about the gold! Damn right I want more money!"

"Keep your voice down, Pearl," said Bertram.

He'd been thinking about things while they talked. She did have a way of putting things together, a quick mind, a knack for hearing what was going on. Giving more money to shut her up might be the best thing for now. Keep her close by until things were settled between the Cowboy Gunmen and the Lobos. Not have her out running her mouth all over the countryside. Hell, he could kill her anytime.

"Why don't you and LaPiers ride along with us awhile, let him heal up and get some blood back in him?" he said. "We can talk about more money. Maybe work things out."

She gave him a dubious look.

"No, I'm serious," he said. "After all, there's plenty of loot to go around and more coming every day."

More loot coming every day? That stirred

her interest, but she played it hesitantly.

"I don't know," she said. "I am so angry with you. Plus, I've got this human scourge dying on me."

"Put it all out of your mind," Bertram said. He smiled. "Give me a chance to make you not angry. As for your scourge, we'll pick up a buckboard along the way. He can lay down in it an' look at the clouds."

She thought about it for a few more seconds and said, "All right. I think it's a good idea, so long as we understand I've got money coming, like everybody else in the outfit."

"Yes, Pearl, I understand," said Bertram. "Let's just say we are off to a new start, you and me."

Kura Stabitz, the Russian Assassin, had kept out of sight since the bank explosion in Esplanade. He'd made it to Gato Saltando the night before the three main Cowboy leaders had arrived. He had shed his pin-striped suit and derby hat in favor of range clothes, tall boots and a faded red sash like the other Cowboy Gunmen. With so many new faces around from all parts of the West, few on the street recognized him.

The ones there who did know him knew him well enough to keep their mouths shut.

Whatever he was doing there, he was doing at the bidding of Nathan Catlow. Enough said. The boots made him a full three inches taller. Another three inches came with the tall-crowned Stetson he wore. A new mustache he'd grown bristled across his upper lip; along with his ever-present spade-shovel goatee, he looked right at home in Gato Saltando.

The fires had been put out and the fighting had deteriorated into name-calling and dirty looks. Townsmen helped to carry wet cases of whiskey, mescal and beer from Pedro's Cantina, and stacked them on a wagon parked in front of the charred, still smoking hotel, in case more fires suddenly flared up again.

As this vital work was going on, two drunken gunmen ventured back into the middle of the stone-tile street and started hurling insults at each other once more. One man wore a red sash; the other had removed his sash and carried it rolled up in the palm of his hand.

"This fight was over too damn soon," one called out. "I still want some answers, or I want some blood!"

"What kind of answers are you looking for, hombre!" Simon Trulock called out from the edge of a boardwalk. His big Colt hung in his right hand, cocked and ready.

"It ain't just me looking," the man said in a whiskey-mescal swirl. He swung his arm around, including everybody. "We all want to know how come when Catlow and his men get word on some big bank to hit, us others won't likely hear about it until it's over."

Another man, one forearm already bandaged and bloody from a gunshot, waved his Colt back and forth and swigged beer from a tall wooden cup.

"It's because you're too stupid to rob a bank, you dumb bastard!" he shouted loudly. "Last time you couldn't find your horse!"

Drunken laughter roared above hooting and clapping.

"You are a lying dog!" a voice shouted in reply.

A gunshot rang out. Bystanders pulled back and once again ran for cover.

A rider came galloping in fast from the edge of town. Recognizing it to be Kura Stabitz in spite of his new wardrobe and mustache, Catlow waved his arm over his head and got the Russian's attention.

Riding headlong into the crowd, scattering people every which way, Stabitz leaned down in his saddle and spoke close to Catlow's ear.

From across the street, Trulock, Wilson Wright and Kelso North stood watching as the drunken gunmen continued to trade insults as onlookers cheered and shouted.

"Something's up," said Trulock.

"Yeah, it looks like it," Wright agreed.

"Hope it's not an Apache flare-up," said North. "They've been quiet up here for a while."

Catlow waited a few seconds after Stabitz rode away out of sight; then he raised his Colt from its holster and fired it twice in the air.

"All my Red Sash Cowboy Gunmen, listen!" he shouted. "I just got word forty or fifty Lobos rode by on the main trail not more than an hour ago. They're headed up to Hanging Man Creek!"

"Then let's get after them!" a Gunman shouted.

Two men who had stood ready to draw on each other raised their hands away from their guns, chest high in a show of peace, and backed away from each other.

In what seemed like only seconds, the crowded street turned empty. Rifles that had been drawn in anger slid back into their saddle boots. Horses were encouraged to drink from a water trough and men who

312

had drunk too much stuck their foggy heads into the cool water to clear them. Then they slung their wet hair back and forth, shoved on their hats and grabbed their reins. A dog stood in the empty street, chewing a goat bone as the last of the Cowboy Gunmen rode out of town.

Catlow waited atop his horse until the group of some sixty men filed past him. They rode to where the tile street ended at the main trail and turned north, toward Cannibal Valley and Hanging Man Creek.

From his saddle, Catlow looked up at a dirt-streaked window on the second floor of the seedy Bella Rosa Hotel, at the room Wilson Wright had moved to after the fire left the Gato Saltando hotel a wet, smoky mess. In a moment he saw Kura Stabitz appear at the window, where he stood only long enough to give Catlow a nod before turning and walking away.

One down, two to go. Catlow smiled to himself and turned his horse toward his army of mounted gunmen.

CHAPTER 23

The ranger and Lars Smith sat at a low fire well back under the cliff overhang. Sam drank his black coffee in silence, knowing from earlier attempts at conversation that the other man was the kind who preferred to be left alone. Any questions the ranger asked had been answered courteously, yet he always felt a chill breeze moving through the replies. He would be glad to get this prisoner back across the border and let the court take him off his hands.

Sam watched the other man sip water from a canteen the three of them had designated specially for him; then Roman Lee stepped in under the overhang, his rifle hanging in his hand.

"You're going to want to see this, Ranger," he said in a serious tone, then immediately turned and left.

Smith stood up, anticipating the ranger would ask him to do so.

Sam set his coffee cup down and picked up the short coil of lead rope that reached up and around the man's waist.

"Let's go," he said, adding, "Put down the canteen. It'll still be here."

Out front they joined Roman Lee at the edge of a sheltering boulder that concealed them from the trails and the game paths below.

"Lobos, I make them to be," Roman Lee offered over his shoulder as Sam and his prisoner came up beside him.

The ranger laid the prisoner's lead rope on the ground and put a boot on it as he took his telescope from inside his shirt. He wiped the lens and focused it on the long string of riders.

"Riding in like cavalry, two by two. Ready to do battle, you suppose?"

Below, the riders moved along at an easygoing pace.

"It wouldn't surprise me," Roman Lee said.

"Whoa now," Sam said, freezing midscan, "here's something new in the mix." He handed Roman Lee the telescope. Watching Roman Lee raise it to his eye, he said, "That's Pearl Whitcomb, this side, third rider back. She's leading a fellow beside her, looks like he had a run-in with a grizzly bear."

"That's Miss Pearl all right," said Roman Lee. "The fellow beside her is LaPiers. He spends most of his time at Pedro's." He handed the telescope back to the ranger.

"I know LaPiers," said Sam. "Those two together prove the devil's quite a match-maker."

"A match made in hell," agreed Roman Lee.

Sam raised the telescope and turned it back along the trail. Behind the riders, a ways back, a small low veil of dust was beginning to rise up from the trail.

"Look like there're more of them coming back there," he said.

"What? They're being followed?" Roman Lee said.

"That, or there's a second wave," Sam said. "Either way, I wouldn't want to be in their gunsights."

"Wait a minute, Ranger," said Roman Lee. "We are in their sights."

"Good thinking, Roman Lee," Sam said.

He collapsed his telescope and stood tapping it on the palm of his dusty hand, considering their situation. There were enough riders down there to cover this place and search them out if need be. But for now there was time to make a run for it; nothing was keeping him from taking his captured prisoner and hightailing it out of there. His and Thorn's job here was done. They'd come to capture the Smith brother cannibals. And they *had* captured them — what was left of them anyway.

This job is done — well done at that, he told himself. *Go home!*

What was he trying to decide here? What was that tugging feeling inside his chest telling him he couldn't leave yet? Not yet. He started to tell himself he couldn't leave until Thorn had returned safely.

But that wasn't true, and he knew it. If Thorn returned with a company of Mexican *federales,* this would all be over. If they sent Thorn back alone, he would see the dust, the many riders here who hadn't been here before; Thorn would see all that and know that Sam, Roman Lee and the prisoner were gone. *Or dead,* Sam thought. *So leave Thorn out of it.* That was what Thorn would tell him if he was here speaking for himself.

Okay! It came to him. That tug in his chest was the tug that gold in large glittering quantities had on a man. The staggering weight of gold. In this case much of it was old gold that belonged to no one and hadn't for hundreds of years. The newer gold, freshly minted, belonged to the French corporations.

The corporations seemed not to care one way or the other, which had a lot of law enforcement thinking the corporations had so much, it didn't matter one way or the other. Many believed the corporations and government leaders themselves were paid off by the ones who'd stolen it. How many killings had this gold brought about?

Sam thought about it. There were too many killings to count, starting at the time when he'd first arrived here, even more if he reflected back to Bad River, where he'd first gotten involved with the Arizona Cowboy Gang while hunting three of their members who were wanted gunmen.

Yes, gold had a way of tugging at a man's chest, be that man a sinner or a saint.

That's enough! Stop it, he told himself. *It's time to go.*

He looked around himself. Without knowing why, and in spite of all he'd done to talk himself out of here, he turned to Roman Lee.

"With a light field cannon, if we were hard-pressed, we could take position in one of the Smiths' sanctuaries and hold off an army if we had to."

Roman Lee gave him a concerned look.

"We don't have a field cannon, Ranger."

"I know," said Sam. "Anyway, it's time to pull up and hightail it out of here."

"I do," the bearded Smith brother blurted out.

Sam and Roman Lee looked at him.

"You do what?" Sam asked.

"I have a cannon." The man nodded at the ground.

"Where did you get a cannon?" asked Sam.

"From one of our visitors," the bearded man said, still nodding. "We kept one as a souvenir. It's in our sanctuary with all our souvenirs."

"With all of your souvenirs?" Sam said somewhere between a statement and a question. "How many souvenirs do you have?"

"We have a lot," said Smith. "Every visitor we ever had, we made sure to get a souvenir. All of them we keep in our sanctuary. Want me to show you?"

Sam pulled Roman Lee to the side and said, "This might be a good way to find out which brother this is. You want to take a look with me?"

Roman Lee whispered in reply, "I hate seeing what's there, but I can't say no."

"We'd take it most kindly if you would," Sam said to the bearded man. To Roman

Lee, he muttered, "Those bandidos will be here in another hour or less, but we can duck and dodge them long enough to get out of here."

"I hope we can, Ranger," said Roman Lee. "But I'm with you. Whatever he's got there, I want to see it."

"Even if it's a field cannon?"

"Most especially if it's a field cannon."

A cloud-shaded grayness moved in over Hanging Man Creek when they arrived at the place where they'd found the first Smith brothers' sanctuary. Except for the sound of the creek, the area around them was as quiet as a tomb, but Roman Lee and the ranger knew the quiet wouldn't last once the riders arrived and settled back into the Smith cabin.

At the spot across the creek where the ranger had heard the man and followed him around the sumac bush into the hillside, the three stepped down from their saddles and scanned the creek bank on both sides before venturing in.

This time they led their horses inside, wrapped their reins around a rock spur and left them there in the grainy light of a low-flamed lantern hanging from a wall peg.

"After you, Lars," the ranger said, holding

firmly to the lead rope around the bearded man's waist.

Both the ranger and Roman Lee realized that this could all be a ruse. More than a few times the ranger had known prisoners who were passive and compliant right up until it came time to leave and head into custody. At that point they'd had a plan in mind to set themselves free no matter what. Knowing what could happen, the two kept a sharp eye on Smith's every step.

"Here," the man said suddenly, stopping almost in midstep. He pointed toward a large door across from what he'd called the supply room, where they had found the butchered bodies.

Passing Roman Lee the lead rope, Sam stepped closer to the big door. "Remember, Lars, no tricks," he said, with the slight twist he always used to let the man know he doubted that Lars was really his name.

"No tricks," the man assured him.

Sam beckoned Roman Lee closer, in case something was amiss, and kept his gaze on Smith as he turned the handle. The man showed no expression out of the ordinary as Sam pushed the heavy door open, unleashing a smell of mildew, musk, old cloth, old books and stale air.

"See? Nothing harmful," said Smith. "Just

all of our souvenirs."

Inside, Roman Lee took a large lantern down from the wall, lit it and held it up. He and the ranger looked around the large room at a seemingly endless jumble of shirts, blouses, dresses, skirts, shoes and coats — men's and women's alike. On rows of wooden tables, they saw hand tools, jewelry, men's watches and women's ornate hairpins.

A series of modeling hands, both male and female, displayed rings, earrings and necklaces, gloves and eyeglasses. Three hands held up handkerchiefs embroidered with family crests or initials.

"This will all be sorted through," Sam said to Roman Lee. "There're people who will be glad to hear about family members who disappeared over the years."

"Yes, this was worth finding," Roman Lee said.

He looked at the Smith brother, who appeared to be lost in wonderment at the surroundings, this room full of remembrances.

"Where's the cannon?" he asked.

"The what — ? Oh, the cannon," said Smith, snapping out of his daze. "Over here."

They followed him, amazed he knew his way among so many intersecting aisles. As they went, displays of clothing and jewelry gave way to more tools, traps, snares, small arms, other weaponry and ammunition.

"And here we have it, gents," the man said finally.

Both Sam and Roman Lee noticed how much livelier and more cheerful he'd become since they had enlisted him in finding the cannon and showing off the rest of the Smith brothers' souvenirs.

"One cannon! With half a keg of powder and cannonballs to boot." He pointed toward the hard dirt floor, where there lay an item wrapped in an army canvas.

"Flip it over," Roman Lee said. "Let's take a look."

The man stooped, almost smiling, then flipped the canvas back and stepped to the side.

"You're right," said Roman Lee. "It's a field cannon, sure enough." It was just a heavy iron cannon barrel, no wheels, nothing else. He hefted it a little. "I'd say it's over two hundred pounds. I reckon a horse can drag it with some rope."

"No need," the man said pleasantly, "I have a cannon skid. A sled, I call it."

He led them farther back and showed them a huge sled from the Franco-Mexican war, built to haul broken cannon back from the battlefield to be rewheeled and repaired.

"I see possibilities here," the ranger said, looking at the cannonballs, the keg and the powder. "Didn't we pass some rifles in a rack back there?"

"We did." Smith nodded. "You're welcome to all you need or want. After I'm gone, this will all lie here until a few hundred more years have passed."

"Maybe so," the ranger said. "But for now let's get this sled out of here and give it some work to do."

The sled pulled easily across the creek at a low gravel bar, and with only slightly more difficulty up a grassy hillside onto the hard dirt trail. The horse that the bearded Smith brother rode became the sled horse. The bearded man, hands cuffed, lead rope still around his waist, stood on the rear of the sled, keeping the weight balanced. The cannon barrel lay longways on the sled. The half keg of powder with the word *Powder* painted on it was tied beside the cannon. The four cannonballs were tied one on each corner of the sled.

When they topped the thin path leading up the last fifty feet to the cliff overhang, Smith brought the loaded sled to a halt. In fairness to the sled horse, Sam and Roman

Lee had each tied three rifles on either side of their horses and carried them to the overhang.

Now they dropped the rifles, gathered the cuffed prisoner by his lead rope and walked him to the edge of the overhang. Looking down at the trail, they saw the dust from so many riders still standing in the air. The column of twos left one side of the trail burrowed like the passing of some great ugly snake.

In the distance, yet closer now, the second rise of dust had grown and thickened as the next group of riders approached.

With his telescope, the ranger searched through the dust and the wavering sun glare and located the Arizona Cowboy Gunmen. First thing, he saw their dusty red sashes swinging down their sides; next, he saw Nathan Catlow at the head of the men, Simon Trulock at his side. Instead of riding in a column of twos, the Cowboy Gunmen had thrown military formation to the wind and spread out, taking up the whole trail.

"You were right, Roman Lee," the ranger said. "This is your bunch coming. Maybe we'll be lucky. This will be a big fight between them, and we'll slip out of here and go home."

"Sounds good to me," Roman Lee said,

"but I'm not going to bet on it."

"Neither am I," Sam said. "But let's hope they chew one another up enough, they'll have no stomach to take on a cannon crew like us waiting up here for them."

The cuffed man sat on the cannon sled, watching as Roman Lee and Sam laid the rifles out in firing position on and above the cliff overhang. Some were aimed directly down on the paths leading up the steep hillside. Other rifles stood leaning against rocks and brush, partially hidden from sight, but giving pause to anyone who might come charging up from any melee going on below.

"It won't stop them, but it might slow them down," the ranger said, patting a hand on the cannon they laid atop a stand of fallen pinyon and stones they'd gathered.

They'd spread the canvas over the stand and laid the cannon atop it, aimed down at the main trail coming up to them.

"If the powder hasn't lost its snap," said Roman Lee, "we could get a round off if we had to."

"We could," Sam agreed, "but after we fired it, we'd spend the rest of the day trying to find it."

"What can we do to stabilize it?" Roman Lee asked.

"Stake it down?"

"With what?"

"Ask our cannibal," the ranger said.

The bearded man on the cannon sled was fidgeting with a wooden tent stake from a bundle they'd found inside the canvas.

"I believe I will," said Roman Lee, and they walked over to the sled.

The man scooped up tent pegs, six in all, and handed them to Roman Lee as if he knew what they'd been discussing.

"Before hammering them in the ground," he said, "wet the spot first and let it soak."

"Well, of course I will," said Roman Lee as if doing so went without saying.

Soaking the ground in spots with tepid canteen water helped some. With no other way to set the pegs, they used the driving butt of one of the rifles. They set the half-empty powder keg beside the gun and stacked four cannonballs beside the open breech.

"There we have it," Roman Lee said with a satisfied look at what appeared to be a deadly field-gun placement ready to do battle.

The buttstock of the rifle they'd used to drive the tent pegs had split. The ranger broke off the part of the butt still barely attached and hefted the long, slim leftover part of the rifle in his hands.

"This is our ramrod if we need it," he said. He leaned the broken rifle against the cannon.

"I sure hope it doesn't come to that," said Roman Lee. "Maybe Thorn will get back and bring a company of Mexican soldiers with him."

"That is my wish exactly," the ranger said. He put his hand on the broken rifle and shook it. "Meanwhile, have faith! They might ignore us altogether, sitting up here like eagles in a nest."

"Yeah, well, I don't have much faith that we'll be ignored," said Roman Lee. "I have wondered if the two of us going down under a white flag and talking to Nathan Catlow might get us off the spot. He wasn't opposed to us coming here to get the Smith brothers."

"I've thought about that too," Sam said. "It might get us off the spot with Catlow, but what about the bandidos?" He gave a thin, wry grin. "Think they'll stop wanting to kill us because Catlow is doing us a favor?"

"It gets no easier, does it?" said Roman Lee.

"No," said the ranger, "but we'll get through it without Catlow's help. Besides, he might not like us knowing about all this going on here. He's so unpredictable, he might want to just kill our cannibal where he stands."

Roman Lee let out a breath. "That's not the worst idea we've had," he murmured.

"Roman Lee Ellison, what an ugly thing to say about the man who just taught you how to drive a tent peg in hard ground."

"With a Franco-Mexican War rifle butt."

"Which you managed to break in the process."

"Cannibals," muttered Roman Lee. "I never want to hunt another one."

They both gave a thought to their situation, to everything that had happened so far, and laughed out loud.

CHAPTER 24

Thorn had a hard four-hour ride ahead of him to the nearest *federale* garrison. Still he knew he needed to stop long enough to water Cochise at the public well of a small hillside village. As Cochise drew water, Thorn saw three tough-looking men in dusty range clothes walking toward him from outside a blighted adobe-and-timber cantina. The three walked abreast, each with a hand on his holstered gun.

Here we go.

Thorn walked to a street cart only a few feet away in the shade of an ancient oak tree and bought four small apples. He paid the vendor and dropped all but one of the small apples into his wide duster pocket. He took out a small knife, sliced a piece of apple and stuck it in his mouth, at which point one of the men called out to him in a fake Mexican accent.

"Señor, do you like our food here and

our water?"

His voice said he was already put out about something. The other two only stared hard at Thorn.

"*Sí,*" Thorn said. He shrugged, knowing this sort of game by heart. "It's not bad, *gracias!*" He tipped the apple toward them. "Sounds like you boys ain't from around here." He smiled.

The three looked at one another; then the one who'd spoken to him dropped his fake accent.

"Okay, here's the deal, hombre," he said in a hostile tone. "We've got ourselves down here drinking and whoring and we spent ourselves broke dry. Now you're going to have to help us out. Give us some money, pronto."

Yep, going just about like I expected.

Thorn finished chewing his bite of apple and picked a fleck of peel from his front teeth.

"I don't have any money, hero," he said with another shrug.

The three had no idea why the man was calling them heroes. Maybe, they thought, he was crazy from the hot sun.

"Then we'll just have to take that dappled stud off your hands," the spokesman said.

"Yep. That's what I would do if I were

you," Thorn said calmly. "It's a much better deal if you can get it done."

He swallowed the bite of apple and offered a slight smile. The three gave him a strange look.

"Now here is the real deal, heroes, so listen up," Thorn went on. "Ordinarily, I'd have already killed all three of you. None of you looks like you're going to live very long anyway. But I'm in a hurry. I've no time for fools today. Turn around and march yourselves back in there. Stay in the shade. Let your brain cool."

The one who'd been talking took an angry step forward.

"Go on him, Jess! Go on him!" said one of the others.

"Don't get stupider than you already are, hero," Thorn warned.

He raised the pocketknife chest high and held the three-inch blade cupped in his long fingers.

"If you don't go on him, I will, Jess," said the other man.

"Shut up, Sebert. I've got him," said the one named Jess. "Get ready to grab that stud so's he don't run off."

The man Sebert took one cautious step after another until he was almost directly behind Cochise. With a little click of Thorn's cheek, the dapple stud let go a powerful kick that lifted Sebert by the front center of his ribs and launched him backward a full flip.

"Holy — !" Jess cried out, seeing his friend writhing breathless in the dirt.

He spun back toward Thorn, but too late. As he reached to draw his gun, Thorn's pocketknife, flashed through the air and buried its three-inch blade in Jess's throat below his Adam's apple.

Thorn watched him try to raise his gun above the top of the holster. In a fast draw Thorn's big Colt came up cocked and fired. He glanced around and saw the third man running from the street.

Thorn walked over to Cochise, who'd gone back to drawing his water. The stud raised his muzzle at the sight and smell of the apple in Thorn's hand. After giving Cochise his treat, Thorn cast a glance at the man on the ground, who was groaning as he scooted away an inch at a time. Thorn chuckled and rubbed the big stud's head.

"What am I going to do with you?" he said affectionately. He gathered his reins, swung up into his saddle and put Cochise forward.

Adios, heroes, he said silently to the two men on the ground, one dead, one kicked within an inch of his life.

■ ■ ■ ■

Kelso North had not seen Wilson Wright since moments before the two of them left Gato Saltando, their men in a column of twos. Tensions were high among the Cowboy Gunmen when word reached them that *Los Lobos* had ridden past town on their way to Hanging Man Creek.

With leadership badly divided, Wilson Wright, Kelso North and Simon Trulock had agreed to keep personal watch on one another for the time being. As little as the three had trusted one another over the past few years, nowadays they trusted Nathan Catlow even less.

"It's clear enough something's gone afoul," Simon Trulock said to Kelso North. "Wilson said he wanted to get something from his room at the Bella Rosa. Said he'd be along two minutes behind me, but I ain't seen him since."

"Neither have I since we pulled out of town," said North.

He looked back toward the trail from Gato Saltando as if the missing Wilson Wright might suddenly appear. Nothing.

"Maybe I'll ride along with you a while longer," North added. "You know, just to keep an eye on things?"

"I don't know," said Trulock. "I'm known to be a bad sumbitch, but I got to admit, I'm not trusting nobody much until we get our leadership in order. No offense."

"No offense taken," said North. "We all know that one of us is going to end up top dog in this gang. Whoever it turns out to be, I'm still a loyal member. We've been friends too long to be so damned suspicious."

"You're right, Kelso," said Trulock. "Hell, come on, ride back with me."

"You sure?" said North.

"I'm sure, come on," said Trulock. "To hell with all this distrust."

North turned to the man riding beside him, who was one of his top lieutenants.

"Take over, Farley," he said to the man. "We're riding back to see what's holding up Wilson Wright."

"Sure thing, boss," said Farley.

"Let's go," North said to Trulock.

They turned their horses and rode back along the wide dusty trail.

Seven miles back toward Gato Saltando, at a place where a smaller trail branched off into a stretch of woodland, the two looked over at the same time and saw a big horse standing saddled and bridled at a hitch rail outside a run-down adobe rancho.

"Is that Wilson's dun?" North asked.

The two of them reined their horses down in a stir of dust.

"It is," said Trulock.

He turned and rode out toward the adobe without another word. North tapped his heels to his horse's sides and followed. Sidling up to Trulock, North drew his rifle from his saddle boot and motioned toward the open front door of the adobe.

"Something's wrong there," he said.

"Yeah." Trulock slipped his Colt from his holster and held it down his thigh. "I'll ride around this side. You take the other?"

"Yep, I've got it," said North.

As Trulock rode out of sight around the back corner, North stepped down and walked his horse to the open front door, which gave a view of the abandoned, dilapidated condition of the interior. He led the horse inside and saw another horse standing in the next room. Glancing around warily, he spoke barely audibly.

"Is that you in there?"

"It sure is," Trulock said quietly, stepping into sight from the back door — Kura Stabitz beside him. "Lay the rifle down."

Instead, North started to swing the rifle toward him. "I levered a bullet up," he said, "so drop your side iron."

"No, you didn't," said Trulock confidently. "You never lever up a bullet. You're too damn lazy to. Now drop the rifle or take one in the eye." He raised his cocked Colt and aimed it at North's face.

"All right, hold on," said North.

He pitched his rifle aside as if knowing he would never again have use for it. He cut a glance at Stabitz.

"You were supposed to be doing this for me, you snake," he hissed.

"Yes, I was," Stabitz said, holding his long knife down his side. "He pays me more. So what could I say?"

"What if I pay you more yet?" said North.

"Is too late now," said Stabitz. Then, after a pause: "How much more?"

"Three hundred dollars," said North. "I've got it right here in my pocket."

Stabitz spread a flat mirthless grin. "Then I kill you and take it?" he said. He looked at Trulock as if seeking approval.

"Nothing to do with me, Kura," Trulock said. "That's between you two."

"Okay, then," said Stabitz. He stepped forward and raised the knife to throw it. "Stand still," he said.

"No, wait!" said North.

But Kura was already in play. He sent the

dagger through the air in a blur and struck North deep in his chest. He sank to his knees and fell backward, his hands clutching the knife handle.

Stepping forward in his new cowboy boots, Stabitz looked down at North and said, "Move your hands. I take the knife and cut your throat."

"No, no! Please," North gasped, clutching the knife handle tighter. "Go away. Leave me here!"

Stabitz reached out a boot, shoved North's hands away and pulled the long knife from his chest. Blood spewed up and fell in a red braid.

"You be all right in a minute," he said to the dying man.

Trulock watched as the Russian finished doing his job. When Stabitz had folded the money he took from North's pocket and put it inside his shirt, they both smiled. Stabitz dragged North's body to a corner of the room and pulled a soiled ragged quilt over it.

"I suppose Catlow would offer you a big fat bonus if you killed me today too," said Trulock.

He kept his hand on the butt of his big Colt as he spoke, but he didn't bother drawing, his attitude being if he couldn't outdraw a throwing knife, maybe he deserved a blade in his chest.

"Yes," said Stabitz, busily wiping his blade clean on North's shirtsleeve. "A thousand dollars he will give me if I kill you now."

"Well?" said Trulock. "What are you waiting for? If you think you can do it, do it."

Stabitz let Trulock see him slip the knife back inside his new leather range vest. He patted it in place. "Only when I am ready," he said.

"Oh, I see," said Trulock, keeping a careful eye on him. He liked the thought that this mean, murdering bastard had at least some level of respect for him. "Are you going to tell me when you are ready?"

Stabitz appeared to consider the question as if he'd never thought of something like that before: telling a man when he was ready to take his life away from him. The idea appealed to him.

"Yes," he replied at length. "I will say, 'I'm ready.' Then I will kill you quick. Too quick for you to do anything about it."

Trulock cast a thin trace of a smile. "That's what I call a sporting chance."

He nodded toward the door without saying whether he would offer Stabitz the same sporting chance.

"Bring his horse," he said. "Let's go break

the news, tell his men we found his dun wandering around out here."

Two of the Leonard brothers, Henri and George, set their horses atop a cliff. Eight more mounted Lobos gathered close and spread along the edge behind them, wild grass and juniper bushes hiding them from the men below. They were all looking down on a campfire where ten Cowboy Gunmen drank coffee and passed a bottle of whiskey around.

"If we kill all of them, do we keep the whiskey?" one man asked in a lowered voice.

"No," George Leonard said quickly. "We were told to scout the area as far as the creek bank, not to get into a skirmish." He backed his horse a step. "Let's go to the cabin and report."

"Report, hell," said the same man. "I don't know about the rest of you, but I'm spoiling for a fight!"

He gave his horse a hard spur. Feeling the sudden pain, the horse jumped a step forward into the same space at the edge that George's horse had just stepped back from. Almost immediately its hoof slipped.

"I'm damn tired — *Aggghh!*"

The man's words turned into a scream as he and his horse tumbled off the cliff. The horse rolled over rock and brush down the steep hillside. The man, less fortunate, went out into the air and touched nothing to slow his fall until he landed directly in the campfire in a spray of sparks, embers and flying hot coffee.

"What the living hell — !" shouted a Gunman, rolling away from the fire as others around him did the same.

Less than fifteen feet way, the fallen man's horse still tumbled, slid, grabbed for hold with its hooves as it neighed loudly.

The Gunmen, backing away, amazed, froze at the sight of the horse, its fall broken here and there by jutting rock and wild saplings on its way down. At the bottom of the steep hill, the horse fell atop a tall pinyon sapling, bent it to the ground, stripped it of all limbs and branches, then rolled off onto the ground in a spray of gravel and dust.

The Cowboy Gunmen remained frozen and wide-eyed as the horse staggered to it hooves and shook itself vigorously, its saddle hanging under its belly. The dazed animal stood splay legged, looking at the men as if seeing humans for the first time. It let out a long whicker under its breath and limped a short distance away.

"Everybody, listen to me," said Elton

Jennings, the leader of the group. "From now on that horse is mine!" He jabbed his finger toward the miraculous survivor.

Two Gunmen dragged the dead man off the fire. Jennings walked over to the horse and examined it thoroughly. Other than nicks, countless cuts and scratches, the horse was all right. Jennings took a big knife from his boot well and cut the conch, letting the battered saddle fall to the ground.

A quick-thinking Gunman had hurried over to a spot that allowed him to see up along the ridge as the fleeing bandidos rode by.

"It was them all right, Elton," he said. "They was too far off to recognize, but there're no other riders up here but them and us."

"Good work," said Elton. "Get everybody settled. We're going up after them."

"We are?" the gunman asked.

"Damned right we are. We all came here to fight. It's time we get to fighting."

CHAPTER 25

At the Smith brothers' cabin, Bertram Leonard, his younger brother Newlin and a few of his top men stood back a good ways from a large fire built inside a low circular stone wall some ten feet in diameter. Women and men from a nearby village had been brought in by wagon to prepare a large meal for the group. In the round enclosure, a fire licked and flared the goat skewered above it.

A guard trotted up to Bertram, rifle in hand, only to be shoved back a step.

"Keep your distance," said the gruff voice behind the hand.

"Easy, Matthew," said Bertram to the one who'd done the shoving. "What is it, Jimmy?"

"Boss!" said the road guard. "He's here! Nathan Catlow under a white flag of truce."

"Holy cats!" said Newlin. "What's going on here?"

"*Gracias,* Jimmy, good work," Bertram said to the young guard. "Go with Jimmy." He gestured at his top men. "Make Catlow feel at ease. I'll be down right away."

To Newlin he said, "This is what I've been working on in secret. I think we can settle our differences on the gold and anything else that's bad between us."

"I hope so!" said Newlin. "I don't like always having to look over our shoulders to see who might be back there wanting to kill us!"

"Keep your voice down, Newlin," his older brother cautioned him. "Some people hear that kind of talk, they think your guts have gone soft."

"The hell they have," Newlin came back in quick defense. "They'll think different if I ever —"

"Settle down, Newt," Bertram said. "I know you're tough as nails. Hell, I taught you to be. Remember?" He gave his brother's shoulder a little shove.

"I remember, all right," said Newlin. "I was just saying, if we can get by without all the killing, I'm all for it."

"Me too," said Bertram.

"I'll be glad to tell George and Henri! Where are they anyway?" He looked around.

"They're out scouting the area for us,"

said Bertram. Seeing a worried look come to Newlin's face, he said, "It's all right. I told them no fighting."

"But what if they get fired at? Then what?" Newlin asked.

"I told them no shooting, no fighting of any kind. I said turn around and hightail it if it comes down to that," Bertram said. "They're both good men. They'll listen to me. They always do."

"Yeah, I know," said Newlin. "I'm just being what folks call worrisome, is all."

"Well, stop it," said Bertram. "We've good things coming if we handle this right. Lots of men on both sides are talking about these two gangs coming together. Imagine what a gang that size would make us."

"We'd be like an army," said Newlin.

"Yes, we would. Let's keep all that in mind and make this thing work."

"Sounds good to me, Bertram," said Newlin. "You don't have to worry about where I stand. Uh-oh," he said suddenly, seeing Pearl Whitcomb walking toward them. "Here comes your friend. I'm getting out of sight."

"Yoo-hoo!" Pearl called out, a colorful parasol twirling at her shoulder.

Oh, hell! Bertram hurried forward, keeping one eye on the trail. He grabbed her firmly by the arm and pulled her aside, positioning himself between her and the trail below. "You need to lie low today!" he said.

Pearl looked around at the village folks setting up the dinner. "Oh? And miss a big party?" Pearl said.

"Catlow and his men are here, Pearl. We're going to try to settle things!"

"Settle things?" She looked appalled at the very thought. "Hold my parasol. Give me your gun! I'll settle things faster than you can say 'Shot him in the head!' "

"Keep your mouth shut, Pearl!" He glanced behind him. "While him and his men are here, I want you and LaPiers out of sight! The money you want so bad? This is how I plan to get it for you! Do you understand?"

"Can I at least get something to drink to take to my human scourge? He's easier to get along with when he's knocked-out drunk."

"Go to your campsite. I'll send some mescal and whiskey for both of you." He could smell the liquor on her breath. "But don't come out, neither of you, until I send someone to tell you Catlow and his men are gone!"

As soon as Pearl was out of sight, Bertram

ordered one of the villagers to take a full bottle of whiskey and two bottles of mescal to her campsite up the hill behind the Smith cabin.

"That should be enough to keep them both knocked out long enough for Catlow and me to talk business," he said to Newlin on their way down the trail to where Catlow waited.

"Gentlemen!" he called out amiably when Nathan Catlow and his guards came into sight. "I hope you brought an appetite. We've prepared a little dinner for you."

Catlow, who was smoking a big cigar, looked hard at Bertram's extended hand before shaking it and then quickly turning it loose.

"I'm not here to eat, Leonard," he said impatiently. "I've heard so much idle talk about our two groups joining forces. Then today I heard you wanted to conversate. I thought I's better see what it's all about before we commence to killing one another here."

"I'm honored you came," said Bertram. "It's no secret that no matter how many men share the leadership of the Cowboy Gunmen Gang, you are always the one at the head of the table."

Catlow liked hearing that, especially today

347

when there would be only one of the three leaders still alive. He relaxed and puffed his cigar.

"I've always appreciated your respectful attitude, Bertram." He sniffed the air and said, "Whatever is cooking back there smells delicious. I am a bit peckish now that I smell something that's as tantalizing as roasted goat."

"Let's eat, then," said Bertram, "all of us. But I have a table set especially for you and me. We can talk while we enjoy our meal."

Catlow eyed him a little suspiciously. "I want my guards nearby," he said. "We heard gunfire on our way here. What do you suppose that was?"

"I have no idea," said Bertram. "We'll set your men's table closer to ours if it suits you."

"Naw, what the hell?" said Catlow. "My six-shooter has kept me alive for years. What's one more night?" He patted his holstered Colt.

When an hour had passed and the afternoon sun began to loosen its grip on the desert hills, the two outlaw leaders had eaten their fill of roasted goat and the side dishes prepared by the village women. They had drunk a half bottle of Mexican whiskey and sipped three glasses of mescal that had been cooled in the rushing water of Hanging Man Creek.

They had discussed several small matters that meant little to either of them. Then, as Bertram refilled their tall wooden mescal cups, he brought up the subject of the stolen gold.

After nearly an hour, Catlow raised a hand and said, "Enough!" The two stared at each other across the tops of the wooden cups. "All this time when you mention the gold, you call it the gold from the bank, or the Esplanade gold. Never once do I hear you call it my gold." He pounded a thumb on his chest. "Call it what it is. It's my gold, Catlow's gold! Or Arizona Cowboy Gunmen's gold!" He glared menacingly at Bertram Leonard. "It's never been your gold or Los Lobos' gold!"

"Whose gold was it before it was yours?" Bertram asked calmly but pointedly.

Catlow shrugged, avoiding an answer. "It doesn't matter," he said. "When I stole it, the gold became mine. That's the law of the outlaw trade." Again, he thumbed himself on his broad chest with a snarl of mescal-lit contempt.

"All right," said Bertram, "by that same reasoning, when I stole it from you, it became mine." He glared back this time with less contempt but invincible resolve.

Catlow fell silent for a moment, then came back with a dark chuff of a laugh. "If that's true," he said, "it will only be yours for as long as it takes me to kill you and take it back."

"And if you can't kill me," said Bertram, "and I kill you instead, it will still be mine."

"We can kick it back and forth all night," said Catlow. "Come morning it will still be mine. We can talk about joining the gangs together, working together, everything else. Still, the gold is mine. Is now, will be from now on."

Bertram let out a breath and pushed his chair back from the table as he wiped his mouth on a linen napkin. "All right, then," he said. "I had an idea that would be good for both of us. But if this is your attitude, I hope you've enjoyed the meal, and I wish you *buenas noches.*" He started to rise.

"Whoa now," Catlow said, waving him down. "I'm a little drunk, and I've been set to kill you ever since you stole the gold. But tell me this idea of yours."

Bertram drew his chair back in to the table. "Here's how I see it, and I believe you're going to see it this way too."

"Try me," said Catlow, getting interested.

"We both know that stolen gold, even legitimate gold, can be sold for only twenty-five percent of its value. For large amounts like we're talking about moving, the price can drop as low as twenty percent unless a railroad handles shipping and security."

"I know all this," said Catlow, unimpressed.

"Now consider that it's stolen, traceable Denver City minted gold coin and it will take a very big investor to even want to make an offer for it."

Catlow thought about it. "All right," he said. "What's your point? That we both know about the gold market? Good for us."

"Ask yourself, Catlow," said Bertram, "knowing the market like I do, why would I make a run at taking all the gold from you unless I had a buyer already set up to buy it from me?"

Catlow got interested again. "I don't know," he said. "Why would you?"

"Because that's exactly what I have: a buyer who's bought the gold from me at next year's price, which they know because they control it."

"I lost my buyers when you stole it from me," said Catlow, working to piece the scheme together in his head. He looked at Bertram intently. "Someone's already bought it from you?"

"That's what I said, Catlow."

"My God," said Catlow, "who is big enough to make this kind of move?" He paused; then he answered himself flatly. "The government, that's who."

Bertram didn't reply to Catlow's guess. "How would you like to partner with the man who has a railroad owner hauling gold for him? Who has a gold-exchange agent handling the paperwork on all the gold, keeping it all looking legal. And people on the foreign-exchange gold markets in case the value shifts fast and you need to dump gold without losing money while you do it."

"All right, hold up," said Catlow. "Maybe you have all these people with you. Maybe you don't. If you do, that's great. But if you don't . . . ?"

"Nothing ventured, nothing gained," said Bertram. "Then you go back to where we've been ever since I took your gold. You'll hunt me down and try to kill me. Meanwhile, if we partner up, I'll give you twenty percent of the gold's value, the same as you would make if you were selling it on your own without the people I just told you taking a cut. Let's face it, Catlow. The world is getting larger and wiser. Every successful business needs good thieves like us working with them. Do we want to be those good thieves?"

"Damned right we do." Catlow gave a dark little laugh and picked up the whiskey bottle from the table. "I'll drink to it!" But he shook the bottle and found it empty. He laughed again, louder this time. "What the hell have I got to do to get a drink here?"

Bertram beckoned one of the villagers over and asked her to bring another bottle of whiskey. When she left, Bertram lit a cigar.

"I believe we are about to become very rich men," Bertram said. "Working together, that is." He smiled, his cigar bowed over a flaring matchstick.

Suddenly they heard a thunder of hooves riding away from the canvas-covered guard station at the bottom of the path leading down to the trail.

"What the hell?" said Catlow.

At the table next to theirs, his men stood up and sprang to flank him. A guard came rushing up the hill from the guard station and yelled, "Bertram! Come quick! This is awful!" He immediately turned around and started back down the hill.

Catlow and Bertram looked at each other, bewildered, and hurried after the guard. Catlow's men surrounded him, running with their rifles cocked and ready for whatever they might encounter.

At the guard station they saw Bertram's men gathered around several bodies that lay on the ground, partially wrapped in bloody canvas.

One of the guards, a newer man called Dick Holsclaw, fell in beside Bertram as they walked the last few yards to the bodies. "Boss, this is bad, powerful bad," he said.

Bandido guards had already moved in close around Catlow and the few men guarding him.

Holsclaw reached down and pulled the canvas covers away from the two badly beaten faces of George and Henri Leonard.

Bertram stood as rigid as steel, his fists balled at his sides.

"And there stands some of the sons of bitches who killed them!" a guard said in a growing rage. "I recognized them. They wore red sashes! I know their names!"

Around Catlow and Bertram, rifle and pistol hammers cocked.

"Stand down!" Catlow said to his men. To Bertram, he said more quietly, "I swear to you, I had nothing to do with this."

"This was the gunfire we heard," said Bertram. "While I was getting ready to welcome you here, your men were out there

354

like wolves, killing my brothers."

"I won't try to deny it was my men who did this," Catlow said, "but so help me God, Bertram, it was none of it under my orders."

Bertram Leonard, his head lowered, cast a sidelong glance at Holsclaw.

"Boss," said Holsclaw, "they rode up fast, holding a white handkerchief. We thought they was part of this bunch" — he nodded at Catlow's guards — "that were bringing fiesta gifts of some sort."

"Go on," said Bertram.

He was fighting an urge to draw his Colt and start shooting. Yet he kept in mind what he and Catlow had just finished discussing.

"Well," said Dick Holsclaw, "they had George and Henri over their horses' backs. One man rolled them off to the ground and said, 'Tell your boss, this is what they got for throwing one of their men off a cliff into our campfire.' "

The men all stood silent. Bertram raised his bowed head slowly and looked at Holsclaw.

"He said what?"

Dick Holsclaw repeated what he'd just said, ending it this time with "That's the whole of it, boss. I have no idea what he meant, and they cut out before I even knew what to ask about it."

Bertram turned his gaze to Catlow.

"Beats the hell out of me," Catlow said, shaking his head in bewilderment.

Up the hill he saw Newlin Leonard walking aimlessly toward the long hitching string of horses. Halfway up the hill was a woman walking down to them, carrying a tray with a tall bottle of whiskey and two wooden decanters standing on it.

It's about damn time, he told himself.

To Bertram he said, "I can't begin to tell you how sorry I am about your brothers. You have my word, when I find out who did this, I will have their heads brought to you in a burlap bag."

Bertram let out a tight breath, still puzzling over a man thrown off of a cliff into a campfire.

"Thanks," he said to Catlow, whose guards had stepped a few feet away and re-formed.

Catlow looked down at Bertram's dead brothers as a guard pulled the bloody canvas back over their faces.

"Look, it might be best if I gather my men and ride out of here easy-like before everybody starts drinking and getting a worse mad-on than they have already."

"You're right," said Bertram. "I understand."

"Yoo-hooo, Catlow!" called the woman

carrying the whiskey tray.

The sound of her voice caused Bertram's spine to stiffen.

"This is for you, Catlow!" she said in a singsong voice.

Catlow grinned and walked toward her. "Obliged!" he said, not fully recognizing the woman's voice.

He was close enough to reach for the whiskey bottle on the tray when Bertram turned toward him and shouted, "Catlow, look out!"

"Drink this, you rotten bastard!" the woman shouted, but she wasn't talking about the whiskey. From beneath the tray, she pulled up a long-barreled Remington six-shooter, cocked it and aimed it.

Pearl? Catlow mused, almost smiling in his confusion. But then his smile froze and fell away. The Remington bucked and fired, once, twice, three times, each bullet hammering him in his chest, his shoulder and then the small of his back after he spun around. He fell to the ground, writhing.

"Ho-ly!" Bertram shouted.

Seeing Catlow go down, Bertram almost reached for his holstered Colt, but he stopped himself, not wanting his move to be mistaken and cause Catlow's men to blow his head off. It didn't matter though.

Every one of Catlow's men fired, almost simultaneously. Pearl hit the ground hard. Whiskey bottle, tray and decanters flew up and landed all around her, mixing with a spray of her blood.

Seeing the Remington twitch in Pearl's right hand, Bertram Leonard hurried over and clamped his foot down over the gun's smoking barrel. He saw several bullet holes in Pearl's clothes and a bullet graze along the right side of her head; yet the only blood he could see oozed from the middle of her chest. His hands held chest high for Catlow's guards to see, he flinched at the sound of a single gunshot from up the long hillside, followed by the loud neighing of a horse in pain.

"He shot Catlow's damn horse!" a voice called out from the hitch rail.

"Shot his horse?" shouted another voice. "Why in hell?"

"That crazy sumbitch!" another man shouted.

"Boss! Quick!" shouted a Cowboy Gunman who came running up to Catlow. "We've got to get out of here. Somebody just now shot your horse!"

"Newlin shot it!" a bystander volunteered.

"Damn it to hell, man! How do I get out

of here if they've shot my horse!" Catlow managed to shout hoarsely. "Get me up! Find me a buggy, a wagon! Anything!"

"Boss, you're hit all over," a man said.

"Where? How many times?" he demanded.

"One in the chest, one in the shoulder. And one in the back! You're bleeding like a stuck hog!"

"Hell! That ain't nothing," said Catlow. "Get me up! Where's Pearl Whitcomb?" He glanced around. "Where did she go?"

"Two of them Lobos scooped her up between them and ran away. I expect she's dead by now!"

"Like hell she is!" said Catlow. "I have learned the hard way, you cannot kill that woman — she won't die!"

One of Catlow's gunmen ran up, carrying a wooden chair. Raising their boss into the seat, four men grabbed the chair legs and carried him up the hill looking the part of a royal being borne on a litter, except for the blood dripping behind him.

CHAPTER 26

It was almost dark when Thorn came racing up the half-hidden game path on Cochise, leading a handsome bay beside him. The ranger and Roman Lee recognized Thorn in the long evening shadows and kept check on the darkening trail behind him as he and the two animals bounded into the campsite. The Smith brother stood round-shouldered beside the low fire.

"Evening there, one of the Smiths," Thorn said, and pitched him a small apple.

The bearded man caught it in his cuffed hands and ran off to the side with it, like a dog defending its dinner.

"Well, Dan'l," said the ranger, "if I didn't know better, I'd think you'd stolen a horse somewhere."

He looked the big bay over. It was a dark chestnut with four white stockings. A well-appointed brass-trimmed military-style saddle lay on its back, military stirrups hanging down its sides.

"I *did,*" said Thorn. "The only way I could get the *federales'* attention was to ride away with the battery *comandante*'s horse. He runs faster than the devil himself!" he added. "I'm talking about the bay, not the *comandante.*"

"What did you do, Dan'l, just take off with this fella like he belongs to you?"

"Yep, I did pretty much," said Thorn, rubbing both Cochise and the *comandante*'s bay on their damp noses. "I told him everything: about the cannibal, the gold, the two outlaw gangs. Nothing seemed to stick with him. I tried two or three times to get him to read the letter from Matamoros. Either he can't read or didn't want to. I thought it best that I didn't stick a gun to his head with so many of his soldiers around."

"I agree," said the ranger.

"I make them about an hour behind me," said Thorn. "I left lots of signs for them to follow." He looked around. "Have I missed anything? Where'd the cannon come from, the rifles and such?"

The ranger gestured toward the bearded Smith brother, who sat by the small campfire chewing on a bite of the apple he held out of sight in his lap.

"He's got a whole room full of souvenirs

in his sanctuary," the ranger said. "Even had artificial hands displaying jewelry and such."

"Are you sure the hands were artificial?" Thorn asked.

"Don't start," the ranger said. "It's gruesome enough thinking of how he got some of his souvenirs."

"I bet it is," said Thorn. "Will this cannon shoot?"

"Hard to say." Sam looked at the cannon with him. "I thought it might be a wise thing to do, point it down this trail in case the Cowboy Gunmen or the Lobos either one comes snooping around here. I have it loaded tight, crammed and rammed and ready to fire," Sam said. "If anybody charges up here at us, I'll peal one off in their faces. Give them something to mull over for the rest of the day."

"Has it been very busy down there?" Thorn asked, looking down on the darkening trails and paths below.

"There've been lots of riders going back and forth," the ranger said. "There was a lot of heavy shooting out there earlier, and it got real busy for a while. But it has settled down some now." He nodded Thorn toward the fire. "Why don't you get yourself some coffee? Give me the Matamoros letter. I'll water this bay and walk him down to the trail. It might be better if I meet the *federales* instead of you."

"Riders coming!" Roman Lee said in a lowered voice, watching the game path leading down to the trail.

"Federales?" Thorn asked. "How many?"

"Not soldiers," said Roman Lee, "two riders, one of them hanging low in the saddle."

"Hola the camp," a weak voice said from the hillside path. "I'm LaPiers from Pedro's. I've got Pearl Whitcomb with me."

"Is she hurt?"

"Shot to hell," said LaPiers. "She might be dying, Thorn. She saw you ride past back there and said to bring her here."

"We're not doctors, LaPiers," said Thorn. "We're cannibal hunters and horse thieves."

"You're what?"

"Never mind," said Thorn. "Who shot her?"

"Catlow's men. They all shot at her. Not many hit her. Are we welcome here or not?"

Instead of answering, Thorn asked, "Why did they all shoot at her?"

"Because she shot Nathan Catlow three times," LaPiers said. When he heard a dark chuckle come from the camp, he said, "It's not funny, damn it."

Thorn collected himself. "No, it's not funny at all," he said. "Bring her up here,

LaPiers. We'll look after her. I'll pour you some coffee too while you tell us about all this shooting."

Turning to Roman Lee and the ranger, Thorn said, "A story like that'll get them into any camp in Mexico. We've got to hear the rest of it."

A minute later LaPiers rode in leading Pearl's horse beside him. Pearl lay forward in the saddle, her face almost down on the horse's neck. As Thorn lifted her down into his arms to carry her to a pallet Roman Lee made for her under the overhang, she looked up at him and whispered, "Did I kill that sumbitch? Did I kill him?"

"You kilt him sure enough, Pearl," LaPiers said, but looking at Thorn he shook his head no.

The bearded Smith brother gave them a thin smile as they passed him seated on the cannon sled, his cuffed hands dangling over his knees.

"What's his story?" LaPiers asked.

Thorn lowered Pearl onto the pallet and said, not loud enough for Smith to hear him, "Let me put it this way: You don't want to get your fingers near his face come suppertime."

"What?" LaPiers looked confused.

Thorn took a patient breath. "He's an

eater of human flesh," he said. "Don't put no part of yourself near our prisoner unless you're prepared to give it up."

Thorn poured water on a cloth and wiped dried blood from Pearl's bullet graze.

"What? Oh, sweet Lord!" said LaPiers, getting it. "A cannibal!"

Hearing him, the Smith brother's eyes turned troubled. He looked down at the ground as if in shame.

"Now you've done it," Thorn said, seeing that the Smith brother had heard them.

"What will he do?" LaPiers asked, his hand slipping down around his gun butt.

"I don't know for sure," said Thorn. He finished wiping Pearl's wounds clean. "It's my first time being around one. Maybe keep apples on hand in case he goes crazy. He seems to like apples."

Sam shook his head, got up from the rock he'd been sitting on and dusted the seat of his trousers.

"It's time I walk down and watch for the *federales*," he said.

"It's over a mile down," said Roman Lee.

"I know, but I'll walk it. There's time to get down there, then water Doc and the bay while I watch the trail if you don't mind. I'll fire a shot when the *federales* get here."

"You got it, Ranger," said Roman Lee.

"When I hear your shot, one of us will bring down the *comandante*'s bay."

Only twenty minutes had passed when the ranger heard the sound of a well-organized column of horses galloping along the main trail toward him. He waved a small lantern back and forth for the *federales* to see, and stood with the lantern on the ground near his feet until they arrived.

The column of horses halted instantly. A voice of authority called out across the quiet of night.

"You there! Lay down your rifle and raise your hands."

"I'm not holding a rifle," Sam replied.

He raised his hands. The Matamoros letter stuck up from his duster's upper pocket. He had decided against holding it up right away.

"*Sargento* Flores!" the voice barked.

Sam stood waiting in silence until a clack of hooves hurried forward and stopped. The rider, a young sergeant, aimed a gun at Sam, who turned his raised hands back and forth slowly, showing they were empty.

"*Capitán* Relano, it is true," the young sergeant called. "He is not holding a rifle."

"Is he the *loco Americano*?" the captain asked.

"Are you —"

"No," said Sam. "I'm not the crazy American. But I work with him."

He slowly lowered his left hand and just as slowly pulled his duster open. The sergeant's eyes looked relieved at the sight of the Arizona Ranger badge on Sam's chest.

"This one wears the badge of an Arizona Ranger, *Capitán*. He tells me he works with the *loco Americano.*"

"He wears the badge of an Arizona Ranger," the captain called out, "but is he an Arizona Ranger, and what is he doing here, *Sargento*?"

Before the young sergeant could answer, Sam called out in clear English, "I'm Arizona Ranger Sam Burrack. I have here a letter signed by the leader of the Matamoros Council that tells everyone why I and the man with me, Daniel Thorn, are here in Mexico, namely to bring wanted criminals back across the border to face American justice."

"Is that the same letter your *loco Americano* wanted *mi comandante* to read?"

"I would say so, *Capitán,*" said the ranger. He ventured a few steps toward the sound of the captain's voice and spoke in a guarded tone. "As important as the letter is the fact that we have found the missing gold that was stolen from the Franco-Mexican Bank of Esplanade. My amigo Thorn would have explained it to your *comandante,* had he only read the letter."

"*Comandantes* do not read, Ranger," the captain said. "They have those who read for them."

"I understand, *Capitán,*" said Sam, detecting a trace of cynicism in the captain's voice.

The captain extended his hand down to the ranger. "The letter, *por favor,*" he said.

The ranger took the letter from his duster pocket and laid it in the captain's gloved hand.

"I have heard much about the gold stolen from the bank in Esplanade, Ranger. If you have found it, you have done a great service to my country, and a great debt of recognition will be shown to you and to your *loco amigo* as well." He smiled and said, "You may lower your hands, Ranger. It is a funny story that your friend thought he must steal *mi comandante*'s horse in order to gain an audience with him."

The ranger lowered his hands and breathed in relief. "Dan'l Thorn has some peculiar ways, *Capitán.* But I think his heart is right. With your permission, I'll fire a shot in the air and signal to have your *comandante*'s horse brought down to you."

Before he had the chance to raise his Colt to fire the shot in the air, the ranger, the captain and all the soldiers turned toward the sound of hard-clacking hooves racing flat out down the path toward them.

"Halt!" the captain shouted, even as he jerked his horse's reins, pulling it back out of the way.

The ranger looked amazed for a second. He saw the *comandante*'s white-stocking bay galloping through the gathered soldiers, who jumped quickly out of its path, and in the bay's saddle, the Smith brother sat wild-eyed, a crazy grin on his bearded face. His lead rope was gathered up in his lap, still tied around his waist.

"Stop that horse!" the sergeant shouted at his men, recognizing the bay's white stockings flashing by him.

"Pursue him, *Sargento!*" the captain shouted, pulling his horse out of the way as another set of hooves came racing down the path.

The soldiers turned their horses and took off after the bay as Roman Lee brought his horse to a halt close to the ranger.

"I don't know where he got it, but he had a key to the handcuffs! He took off the cuffs, grabbed the bay and lit out!"

"Where's Thorn?" Sam asked.

"He and LaPiers are still cleaning Pearl's bullet wounds," said Roman Lee.

"Good," the ranger said. "He needs to stay out of these soldiers' sight until we get that horse back. Ride me up. I'll take Doc and catch up with them."

At the campsite, Pearl Whitcomb had been washed and rebandaged. She was on the pallet, leaning back comfortably against a saddle.

"*Hola,* Ranger," she said in a weak voice. "Are you surprised to see me?"

In spite of her condition she had a faint glint of victory in her eyes.

In a hurry, the ranger said, "You're always full of surprises, Pearl. Glad to see you're alive."

"I said I would kill him," she murmured.

"Yes, you did," said Sam. "That is a fact."

He saddled Doc and got ready to ride.

"Ranger," said Thorn, "I hope I didn't ruin nothing for us down here, stealing the *comandante*'s horse. I couldn't get him to read the letter. If he wouldn't read the letter, he would never believe we found the stolen gold."

"You might feel better knowing the captain has read the letter, and he listened to me tell him about the gold. I speculate this place will be crawling with soldiers pretty quick."

Thorn looked relieved.

"Then you and I are good on what I did?"

"As good as we're ever going to be, Dan'l." Sam looked over at the handcuffs lying on the cannon sled, a key sticking out of one of them, and said, "How do you suppose he got ahold of a key?"

"When we were in his second sanctuary?" suggested Thorn. "That's probably why he was so happy going there."

"I think you're right," said the ranger, swinging up into his saddle. "I've got to go. It'll be daylight in another hour."

"Adios, Ranger. Bring that cannibal back," Thorn said, touching his hat brim.

CHAPTER 27

Early sunlight had broken over the eastern horizon when the ranger first caught sight of the dust the column of soldiers had left in their wake. He stopped, raised his bandanna over his nose and mouth and rummaged through his saddlebags. He took out a shirt, wrapped it loosely around Doc's muzzle and tied the sleeves together.

Even so, when he saw the soldiers' dust rising high and drifting to his left, he veered Doc over to the right to make breathing a little easier for both of them. Seeing the dust fall and the soldiers standing beside their horses on the side of the road, the ranger pushed harder, hoping to gain ground out of the dust.

The soldiers had just remounted when he came galloping into their midst and the sergeant raised a hand and called out, "Column, halt!"

"You have no business here, Ranger," the

sergeant said. "My men and I have ridden all night. We have this under control!"

"I know you do, *Sargento,*" said the ranger. "But he is my prisoner. I would feel responsible if he did more harm."

"*Sí,* I understand." Taking a calming breath, the sergeant said, "*Mi capitán* and two guards rode back to tell what has happened out here. He told me to tell you when I see you. And now I have told you."

"*Gracias,*" said the ranger. "Should I wait for you and your men or ride out ahead to scout for you?"

"I don't need a scout," the sergeant said. "The bay's tracks are clear. He stays on the trail. But you may ride ahead and look for him."

"I think I will, *Sargento,*" said Sam. "If you hear two rifle shots, it means I have found him."

The sergeant nodded and watched him ride away.

The ranger had followed the clear hoof tracks for no more than two miles when they turned off the main trail and headed for a line of low desert hills in the near distance.

He rode cautiously, knowing that whoever might be in the low hills had a great advantage. They were settled in behind good rock cover, and they had the whole barren desert flats laid out below them. *Yes, this is a time to be cautious, even more cautious than usual,* he thought. Then, as if on demand, he caught the glint of sunlight off a gun barrel, and without making a show of it, he eased Doc over slowly until the glare was at their backs. They rode on.

Twenty minutes passed with no more sun glare. Sam wanted to raise his telescope and look things over, yet to do so was to alert the Smith brother that he had a telescope, if this was a Smith brother and if he didn't know it already.

Riding on, Sam spotted the first cover on the flats below the hill line, a large, rough sandstone land stuck on the desert floor. In the sand the bay's hoofprints were clear, but Sam knew that could change as soon as the bay climbed up from the sand and onto the rocky hill line.

Sam made it to the sandstone rock and paused. He looked all over the rising hills and saw for the first time a tall leafless tree standing amid a cluster of rocks and fall branches. There was something high up in the tree that he couldn't make out, and — there — stopped cold, the *comandante*'s bay standing relaxed in a strip of pinyon shade, its reins hanging to the ground.

374

All right, easy does it, the ranger thought. He slipped down from the saddle, leaving Doc's reins hanging free in case things didn't go right. He judged the bay and the tall, leafless tree to be around twenty yards away. With his rifle in his hand, he eased along from one cover to the next without incident.

But when he found himself looking up at the tree from a different angle, his heart sank. Smith swung ever so slowly at the end of the rope that had been tied around his waist when he made his getaway. Sam let out a tense breath.

The chase was over. He was sorry to see his prisoner hanging dead, most likely by his own hands, although he saw no way the man could have climbed up there. Either way, he never liked losing a prisoner. And as prisoners go, this had been a good one. Now, how to get the body down? He thought about it as he gathered Doc and the bay and put them in an area with more shade.

He checked his rifle and circled the tree in slow steps, looking for the best place to take a firing position. There was no other way for him to get the body down except to shoot through the rope.

All right, there was no putting it off. He

found a rock waist high, lowered himself behind it, propped his elbows on it and took close aim. He knew the shot was not impossible, yet it was highly improbable at this time of day, at this angle of the sun. Okay, he would hit it, but how many shots was it going to take?

He seated the butt plate in the pocket of his right shoulder and took aim. He took a deep breath and let it out slowly. *This isn't as bad as I thought. . . .*

He took another breath, let it out slowly, easily, and as he finished letting it out, he stopped his breathing and pulled back on the trigger.

In his rifle sight, he saw the rope fly apart as a bullet sliced through it. *Strange!* He saw the body plunge down. Then and only then did he hear the delayed blast of the rifle shot in the low hills over his right shoulder. It echoed across the barren desert floor and rolled off along the hilltops. It was not his own shot. He had not yet pulled the trigger all the way.

The ranger recognized the sound of the blast. It was that same powerful sound he'd heard the day Shelby Burnes had been killed and that same kind of incredible shot in the one thin break in the cloud cover.

Smith's body lay on the ground less than

fifteen feet from him. His dead eyes were open wide and upturned, his mouth agape. His feet were bare. The soles were scraped black and dirty from climbing. So were his palms.

Maybe he did *climb up there and hang himself,* Sam thought. Maybe whoever had made the shot had also found a way to slip this one the key to the handcuffs. *The other Smith brother? The one who was supposed to be dead?*

Leave it alone, Sam told himself.

Here was what had happened. He and Thorn had come here to take back a couple of cannibal outlaws, the Smith brothers. One was already dead; the other one had hanged himself. How much simpler could it be? The gold, for better or worse, would go to the Mexican government.

Sam smiled to himself and thought, *If they can find it.*

He scooted a few feet farther away from the body and scanned the low hills without his telescope. In this light breeze, the smoke would have dissipated by now, he told himself. Even as he scanned the low hills again, he raised his Winchester, the hammer already cocked, ready for the shot he didn't have to make.

He fired the rifle straight up, levered

377

another round and fired it. Two shots back to back. For whatever reason, he felt no danger from whoever was up there, whoever had just shot the Smith brother down from the tree. He leaned back and looked over at Doc and the bay. He had a feeling there would be a lot more going on here regarding the hidden gold, both the old and the new. Would he and Thorn, and maybe even Roman Lee, come back into the mix if the Mexican government asked for them?

Sure, the ranger thought to himself. *Why not?*

ABOUT THE AUTHOR

Ralph Cotton is the author of dozens of Western and crime novels. Prior to becoming a writer he was, among other things, an ironworker, a commercial seaman/second mate, a teamster, and a lay minister with the Lutheran Church of America.

The employees of Thorndike Press hope you have enjoyed this Large Print book. All our Thorndike, Wheeler, and Kennebec Large Print titles are designed for easy reading, and all our books are made to last. Other Thorndike Press Large Print books are available at your library, through selected bookstores, or directly from us.

For information about titles, please call:
(800) 223-1244

or visit our website at:
gale.com/thorndike

To share your comments, please write:
Publisher
Thorndike Press
10 Water St., Suite 310
Waterville, ME 04901